THE EXPLOSION BLEW AWAY THE EMERGENCY LIGHTS.

Before Jake could react, the world fell out from under him. Blood rushed to his head, as if he were plummeting down a well. He knew something was staring at him out of that darkness.

Then it began to move.

A few words scraped into his mind, like fingernails digging at the lid of a stone coffin.

"Come to me . . ."

JAKE RANSOM
AND THE SKULL KING'S SHADOW

JAMES ROLLINS

HARPER

An Imprint of HarperCollinsPublishers

Library of Congress Cataloging-in-Publication Data
Rollins, James.
    Jake Ransom and the Skull King's shadow / James Rollins. — 1st ed.
        p. cm.
    Summary: Connecticut middle-schooler Jake and his older sister, Kady, are
transported by a Mayan artifact to a strange world inhabited by a mix of people
from long-lost civilizations who are threatened by prehistoric creatures and an evil
alchemist, the Skull King.
    ISBN 978-0-06-147381-4
    [1. Space and time—Fiction. 2. Adventure and adventurers—Fiction.
3. Brothers and sisters—Fiction. 4. Prehistoric animals—Fiction. 5. Archaeology—
Fiction. 6. Mayas—Antiquities—Fiction. 7. Indians of Central America—
Antiquities—Fiction. 8. Science fiction.] I. Title.
PZ7.R6498Jak 2009   2009014570
[Fic]—dc22   CIP
                                                                               AC

Typography by Hilary Zarycky
10 11 12 13 14   CG/CW   10 9 8 7 6 5 4 3 2
❖
First paperback edition, 2010

For all my nieces and nephews:
Katherine, Adrienne, R.J., Mack, Alexandra, and Nadia.
May all your worlds shine with wonder and magic.

ACKNOWLEDGMENTS

This adventure with Jake Ransom was an exciting journey into the unknown for me, a departure from the familiar—but as usual, I didn't head out into the woods alone. Friends and family, a long list of them, were at my side from the first step to the last. First, I must acknowledge my entire critique group: Penny Hill, Steve and Judy Prey, Dave Murray, Caroline Williams, Chris Crowe, Lee Garrett, Jane O'Riva, Michael Gallowglas, Denny Grayson, Leonard Little, Kathy L'Ecluse, Scott Smith, and our newest and youngest member, Sally Barnes. I'd also like to give a special shout-out to Steve Prey and Janice Prey-Wolfe for all their help with the map and its artwork. Beyond the group, Carolyn McCray and David Sylvian have marched to either side of me and kept the road clear of all obstacles. And finally, a special thanks to everyone at HarperCollins, especially my editors, Ruth Katcher, who started this journey with me, and Barbara Lalicki, who finished it. And I'd be remiss not to thank two other people who have been with me every step of the way: my agents, Russ Galen and Danny Baror. And as always, I must stress that any and all errors of fact or detail in this book fall squarely on my own shoulders.

CONTENTS

Prologue 1
Grave Robbers

Part One
Three Years Later
1 *School Daze* 13
2 *An Unexpected Invitation* 25
3 *Mr. Bledsworth's Show* 41
4 *The Black Sun* 52

Part Two
5 *Land of the Lost* 73
6 *Broken Gate* 87
7 *Calypsos* 98
8 *Strangers in a Strange Land* 109
9 *The Council of Elders* 120
10 *The White Road* 132
11 *The Alchemist's Apprentice* 148
12 *Bornholm Hall* 161
13 *The First Tribe* 174
14 *A Midnight Intruder* 187
15 *The Crystal Heart of Kukulkan* 200

Part Three

16 *Game Day* 221

17 *First Skirmish* 230

18 *Race Across Town* 240

19 *Death Trap* 249

20 *I See You . . .* 261

21 *Rumor of War* 269

22 *First Blood* 280

Part Four

23 *Whistling in the Woods* 293

24 *Shadow in the Machine* 303

25 *World Enough and Time* 315

26 *The Long Count* 326

27 *Serpent Pass* 338

28 *Last Stand* 347

29 *Fire and Shadows* 357

30 *Time and Time Again* 374

A Note from the Author 395

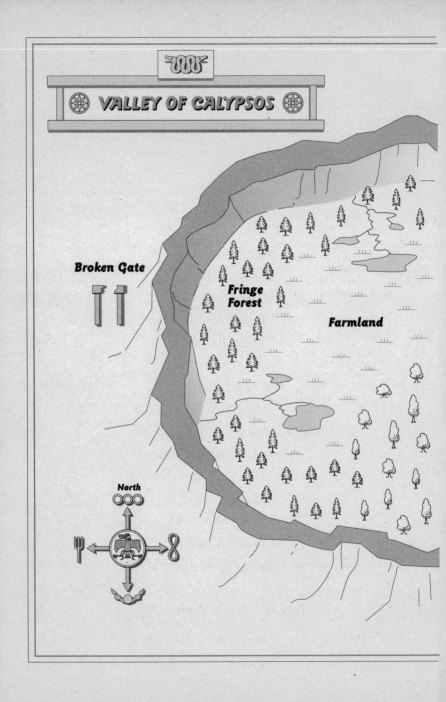

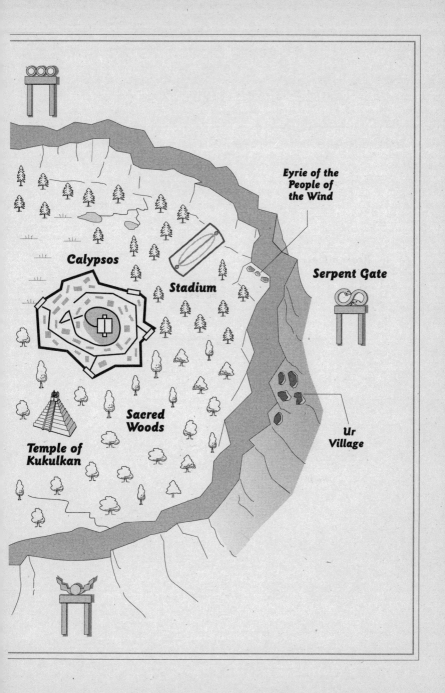

Eyrie of the
People of
the Wind

Calypsos

Stadium

Serpent Gate

Sacred
Woods

Temple of
Kukulkan

Ur
Village

JAKE RANSOM
AND THE SKULL KING'S SHADOW

GRAVE ROBBERS

The man fled down the steep slope of the jungle mountain. His boots slipped in the muck of wet leaves and slick mud. Clinging branches and snagging thorns sought to catch him, but he ripped straight through them.

Must not stop . . .

As he reached a sharp switchback in the trail, he fought to keep from tumbling headlong over the cliff that bordered the path. He swung an arm out to catch his balance and skidded in the mud around the turn. His other hand clutched the paper-wrapped parcel to his chest. Despite the near fall, he sped faster. He glanced back over his shoulder.

Fires still raged atop the mountain's summit.

The natives called the place Montaña de Huesos.

The Mountain of Bones.

It was a cursed place, shunned by all. The peak rose from the dark emerald jungles of the Yucatán Peninsula, where Mexico bordered its southern neighbor of Belize. Swamps and deep pitfalls challenged all who dared approach it, while mosquitoes and biting flies plagued anything that moved. Thick forests and vines crusted over the mountain in an impenetrable mass, hiding its true heart from prying eyes. The peak overlooked a lake where crocodiles floated like broken logs. From its forest canopy, gray monkeys with white faces stared down, strangely silent, like small ghosts of old men. Elsewhere, shadowy jaguars prowled its deepest glades. When it rained, which was often, waterfalls and cataracts flowed down the mountain's sides like molten silver.

It was a sight to behold.

But a rare one.

Few people had ever set eyes on the giant mountain; even fewer had ever walked its slopes. And only *one* man knew its secret.

He had learned the truth.

The Mountain of Bones . . . was no mountain.

Clutching his package, the man hurried down the dark jungle path. The ghostly monkeys barked softly at his limping passage as if encouraging him to run faster. The stub of a broken arrow stuck out of his thigh. Fiery agony lanced through his leg with every other step, but he had to keep going. The hunters were closing tightly around him.

His name was Henry Bethel.

Dr. Henry Bethel.

Professor of archaeology at Oxford University.

He and his dearest colleagues, Penelope and Richard Ransom, had spent the last three months of the rainy season excavating the top of the Mountain of Bones. They had uncovered a tremendous cache of pristine artifacts: a silver jaguar mask, a crown of jade and opal, small carvings of onyx and malachite, a twisted golden snake with two heads, and many other priceless objects from the Classic period of the Mayan civilization.

They had found the items in a stone tomb atop the mountain. Even as he fled now, Henry remembered Penelope Ransom being lowered on a rope into the tomb for the first time. Her flashlight's glow had illuminated the subterranean crypt and the giant sarcophagus it held inside. Atop the coffin's carved limestone lid, the most magnificent artifact rested: a two-foot-tall gold pyramid, topped by a chunk of jade carved into a curled snake with outstretched wings—like a dragon. The sculpture depicted a creature out of legend.

Kukulkan.

The feathered dragon god of the Maya.

The tomb was the discovery of a lifetime.

And word had quickly spread.

Drawn by the rumors of gold and treasure, the bandits had attacked two hours ago, as the sun sank. Under the cover of twilight, the archaeological camp had been quickly subdued by rifles, machetes, and barked threats. When the attack had first started, Henry had rushed to the Ransoms' tent, only to find it empty. He didn't know what had happened to Penelope and Richard.

He still didn't.

All he knew was he had to get the package to safety.

The Ransoms had left specific instructions.

He risked another glance up. He could no longer see the flames from the burning camp. The attackers had torched the entire site, even blowing up the petrol tank to the generator.

The crack of a rifle shot echoed down from the summit.

Startled, Henry flinched, and his left boot heel slipped. His legs went out from under him. He struck his backside hard and began a treacherous slide down the remainder of the mountain's steep slope.

He dug his heels, but the muddy ground proved too slippery from the day's rain. Wet palm fronds slapped his face, and half-buried rocks pounded his spine. A branch of a thorny bush tore a fiery path across his cheek.

Still, he hugged the parcel tightly to his chest.

The mountain's slope suddenly ended, and Henry shot off the edge. He went airborne with a small cry of surprise. Plummeting feetfirst, he splashed into a small murky pool at the foot of the mountain. It was shallow, waist deep. His boots struck the pond's sandy bottom and jarred his teeth together with a loud clack. Still, he kept hold of the package. He lifted it above his head to keep it dry.

Just a little farther . . .

The lake and boat lay only a half mile away.

He took a deep breath and attempted to slog out of the pool—but his legs refused to obey. His boots were trapped in the muddy bottom of the pool, sunk to the ankles. He twisted and yanked, but the sucking muck held him in an inescapable grip. His efforts only wormed his legs even deeper. He felt the mud and sand climb up past his calves to his knees.

No . . .

The level of the water quickly rose up his chest. The chill of the pool sank to his bones. He knew the danger he had fallen into.

Quicksand.

He clutched the package above his head. What to do? Tears of frustration and fear misted his sight. In that moment, the rational part of his brain dropped away, replaced by raw terror.

Henry stared up at the cursed mountain.

Montaña de Huesos.

The Mountain of Bones.

And now his bones would join all the others.

He had failed the Ransoms.

With Penelope and Richard vanished, no one else knew the truth. He watched the moon climb over the sharp edge of the mountain. He shivered at the sight, and even this small motion hurried his descent into the quicksand. Mud climbed to his waist, the water to his neck.

The secret would die with him.

Sensing his doom, he craned up at the mountain.

A mountain that was no mountain.

From his deadly vantage, the truth seemed so obvious now. The sharp lines, the steep slopes, the blunted summit. Though the mountain appeared to be some natural hill, he knew the ages had buried its true heart under centuries of mud, leaf, vine, and snaking roots.

In his mind's eye, Henry peeled and stripped the piles and tangles away to reveal the hidden heart. He pictured the four sides, the nine giant steps, and the flat summit thrust up toward the rising sun.

A Mayan pyramid.

The ancient structure lay buried within the false mountain.

But that was not its deepest secret.

Not by far.

Henry fingered the twine that snugly wrapped the parcel. He sent out a silent apology and prayer to Richard and Penelope Ransom.

As water climbed to his lips, he tasted the sandy water. He spat and choked. His vision blurred. Lights danced before his eyes.

No, not lights . . .

His vision sharpened despite his panic.

Torches approached through the boggy jungle. Flames flickered. Dark shadows shed to reveal a dozen warriors. They were half naked, dressed in loincloths. Ashes and black paint daubed their faces. Some came forward with drawn bows, flint arrows pointed toward him. Others had rifles shouldered.

The hunters had found their prey.

From out of their midst, a larger figure pushed forward. The leader of the bandits. But Henry knew the bandits were no more bandits than Montaña de Huesos was a simple mountain.

The attackers also hid a darker secret.

Henry heard a familiar *whump-whump* echoing from off in the distance. Helicopters were sweeping toward the burning campsite. Military helicopters. Henry had managed to get out a Mayday on the radio before escaping.

If only they'd come sooner . . .

The bandits' tall leader strode forward and lowered to one knee.

Henry struggled to see the man's face, but the torchlight seemed to shun his form. Wearing a longcoat and slouched hat, he was more shadow than man.

He reached out a wooden pole with a wicked steel

hook at the end. Henry knew the man was not offering to pull him out of the quicksand. He was after the package. Henry attempted to yank it under the water, but he moved too slowly. The man lunged out with the pole and snagged the package from his fingertips.

Henry struggled to regain it, but it rose beyond his reach.

The bandits' leader climbed to his feet. With a skilled flip, the package sailed high and landed in his open palm. For just a moment, Henry caught a glimpse of bony fingers with nails sharpened to points.

Like claws.

Then the man tossed aside the pole and started to leave.

"Thank you, Dr. Bethel," came a hoarse whisper, strangely accented. "You've proven most resourceful."

Henry strained his neck as far back as it could reach. His lips rose above the water. He spat his mouth clear.

"You'll never have it!" Henry's choked words were followed by a bitter laugh of satisfaction.

The leader swung back toward him. From beneath his hat, his eyes appeared like polished shadows, brighter than the cloaking darkness, sinister, unnatural.

As Henry sank beneath the pond's surface, those strange eyes focused on him and narrowed. The waters grew colder under that questioning gaze.

As the water swamped over Henry's head, he answered silently the dark suspicion of the leader. *You're too late.*

He heard the leader cry out. Henry imagined the man ripping into the package he had guarded so bravely. He knew what the man would find: only dried-out palm fronds, folded and bundled.

Through the drowning waters, Henry heard the scream of bright anger from the bandits' dark leader. The man had finally realized *nothing* was what it seemed here in the shadow of the Mountain of Bones.

Not bandits, not the mountain . . . not even a package tied in twine.

All a trick.

The purpose of Henry's flight was to blaze a false trail, one to lure the hunters away from the *true* path. As darkness descended and Henry sank into the jungle's final and eternal embrace, a smile formed on his lips.

The secret was safe, headed to where it belonged.

To be hidden until it was needed.

No one paid attention to the small Mayan boy as he climbed the two steps to the post office in Belize City. He carried a twine-wrapped parcel in his hands. Behind him, the ocean glinted brightly. It had taken the boy and his grandfather a full month to reach the coast. They had to be careful, wary, and watchful.

His grandfather knew all the old paths, the secret ways of their ancient people. He had taught the boy much on the long journey—how to soothe a toothache by chewing on the sap of the *chicle* tree, how to start a fire with flint and tinder, how to walk a jungle and not be heard.

But the most important lesson was unspoken.

To honor one's promise.

The boy lifted the package toward the mail slot. He longed to look inside, but promises had been made. So instead he stared at the address written on the brown paper wrapping. He sounded out the letters.

"North Hampshire . . . Connecticut."

He imagined the long journey the package would take. He wished he could follow it, too. Fly off to some exotic land.

The boy traced a finger over the top line:

Master Jacob Bartholomew Ransom

So many names for one person. With a shake of his head, the boy tipped the package through the slot. It struck the bottom with a satisfying thunk.

With the promise fulfilled, the boy turned away. *"Master Jacob Bartholomew Ransom,"* he whispered as he headed down the post office steps.

With so many names, surely he must be someone very important.

Maybe a distant prince or lord.

Still, the question nagged him—and would for many years.

Who exactly was Master Jacob Bartholomew Ransom?

PART ONE

Three Years Later

1

SCHOOL DAZE

From his school desk, Jake Ransom willed the second hand on the wall clock to sweep away the final minutes of his sixth-period history class.

Only another twenty-four minutes and he would be free.

Away from Middleton Prep for a whole week!

Then he could finally get some *real* work done. He had already mapped out his plans for each day of the weeklong vacation break: to explore the rich vein of shellfish fossils he had discovered in the rock quarry behind his house, to attend a signing by one of his favorite physicists, who had a new book out called *Strange Quarks and Deeper Quantum Mysteries*, to listen to the fourth lecture by a famed anthropologist on the cannibal tribes of Borneo (who knew sautéed eyeballs tasted sweet?)—and he had so much more planned.

All he needed now was the school's last bell to ring to

free him from the prison that was eighth grade.

But escape would not come that easy.

The history teacher, Professor Agnes Trout, clapped her bony hands together and drew back his sullen attention. She stood to one side of her desk. As gaunt as a stick of chalk, and just as dry and dusty, the teacher peered over her fingertips at the class.

"We have time for one more report," she announced.

Jake rolled his eyes. *Oh, great . . .*

The class was no happier. Groans spread around the room, which only hardened her lips into a firmer line.

"We could make it *two* more reports and stay after the last bell," she warned.

The class quickly quieted.

Professor Trout nodded and turned to her desk. One finger traced a list of names and moved to the next victim in line to present an oral report. Jake found it amusing to watch her thin shoulders pull up closer to her ears. He knew whose name was next in line alphabetically, but it had somehow caught the teacher by surprise.

She straightened with a soured twist to her lips. "It seems we will hear next from Jacob Ransom."

A new round of groans rose. The teacher did not even bother quieting them down. She plainly regretted her decision to squeeze in one more report before the holiday break. But after almost a year in her class, Jake knew Professor Agnes Trout was a stickler for order and rules. She cared more about the memorization of dates and names than any real understanding of the flow of history. So once committed to her course of action, she had no choice but to wave him to the front of the class.

Jake left his books and notes behind. He had his oral report set to memory. Empty-handed, crossing toward the blackboard, he felt the class's eyes on him. Even though he had skipped a grade last year, he was still the second tallest boy in his class. Unfortunately it wasn't always a good thing to stand out in a crowd, especially in middle school, especially after skipping a grade. Still, Jake kept his shoulders straight as he crossed to the board. He ignored the eyes staring at him. Not one to set fashion trends, Jake wore what he found first that morning (clean or not). He ended up with scuffed jeans, a tattered pair of high-top sneakers, a faded green polo shirt, and of course the mandatory navy school jacket with the school's insignia embroidered in gold on the breast pocket. Even his sandy blond hair failed to match the current razored trend. Instead it hung lanky over his forehead.

Like his father's had been.

Or at least it matched the last picture Jake had of the senior Ransom, now gone three years, vanished into the Central American jungle. Jake still carried that photograph, taped to the inside of his notebook. It showed his parents, Richard and Penelope Ransom, smiling with goofy happiness, dressed in khaki safari outfits, holding up a Mayan glyph stone. The photo's edges were still blackened and curled from the fire that burned through their hilltop camp.

Taped below it was a scrap of parcel paper. On it, written in his father's handwriting, was Jake's name along with the family address for their estate here in North Hampshire, Connecticut. The package had arrived six weeks after the bandits had attacked his parents' camp.

That had been three years ago.

It was the last and only contact from his folks.

Jake fingered the thin cord around his neck as he reached the front of the class. Through his cotton shirt, he felt the small object that hung from the cord and rested flat against his chest. A last gift from his parents. Its reassuring touch helped center him.

To the side, the teacher cleared her throat. "Class, Mr. Ransom will be teaching us . . . well . . . I mean to say his oral report will be on . . ."

"My report," he said, cutting her off, "is on Mayan astronomical techniques in relation to the precession of the equinoxes."

"Yes, yes, of course. Equinoxes. Very interesting, Mr. Ransom." The teacher nodded, perhaps a bit too vigorously.

Jake suspected Professor Agnes Trout didn't fully understand what the report was about. She backed toward her desk, as if fearful he might ask her a question. Like everyone else, she must have had heard the story of Mr. Rushbein, the geometry teacher. How after Jake had disproved one of the teacher's theorems in front of his whole class, he had suffered a nervous breakdown. Now all the teachers at Middleton Prep looked at Jake with a glint of worry. Who would be next?

Jake picked up a piece of chalk and wrote some calculations on the board. "Today I'll be showing how the Maya were able to predict such events as the solar eclipses, like the one that will occur next Tuesday—"

A balled-up piece of paper struck the board near his hand and caused the piece of chalk in his fingers to snap with a loud squeak on the board.

"Were they able to predict that?"

Jake knew the voice. Craig Brask. A linebacker for the junior varsity football team. While Jake had skipped a grade, Craig had been held back. Ever since, Jake had become the target for the beefy troglodyte.

"Mr. Brask!" Professor Trout declared. "I'll have no more of your shenanigans in my classroom. Mr. Ransom listened to your report with respect."

With respect? Craig's report had been on Custer's Last Stand. He even got the ending wrong: *The injuns got whooped good!*

As the few snickers finally died down, Jake took two steadying breaths and prepared to resume his report. In preparing for his report, Jake had delved deeply into how the Maya were skilled astronomers, how they understood the grand movement of the cosmos. Such research made him feel closer to his parents. It had been their life's work.

But now, standing at the chalkboard, Jake sensed the boredom of the class behind him. With a small shake of his head, he picked up the eraser and wiped away the calculations he had already written. That wasn't what the class wanted to hear. He turned to face them, cleared his throat, and spoke boldly.

"It is well known that the Maya practiced ritual human sacrifice. They even cut out their victims' hearts—and ate them."

The sudden change in topic shocked away the bored looks of the class.

"That's so sick," Sally Van Horn said from the front row, but she sat straighter in her chair.

Jake drew an outline of a human body on the chalkboard and went into great detail about the method of ritual sacrifice: from types of knives used in the slaughter to the way the blood was collected from the altar in special bowls. By the time the bell rang, no one moved. One student even held up his hand and called out, "How many people did they kill?"

Before Jake could answer, Professor Trout waved him to stop. "Yes, very interesting, Mr. Ransom. But I think that's enough for today." She looked a little green, possibly after Jake's description of how the Maya used bones and intestines to predict the weather.

Jake hid a small smile as he dusted the chalk from his hands and returned to his desk. A few students clapped at the end of his report, but as usual, he was mostly ignored. He watched the others leave, clutched in groups of two or three, laughing, joking, smiling.

New to the class, Jake hadn't made any real friends. And he was okay with that. His life was full enough. Determined to follow in his parents' footsteps, he had to prepare himself—mind and body—for that goal.

Reaching his desk, he collected his backpack and saw that his notebook was still open. He paused just a moment to look at the photograph of his parents on the inside cover, then closed the notebook, shouldered his backpack, and headed toward the door.

At least he was done with school for a week.

Nothing could go wrong from here.

Jake hurried down the school's marble steps in the bright April sunshine and headed to his mountain bike.

Bright laughter drew his attention to the left. Under one of the flowering dogwoods in the school yard stood his sister, Kady. She leaned on the trunk of the tree, dressed in the yellow and gold of the senior cheer squad. A match to the three other girls gathered around her, though clearly she was their leader. She also held the full attention of half a dozen upper-class boys, all wearing letterman jackets.

She laughed again at something one of the boys said. She tossed her head in a well-practiced flip, sending out a cascade of blond hair, only a few shades lighter than Jake's. She stretched out a leg as if limbering up, but mostly, Jake knew, it was to show off the length of her leg and the new silver ankle bracelet. She was trying to gain the attention of the captain of the football team, but he seemed more interested in a shoulder-punching contest with a fellow teammate.

For just a brief moment, Kady's eyes caught Jake's approach. He watched them narrow in warning, marking off forbidden territory.

Jake skirted away. He quickened his steps, prepared to take a wide swath around the gathered elite of Middleton Prep. It was because of such a concentrated effort that he failed to see Craig Brask until he was almost on top of him.

A large arm shot out and slammed a palm into Jake's chest. Fingers curled into his shirt. "Where do ya think you're going?"

Craig Brask stood a head taller than Jake and twice his weight. His classmate's red hair was shaved to a stubble, and his face had so many freckles it looked like he was always blushing. He had the sleeves of his school jacket rolled up to expose his apelike forearms.

"Let me go, Brask," Jake warned.

"Or what?"

By now, others gathered. Snickers rose from the crowd.

As Craig turned to grin at his audience, Jake reached up and grabbed Craig's thumb in a lock and twisted it. Over the past three years, Jake had studied more than just ancient civilizations. He had readied his body as much as his mind by taking Tae Kwon Do classes three times a week.

Craig gasped as Jake broke his hold. The large boy stumbled back.

Not wanting the fight to escalate, Jake turned and headed for his bike. But Craig lunged and grabbed the back of Jake's collar, not letting him leave.

Jake felt the thin braided leather cord around his neck snap under the pressure. The weight suspended from it slid down his belly where his shirt was tucked into his jeans.

Anger flared, white hot and blinding.

Not thinking, Jake turned and snap-kicked Craig in the chest.

Craig flew back and landed flat on his back. Jake's anchoring foot slipped in the grass, and he fell hard on his backside, jarring his teeth.

Someone called out, "Kady, isn't that your brother?"

Jake glanced over a shoulder. The elite of Middleton Prep all turned in their direction, including the captain of the football team.

With a frown, Randy White headed over. Taking his lead, the others followed in tow, including Jake's sister.

Reaching them, Randy pointed at Craig's nose. "Brask, leave the kid alone." The command in that voice did not invite debate.

Craig rubbed at his bruised chest and scowled.

Randy offered Jake a hand up, but he managed to gain his feet on his own. He didn't want any help. He brushed off the seat of his pants. Randy shrugged and turned away, but not before mumbling, "Weird kid."

As the elite drifted away, Kady remained. She caught Jake by the elbow and leaned close to his ear. "Quit trying to embarrass me," she hissed between clenched teeth.

Embarrass you?

Jake shook free of his sister's grip and returned her glare, eye to eye. Though they stood the same height, Katherine Ransom was two years older.

Jake's face went even redder than during the fight. Unable to form words, he freed the broken cord from under his shirttail. The object that hung from it dropped into his open palm.

A gold coin. Actually it was only *half* a coin, the whole having been broken jaggedly in two, a Mayan image engraved on each half. The sunlight glinted and caught Kady's eye. Her left hand rose to her own throat. Her half of the same coin hung from a fine gold chain around her neck.

The two coin pieces had been mailed in the parcel three years ago, along with their father's camp diary and their mother's sketchbook. Neither knew why the package had been sent or who had mailed it. Since then, the gold tokens never left Kady's or Jake's neck.

Jake stared down at the piece in his palm. Sunlight reflected off the burnished gold, making the symbol on his half of the coin shine brightly. The symbols were called *glyphs*.

The glyph on his coin represented the Mayan word *be* (pronounced BAY) or, in English, *road*.

For the thousandth time, Jake wondered what it meant. It had to be significant. Turning his back on his sister, he shoved the coin into his pocket and strode stiffly toward his chained-up mountain bike.

He was soon pedaling away. How he wished he would never have to return to this lame school.

But he shook his head.

No, his heart was too full of *one* wish to bother with any others.

One hand lowered to his pants pocket as he pedaled.

He rubbed his palm over the coin through the jeans, shining it like Aladdin's lamp.

There was room for only one wish in Jake's heart: to discover what had happened to his mother and father.

It was why he worked so hard.

If he ever hoped to learn the truth about his parents' deaths—to discover why they'd been killed—he must first become like them. Like father, like son. Follow in their footsteps.

With a renewed determination, Jake lifted out of the seat and fought his bike up the long hill toward home.

Nothing else mattered.

2

AN UNEXPECTED
INVITATION

Just the smallest tap . . .

Jake lay on his belly as the sun baked his back. He had been down in the quarry behind his house the entire Saturday. The slab of rock under him was mostly flat, but by now, every slight bump in the surface had grown into a sharp knob.

His lips were stretched in a hard grimace—not from pain, but from his painstaking concentration.

Mustn't harm the sample.

The Paleozoic-era fossil looked like a cross between a squashed crab and some alien spacecraft. He could even make out a pair of tiny antennae.

It was a rare find for the area. It stretched almost three inches long, an outstanding example of *Isotelus maximus*, more commonly known as a giant trilobite.

An amazing find!

Jake held a small pick-chisel in one hand and a tiny

hammer in the other. One more good tap should free the fossil from the surrounding rock. He could then take it back to his room and perform a more delicate cleanup under proper conditions.

He positioned the chisel, took a steadying breath, and lifted the hammer. He wanted to close his eyes, but he doubted that would help.

Here we go . . .

He swung the hammer and—

"CALLING, MASTER JAKE!"

—startled, he struck his thumb a good blow, right on the knuckle.

"CAN YOU HEAR ME?"

The squawks were coming from the two-way radio balanced on a rock near his elbow.

Jake shook his injured hand and rolled to his side. He picked up the radio and pressed the transmit button. "What is it, Uncle Edward?" he asked with exasperation.

"DINNER IS ABOUT TO BE SERVED."

Dinner?

"AND I SUSPECT YOU'LL NEED TIME TO CLEAN UP."

Jake glanced to the sky and finally noted how low the sun had sunk and how long the shadows had grown. Lost in concentration, he had not realized how late it had become.

He raised the radio to his lips. "Okay. I'll be right there."

He took an extra moment with chisel and hammer to free the trilobite fossil, then pocketed it. Finished, he rolled onto his back, only to find slobbering jowls and a big black wet nose hanging over his face. Hot breath panted down at him. A dollop of drool landed on his forehead.

Ugh.

Jake reached up and pushed the basset hound's face away from his own. "Phew, Watson. That breath could kill a dragon."

Jake sat up.

Ignoring the insult, Watson dragged a long wet tongue across Jake's cheek.

"Yeah, that's better. Share the germs."

Still, Jake grinned and gave the old dog a rough scratch behind his floppy left ear, which got the hound's rear leg kicking happily. Watson, going on fourteen years, had been a part of the Ransom family longer than Jake. Jake's mother had rescued Watson from a British breeder of foxhounds who was going to drown the dog as a puppy because he was born with a crooked front leg. Watson still walked with a bit of a limping swagger, but as his mother always said, *It's the warts that make us who we are.*

Still, bum leg or not, if Watson saw a squirrel, he could take off after it like a furry bolt of lightning. Jake kept a dog whistle handy to keep from losing the hound in the woods. Especially because Watson's eyesight was getting weaker with age.

"C'mon, Watson. Let's get some food."

The last word got the hound's tail wagging again. His nose lifted in the air, sniffing. *That* sense certainly hadn't gotten any weaker with age. He probably already knew what Aunt Matilda had cooking on the stove.

Jake stared down at another two fossils he wanted to collect. They would have to wait until tomorrow. The light was getting bad, and he didn't want to make any mistakes. That's what his father taught him. An archaeologist needed patience. He heard his father's voice in his head: *Don't rush history . . . it's not going anywhere.*

Taking that advice, Jake gathered his tools and set off with Watson. He climbed out of the old quarry and headed home.

Ravensgate Manor spread ahead of Jake, fifty-two acres of rolling hills dotted by forests of sugar maples and black oaks.

Jake headed down a wood-chip-strewn path. The estate went back generations, to the first Ransom to set roots here shortly after the signing of the Declaration of Independence. He had been a famed Egyptologist, and each generation continued in the footsteps of the founder, all explorers in some manner or another.

As Jake rounded a bend, he spotted home.

In the middle of a sprawling English garden stood a small mansion of stone turrets and timbered gables, of slate roofs and copper trims, of stained-glass windows and brass hinges. Off near the front, a circular driveway of crushed stone led out to the main gate, whose pillars supported a pair of carved stone ravens, namesakes of the estate.

Since his parents had vanished, the house itself had grown more forlorn. The ivy had grown thin and yellowing in patches, a few tiles were missing from the roof, and a section of windowpanes had been patched with tape and board. It was as if something essential had been stolen—from the land, from the house, but mostly from Jake's heart.

With Watson at his side, Jake headed to one of the back doors. He pushed inside the house to a small red-tiled mudroom, where he knocked the dust from his shoes and patted down his clothes. He hung up his specimen bag and tools on a hook by the door.

A head popped in from the next room. Aunt Matilda. Her wrinkled face was framed by white curls, mostly bunched under a baker's cap. She didn't step fully into the room. She seldom did. Aunt Matilda seemed always too busy to move her entire body into one room.

"Ah, there you are, my dear. I was just spooning up the soup. Best you hurry and clean yourself up." A small frown of concern tightened the corners of her lips. "And where might that sister of yours be?"

The question was not truly meant to be answered, especially by Jake, because he and Kady seldom kept company anymore. It was merely a complaint to the universe.

"I'll wash up and be right back down, Aunt Matilda."

"Be quick about it." She vanished away, off to oversee the cook and two maids. But her head popped back into view. "Oh, Edward would like you to stop by the library before dinner. Something's arrived in today's post."

Curiosity hurried Jake's pace. Significantly less interested, Watson wandered off to search for scraps in the kitchen.

The library was just off the main foyer. To reach it, Jake headed down the manor's central hall that stretched from the back of the house to the front. One wall was hung with oil portraits of his ancestors, men and women, going back to the original Bartholomew with his heavy mustache and sun-squinted eyes, posed next to a camel. Every portrait looked down across the central hall to its own private display cabinet.

Cabinets of Curiosities, his father called them.

Each leaded-glass display contained artifacts and relics from that ancestor's adventures: beetles and butterflies pinned to corkboard, gemstones and mineral specimens, tiny bits of pottery and carved figurines, and of course, enough fossils to fill an entire museum, including a tyrannosaurus egg, partially hatching.

Jake turned under the next archway into the main library. Shelves of books climbed two stories, accessible by a pair of tall ladders on wrought-iron rails. The far wall contained a fireplace tall enough to walk into without bending over. A small fire crackled cheerily, shedding a welcoming warmth into the room. His father's massive oak desk occupied one corner. The remainder of the furniture was a collection of overstuffed chairs and sofas, encouraging someone to collapse into them and become lost in the worlds contained between the covers of one of the books.

Uncle Edward stood beside the desk.

"Ah, there you are, Master Jake," his uncle said. He turned on a heel. His back was straight, his manner stiff, but his eyes were never cold, even now, when pinched with some slight concern. A pair of small reading glasses rested at the tip of his nose. He held a large yellow envelope in his hand. "This arrived today. Mailed from England. From London's Blackfriars district."

"Blackfriars?"

A nod answered him. "One of London's oldest financial districts. Banks and whatnot."

Uncle Edward should know. He had grown up in London. In fact, Edward and Matilda were not truly Jake's aunt and uncle. Their family name was Batchelder. They'd been friends of Jake's grandfather and had managed Ravensgate Manor for three generations. It was whispered that Edward had once saved Jake's grandfather's life during World War II, somewhere in Africa. But no one would ever tell the whole story.

With no surviving relatives to look after Jake and Kady, Uncle Edward and Aunt Matilda had become the children's guardians, while continuing to oversee the estate. The pair were as doting as any parents and sometimes as stern. But mostly the entire household seemed to be waiting, holding its breath for the manor's true masters to return.

Uncle Edward crossed to Jake and held out the sealed envelope.

Jake accepted it and stared down at the top name.

Master Jacob Bartholomew Ransom.

Below it was his sister's full name.

Jake felt a chill. The last time he had seen his name written in full, it had been on the package with his father's handwriting, a parcel that still carried a tinge of doom about it.

Now here the name was again, only typed neatly and coldly.

Uncle Edward cleared his throat. "I didn't know if you would like to wait until your sister returns to—"

Jake ripped the tab and peeled open the envelope. No telling when Kady would return.

Jake heard a low growl behind him. He turned and found Watson stalking into the room. The dog's hackles were raised and his nose was in the air. Plainly Watson had been scolded out of the kitchen and had come to find Jake for consolation. But his keen nose must have caught wind of the mail, perhaps smelling something only the dog's keen sense could pick up. Watson approached no closer. He circled slowly with a low growl of warning.

"Hush, Watson . . . it's all right."

Jake shook out the contents. A colorful brochure and a few other items slipped between his fingers and fluttered to the hardwood floor. Watson skittered back a step. Jake did manage to catch the largest sheet of stiff linen paper. It was yellowish and embossed deeply with the blackest ink.

Uncle Edward had knelt down and gathered the loose papers, including a cover letter. He glanced through them as Jake read over the invitation twice.

"There are airline tickets," his uncle added. "Two. For you and your sister. First class. And what looks like room reservations at the Savoy. A very expensive hotel."

Jake scrunched his brows and read the most intriguing line. "'Mayan Treasures of the New World.'"

Uncle Edward unfolded the brochure. Photos of gold and jade objects adorned what appeared to be a museum advertisement for the exhibit. "It's from the British Museum," he said. "How very strange. The flight tickets are for the day after tomorrow. Monday. And according to the brochure,

We kindly extend a Gracious and Grand

Invitation to

Master Jacob Bartholomew Ransom

and

Mistress Katherine Edwina Ransom

To Attend the Auspicious Opening of an

Exciting New Exhibit at

The British Museum

London, England

Mayan Treasures of the New World

Humbly and Sincerely sponsored by

Bledsworth Sundries and Industries, Inc.

the first day of the exhibit is on that Tuesday."

"Tuesday?" Jake said, noting another oddity. He remembered his talk at school yesterday about the Mayan calendar—and the Mayan prediction for that day. "That's the day of the solar eclipse. In London, it will be a *total* eclipse."

He couldn't keep the excitement from his voice.

"I don't like this," Uncle Edward said, deepening the

lines across his forehead. "Such short notice. Only two tickets. For you and your sister."

"Kady and I are old enough to travel by ourselves. And aren't you always telling me I should see the British Museum one day?"

Uncle Edward's frown only grew larger. "Before we even consider it, I must make some calls. There are a thousand details to attend. We must address . . ."

Jake grew deaf to his uncle's words. Instead his eyes fixed on one of the pictures on the unfolded brochure. He reached and slipped it from his uncle's fingers. In the center of the page was a photograph of a gold snake decorated with jade and rubies. It was bunched up into a figure-eight, but at each end was sculpted a head, one with its jaws open, bearing fangs, and a second that was closed with a small forked tongue protruding.

Jake stared at the image. He felt the room tilt under his feet, and his breath grew shallow and fast.

He recognized the two-headed snake.

He had seen a drawing of it in his mother's sketchbook, even read a detailed description of it in his father's field notebook. Both books—two halves of their joint diary—had arrived with the broken gold coin. All were contained in the parcel addressed in his father's handwriting. But the package had come with no note, no further explanation.

Jake finally lifted the brochure and pointed. "This is one of the artifacts from Mom and Dad's dig." He glanced through the brochure. Other items also looked familiar, but he wanted to compare them to the sketches in his mother's sketchbook.

Uncle Edward moved closer. "I thought the artifacts were all locked up in some vault in Mexico City."

Jake nodded. Shortly after the bandits had attacked his parents' camp, the Mexican military had flown in and locked down the site. It was unknown how many items were stolen or what became of the bodies of Jake's mother and father. Another colleague had also gone missing. Dr. Henry Bethel.

But the military did recover most of the Mayan artifacts. Due to their value as national treasures, they had never left Mexico.

Until now.

The London museum had them on loan for this exhibit.

Mayan Treasures of the New World.

"No wonder they invited you," his uncle said at his side as he read over Jake's shoulder. "The son and daughter of the team who discovered the artifacts."

Jake could not take his eyes off the brochure. A finger traced the curves of the two-headed snake. Surely his parents had also touched it, unearthed it with their hands.

"I have to go," Jake said with a fierce determination in his voice.

Uncle Edward placed a reassuring hand on his shoulder.

Who knew when he'd get another chance before the relics were all locked up again? Jake felt tears begin to well. To be that much closer to his parents.

The crunch and squeal of tires sounded from the front of the house. Laughter and shouted good-byes echoed to them. A moment later, the door swung open and Kady swept inside. She turned and waved to her departing ride, using her whole arm.

"I'll see you tomorrow, Randy!"

She came in and discovered Jake and Uncle Edward staring at her. Seeing the expressions on their faces, a single line of worry etched her perfect forehead.

"What?" she asked.

"Well, I'm not going," Kady declared.

Jake watched her tick off her reasons on her fingers.

"I have Jeffrey's pool party on Sunday. Then there's cheer practice on Monday . . . followed by another party. And that doesn't even count the *two* parties on Tuesday."

She finished with a slight stamp of her heel. "And I'm certainly not giving up all that just to babysit Jake at some boring museum."

Jake felt his face growing hotter. She had hardly taken a breath to listen to them. His heart pounded. He knew that if Kady didn't go *he* wouldn't be going. Uncle Edward would not let him travel alone.

"Kady! It's Mom and Dad's artifacts!"

She swallowed. Her eyes darted to the brochure and away again. Kady was far better at drawing and art than Jake. She had studied their mother's sketchbook at length. Or at least she had when the books first came in the mail. For the past two years, she hadn't bothered to look at them again.

But Jake had noticed the slight tremble to Kady's hands when she'd first looked at the brochure. She also had recognized the double-headed snake.

"I don't know," she said. "I still have too much to do."

Jake turned to Uncle Edward with a pleading expression.

His uncle only shrugged. He plainly still questioned whether they should go. Especially without Kady's cooperation.

"Are these *first*-class tickets?" Kady suddenly asked. She shifted the papers in her hands. "And a penthouse reserved at the Savoy?"

Sensing a chink in her armor, Jake changed his approach. In all his excitement, he'd forgotten with whom he was dealing here.

"It's . . . I'm sure, a big deal," Jake said cautiously. He waved to the tickets. "Look at the expense. And they even timed it to the solar eclipse. I guess it's all just a stupid publicity stunt. Still . . ."

He noted how her shoulders twitched at the word *publicity*.

"I'm sure there will be cameras," he pressed. "News crews, television stations, possibly celebrities."

Her eyes grew brighter. She took another look down at the invitation.

As Kady took the bait, Jake set the hook. "Besides," he said, "think of all the shopping . . . all the newest European fashions that haven't reached the North Hampshire Mall. You'll be the first to wear them."

Kady glanced down to her shoes. "Wellllll, maybe a short trip. It might not be *that* bad."

Jake glanced at Uncle Edward.

The man shook his head. Uncle Edward knew when he was defeated. He might succeed in stopping Jake, but he'd never be able to come between Kady and a camera.

"Then I guess I'll have to check into the arrangements," he said.

Kady nodded, and Jake sighed with relief.

There remained only one last holdout.

Watson still sat near their father's desk with his hackles raised. The basset hound's eyes remained fixed on the discarded yellow envelope. From the old dog's throat a low growl still flowed.

3

MR. BLEDSWORTH'S SHOW

Jake had never been in a limousine before. He never imagined the sheer size inside. It felt like he was in the belly of a black jetliner, flying low over the ground.

The limousine whipped through the narrow avenues and confusing roundabouts of London. Car horns blared and a few pedestrians shook fists at the massive vehicle. They were running late.

Jake pressed his cheek against the darkly tinted window. He tried to get a peek at the sky.

"Don't worry," Kady said next to him. With her iPod's earbuds in place, she shouted a bit to be heard. "You won't miss the eclipse."

Kady returned her attention to the tiny compact mirror in her hand. She was checking her face again after an entire morning in their suite's bathroom, performing unfathomable experiments with lip gloss, moisturizers, hair gels, eye shadow, lash curler, and a blow dryer—and even something that left glittering dust on the bathroom's marble counter. Still, like any good scientist, Kady was never done tinkering with her work.

Jake ignored her and searched the blue sky. The sun shone like a yellow bruise through the tinted window. The moon waited, ready to begin its inevitable sweep across the sun's face, turning day into night.

Jake's left knee jumped up and down with excitement.

Also a little worry.

There was another force just as unstoppable as his sister.

Near the horizon, black clouds stacked high into the sky. Flashes of lightning sparked deep within the heart of an approaching thunderstorm. It was a race against time. If the storm blotted out the view of the eclipse, Jake would be crushed.

The limousine bumped around an especially sharp turn. Tires squealed. Jake was thrown away from the window. Ice clinked in a crystal glass. A huge hand caught Jake and righted him in his seat.

A rumbling voice scolded with a clipped English accent. "Young sir, if you'd like to see the sky, perhaps I can assist you before you break your neck."

Jake had almost forgotten Morgan Drummond shared their limousine, which was surprising considering the man's size. His body filled the entire front half of the limousine's passenger cabin. He was all muscle with craggy features. He wore a double-breasted black pinstripe suit, a veritable *tent* of a suit, but still his biceps strained the fabric with every motion. He looked more like a drill sergeant than the head of security for Bledsworth Sundries and Industries, Inc., the sole sponsor for the Mayan exhibit.

Drummond tilted toward Jake. He reached a thick finger to a row of buttons near Jake's elbow and pressed one. The limousine's moonroof glided open. Through the glass, the sky appeared.

As the limousine barreled past a double-decker bus, the passengers on the upper deck glanced down over the top rail and into the limousine below. Jake found himself staring up at the faces like a goldfish in a fishbowl. Hands pointed. Jake waved back, but there was no response.

"Privacy glass," Morgan Drummond explained. "They can't see you."

The large man settled back into the shadows of his seat. For someone so mountainous, he had a strange ability to fade into the background. Jake did note a tiny flash out of the darkness as Drummond leaned back. It came from the man's tie tack. It was a chunk of polished gunmetal steel fashioned into the symbol for Bledsworth Sundries and Industries Inc.

A griffin.

The mythological monster had the head, wings, and claws of an eagle with the body, hind legs, and tail of a lion. With a black jewel for an eye, it was shown reared up as if ready to tear into some cowering prey. Some said

it also represented the corporation's business practices: attacking the weak and devouring them whole.

Jake had read up on the corporation during the flight from Connecticut to London. No one could quite say where or when the company had first started. It was hinted that its "sundries and industries" stretched back to medieval times. There were rumors that the Bledsworth family made their first fortune by selling false potions to protect against the Black Plague. They were also the ones who collected the dead bodies of the victims, piling them up on carts and selling off body parts for medical research. Truth or not, the Bledsworths came out of the Dark Ages with more gold than the king of England. Now considered fairly reputable, they owned an entire block in the financial center of Blackfriars.

Jake sat straighter and cleared his throat. He asked the question that had been nagging him since he landed in London. "Mr. Drummond, sir, why is your company sponsoring the museum exhibit?"

A heavy grumble answered him. It sounded little

pleased with his question. But even Kady lowered her compact mirror and removed one of her iPod's earbuds to hear his answer.

Morgan Drummond sighed. "It's very expensive to put on this show. The extra guards, the electronic security . . . it cost the corporation a fortune just to convince the Mexican government to allow these national treasures to be taken out of the country."

From the tone of his voice, the man was not happy that his company was spending so much money on something so frivolous.

"Then why is the corporation doing it?" Jake asked.

Drummond leaned closer. "Mr. Bledsworth insisted. And no one goes against Mr. Bledsworth."

Jake frowned. He had read all about the reclusive head of the corporation: Sigismund Oliphant Bledsworth IX.

In his nineties, the man represented the ninth generation to carry the Bledsworth family name—but unmarried with no children, he would be the last. Only a few photographs existed of Sigismund Oliphant Bledsworth IX. Jake could find only one on the computer, taken when Bledsworth was a much younger man: a stick of a man in a British military uniform. Like his medieval ancestors, his past was clouded with rumors of misdeeds—stories of stealing art treasures from France and Germany during the confusion of war. He had also been stationed in Egypt.

But after World War II, all sightings of the head of Bledsworth Sundries and Industries dried up. He had become more ghost than man.

Jake's brows pinched. "But what's Mr. Bledsworth's interest in putting on this show?"

"You truly don't know?" Morgan Drummond asked.

Jake shrugged, turned to his sister, then back to the large man. "No."

"Mr. Bledsworth felt obligated. A debt to be paid."

"A debt?"

"To your parents."

The air suddenly grew heavier in the limousine. Jake found it harder to breathe.

Drummond leaned back in his seat and dissolved back into the shadows. "Who do you think financed your parents' Mayan dig? Who do you think sent them in the first place?"

Jake frowned. *Mr. Bledsworth?* Could it be true? Had the mysterious head of Bledsworth Sundries and Industries paid to have his mother and father explore the Mayan peak known as the Mountain of Bones?

Why?

The chauffeur called from the front as the limousine slowed.

"We've reached the museum, sir."

Flashes and camera lights blinded as Jake and Kady exited the dark interior of the stretch limo. Jake took a step back in shock, but he had nowhere to retreat. Behind him, Morgan Drummond unfolded his large bulk and rose up like a wall.

"Just keep moving," he muttered under his breath.

Drummond herded them forward through a crush of reporters on the sidewalk in front of the museum. The news crews and onlookers were held back behind two black velvet ropes that framed a red carpet. Ahead, the British Museum towered behind marble pillars, looking like a massive bank vault. A giant banner hung across the pillars and boldly announced the exhibit.

Mayan Treasures of the New World

Jake noticed many people wore special goggles to view the coming eclipse.

He looked up to the sky. Of course, he should've known better. The moon was already beginning to cross the sun's face. The blinding corona stung his eyes. He glanced away before it could damage his sight. To the south, a spate of lightning flashed, followed by a rumble of thunder. The storm was still blowing up along the Thames River and threatened to wipe out the rare sight.

"Aren't they darlings?" a matronly woman called out.

"Spittin' images of their mum and da."

"And look at those cute outfits."

"Regular little explorers, they are," another chuckled.

Jake became conscious of his clothes. Courtesy of the

Bledsworth corporation, the pair had been tailor-fitted at an expensive shop on Savile Row, famous for its custom clothiers. Jake wore safari pants and a long-sleeved shirt, both khaki in color, along with a vest (with pockets everywhere, some zippered, some buttoned, some pockets inside other pockets). He also had a pair of hiking boots made of waterproof GORE-TEX and a matching backpack. They'd wanted him to wear a safari hat, too, but he refused.

Kady loved the hat. It sat jauntily on her head. More cameras flashed. She tilted on a hip and coyly twined a finger in one of her hat's ties.

Jake rolled his eyes and continued toward the museum.

The shouts and calls became a wordless blur. He just wanted to get inside, away from all the commotion. Bledsworth Sundries and Industries, along with the museum, had organized a media blitz: newspapers, television, even posters on the sides of buses and subways. All to promote the exhibit. The story of the disappearance of Jake's parents had been big news when it had first occurred, a story of gold and bandits and murdered archaeologists. The papers pumped it up again. Everyone had soon learned of the orphaned Ransoms. And now to have the kids here, for the opening of the exhibit, had brought out everyone with a camera.

Morgan Drummond kept close to Jake's shoulders and

encouraged Kady to keep moving with the flat of his hand at her back. His voice boomed to the crowd. "We're running late! There'll be time for more photos after the event!"

Murmurs of disappointment dogged their steps.

But Jake noted how Drummond glanced to one member of the audience, fixing him with a stare. At the ropes stood a toad of a man, squat and dressed all in green, munching on a doughnut. His eyes were buried under bushy eyebrows. His lips were puffy and dusted with powdered sugar. He also had a camera around his neck, but it just hung loose. He didn't bother raising it as they passed.

He only gave the smallest nod toward Drummond, who hurried them faster.

At long last, Jake and Kady crossed under the banner and into the museum's interior. Apart from the guards in blue uniforms, the lobby was deliciously empty. Kady glanced outside with a longing look.

"There's a ribbon-cutting ceremony in the Queen Elizabeth Court," Morgan Drummond said as he led them past a gift shop and across the polished marble floor.

"Will there be more cameras?" Kady asked, flipping open her compact mirror with the skill of a knife thrower.

"Just the television news and the London *Times*," Drummond said. "The museum is hosting an exclusive event, limited to the largest contributors. And even they had to pay a hefty fee to attend the ribbon cutting."

"Does your company get a cut from that extra fee?"

Drummond frowned down at Jake as if he had asked a rudely stupid question. "Of course we do. We'll have to collect a small fortune just to break even on this exhibit." A certain huffiness entered his voice. "Why do you think you two were invited here? It's not dusty artifacts that draw a good crowd. Stories get people in the door. Like your . . . well, the tragedy surrounding . . ." The large man suddenly seemed to realize to whom he was talking. He became a tad tongue-tied. He had the decency to blush around his collar and rub at his neck.

Jake's own face heated up, but not with embarrassment. One hand balled up into a fist as the full realization struck him. The invitation to come here wasn't to publicize and celebrate their parents' achievements, but to take *advantage* of their tragedy: to turn their loss into cold, hard cash for Bledsworth Sundries and Industries. Jake suddenly felt both foolish and angry. He and his sister had been flown all the way to London to dance like puppets for the crowd, to sell more tickets.

Kady seemed unfazed by the revelation. She pranced onward, eager for the next dazzle of flashbulbs and attention.

"Through here," Drummond said, and held a door for them.

As Jake stepped through, an amazing sight opened. A giant inner atrium stretched a full two acres, all paved in marble.

"The Great Court," Drummond declared. He reached into a pocket and handed out glasses with black lenses. "Eclipse goggles. You'd better wear these."

As Jake put on the goggles, he continued across the floor. The wings of the museum surrounded the vast courtyard on all four sides. Sweeping staircases led up to other levels. But what truly captured Jake's attention was the roof that enclosed the courtyard itself. It was composed of triangular sections of clear glass that seemed to float above their heads, weightless and bright with sunlight.

Jake craned his neck and stared up through the glass roof.

The tinted goggles allowed him to stare into the full face of the eclipse without fear of being blinded. Already the moon half covered the sun. The total eclipse was not far off.

Thunder rumbled. Jake turned and looked to the south. The front edge of the storm rolled into view.

Would it hold off long enough?

4

THE BLACK SUN

In a hidden corner of the museum courtyard, Jake leaned against a giant stone head from Easter Island. The statue's heavy brow and sharp nose had been carved from black basalt. Jake matched its stern expression as he spied on the audience.

Dressed in tuxedos and party dresses, the guests carried glasses of champagne. A waiter with a silver tray passed among them with caviar on toast points. One woman sported a diamond tiara on a tall pile of white hair. Was she royalty?

Off to one side, Kady basked within a television camera's spotlight. A reporter held a furry microphone toward her nose.

"So tell the viewers of BBC One," the reporter asked, "are you excited to visit the exhibit?"

"Oh, certainly," Kady answered, and turned slightly. Jake knew she was trying to highlight her best side, or at least that was the side she'd decided this morning was her best for television.

His sister continued her interview with much waving of her hands. She made sure she bounced on her toes a bit to get just the right flounce from her well-groomed curls.

Jake crossed his arms. Morgan Drummond's revelation about the true purpose of their attendance here still irked him. *Just to sell more tickets.* He unfolded his arms and tugged at the safari vest. He was tempted to rip it off and storm out of here. But then what? And he still had to consider his sister. Kady clearly wasn't going anywhere.

Jake turned in the opposite direction. Beyond the crowd, he spotted a thick red ribbon across the top of a stairway that led to the second level. A man in a top hat held an oversized set of scissors that looked like garden shears.

"The museum curator," Morgan Drummond said at Jake's elbow, startling him. The large man had crept up behind him. "It won't be much longer. It'll be over before you know it."

Though the words were whispered, they sounded vaguely like a threat. Maybe because they were accompanied by another rumble of thunder.

Jake shrugged and moved out of Drummond's shadow. He stared up toward the sky again. The moon was almost completely in front of the sun. Even with his goggles, the sun's corona around the edge of the moon blazed and made his eyes ache.

Jake blinked and turned as a bell chimed, starting the official event. *Finally!* He felt his heart thump harder. All eyes were drawn forward as the museum curator held up an arm to silence the murmur in the crowd.

The camera lights, shining on Kady, were suddenly extinguished. She sagged as if she were a plant shut out from the sun.

"Here we go," Drummond said.

The curator lifted his scissors. "If we could have the Ransom children up here with me!" he called out. "It is only appropriate that they be here for this auspicious occasion. In honor of their parents, Drs. Richard and Penelope Ransom."

Morgan Drummond pulled Jake out of hiding and into the limelight. They collected Kady on the way to the stairs.

A smattering of applause encouraged them up the steps.

The curator continued, "I'm sure everyone knows the story of the Ransoms, how they discovered the Mountain of Bones, one of the most remote and inhospitable Mayan archaeological sites. Surmounting all manner of obstacles—from man-eating jaguars to malaria-bearing mosquitoes—they explored a magnificent tomb full of relics priceless to history and to our understanding of the ancient Maya. The British Museum, along with the generous and philanthropic support of Bledsworth Sundries and Industries"—the curator nodded to Drummond as he climbed the stairs with Jake and Kady— "are proud to present in public for the first time the *MAYAN TREASURES OF THE NEW WORLD!*"

Another burst of thunder followed his pronouncement.

As Jake and Kady reached the top of the stairs, the curator pointed to the skies and yelled, "Behold!"

All the lights were turned off in the courtyard.

Jake gaped upward. It was happening!

The moon moved an imperceptible amount and fully covered the sun. The eclipse had gone total. The sun's corona shot dazzling rays around the darkened moon, as if a black sun blazed in the heavens.

Jake held his breath in wonder.

Under the glow of the eclipse, the room dimmed to an eerie twilight. The courtyard's marble surfaces took on a silvery sheen, as if the floors and walls glowed with an inner light.

The curator spoke into the darkness. "The Maya themselves predicted this eclipse through their ancient astronomical studies and calculations. We chose this celestial moment to open the exhibit." He turned with his giant shears. "Mr. Ransom, would you like to help me?"

A spotlight flared and flooded the top of the steps.

Jake tore his gaze from the skies and down to the red ribbon. He knew the hallway to his parents' treasures lay beyond this thin ribbon. He nodded, anxious to move on. "Let's do it."

The curator grinned and held up a hand, signaling Jake to wait stiffly as cameras flashed below. Kady stood with her arms crossed tightly across her chest. Jake knew he would pay later for stealing her attention now.

Like he had any choice.

Jake grasped one half of the scissors and together with the curator cut the ribbon with one swift snap.

As the shears closed and the ribbon fell away, a blinding crackle of lightning shattered across the sky. Thunder immediately boomed. The roof overhead rattled with the close impact. The audience was struck into a frightened silence—then patters of soft laughter followed.

The curator winked at Jake. "Well, we couldn't have timed that any better, could we, lad?" He took the shears and straightened.

Jake turned to stare up at the sky. Storm clouds rolled over the view of the eclipse and blotted it out. A deeper twilight swallowed the courtyard.

The curator lifted an arm toward the audience. "Everyone stay where you are. We'll get the lights back up in the courtyard in a moment. While we wait, maybe it's best we let the Ransom children enter the exhibit first, to have a private moment among the treasures that their parents discovered."

Murmured *Ahs* and *How touchings* flowed up from the

audience, along with some soft clapping.

One voice, though, rose above the others, full of scorn. *"The treasures their parents discovered?* Bah! More like *stole!"* The last word cracked across the courtyard like a rifle shot.

Stunned silence followed.

The man continued, "What about the rumors that the Ransoms are still alive in South America! That they staged their vanishing so they could abscond with the most valuable of the treasures!"

Jake's heart climbed to his throat. His cheeks burned with anger.

"Hear, hear," said the curator. "We'll have none of these foul aspersions—"

He was cut off with a bellow. "Richard and Penelope Ransom are nothing more than right common thieves, I tell you!"

Lights flickered back on in the courtyard.

Jake took off his eclipse goggles and picked out the man in the crowd. It was the toadish reporter from outside, the one who had been eating a doughnut.

Jake took a step forward, ready to leap down and make the man take back his words—but a large palm stopped him and pushed him up onto the second-floor landing.

Morgan Drummond gently shoved Kady after him. "No need for you to hear this ugliness. Go on into the exhibit."

Behind him, the curator called for security. The exhibit's guards ran past Jake and Kady and pounded down the stairs.

Still, he raved on. *"Thieves! Charlatans! Blood is on the Ransoms' hands!"*

Each utterance was a knife to Jake's heart.

Drummond gave him a push. "Go. I'll join you in a bit."

Kady glanced at him. Her eyes were wide, stunned, scared. "Jake . . ."

He had to get her away. "Let's get going."

They hurried into the room across the landing. Jake stumbled along, half blind with anger. He was well into the exhibit before his brain finally registered the wonders around him.

He stopped. Kady did, too.

"It's Mom and Dad," Kady said.

They had both halted in front of a giant poster. It was the same as the picture Jake had in his notebook. Their parents smiled goofily into the camera, dressed in muddy khakis and bearing aloft a block with Mayan carvings on it.

Behind him, shouts still echoed from the courtyard.

More lies about his folks.

Jake stared up into the faces, blown up to life size. It was too much. He turned away. A particularly loud bellow reached him.

"Murderers and thieves!"

At that moment, Jake remembered something: how the toadish man had nodded to Morgan Drummond as they had entered the museum.

It was as if the two had known each other.

The nod.

Like it had been some planned signal.

Jake remembered Drummond's earlier revelation. Could this outburst be just another way to whip up more publicity for the show, to create some controversy around the exhibit, to sell more tickets?

Or was it something more sinister?

For another three minutes, Jake wandered through the exhibit, lost in his thoughts. Kady also circled the room. She kept her arms hugged tightly around her chest, as if fearful of touching anything. They moved through the room in separate orbits, like two planets that dared not cross paths.

As Jake walked in the room, his worries began to fade. Wonder cooled the heated pounding of his heart. All around he spotted artifacts and relics as sketched or described in his parents' books, like the double-headed snake from the brochure. In person, the strange serpent was even more dazzling, brightly lit under halogen lights. The snake's eyes were rubies. The scales were carved with great detail into the gold. The fangs were made of slivers of ivory or perhaps bone.

Jake reached into his vest and pulled out his father's field logbook and his mother's leather-bound sketchbook. He had wanted both books with him when he visited the museum. He opened his father's log and read the entry for the double-headed snake.

Clearly from the intricate curling of the serpent into a figure eight, the relic must represent the Mayan belief in the eternal nature of the cosmos. From the craftsmanship, the work must represent the high Classic period. I can only imagine . . .

Jake read onward, hearing his father's voice in his head as he continued through the exhibit, stopping in front of each object. As he wandered, each piece brought him closer to his parents. Had his mother polished the silver jaguar over there? Had his father counted the number of circles, like tree rings, that made up the Mayan calendar wheel?

Jake remembered lessons taught to him as a young boy . . . by his mother, by his father. And not just about archaeology. He remembered his mother teaching him how to tie his shoelaces.

The rabbit dives into the lace hole and pops back out. . . .

He found his feet slowing. Though he was thousands of miles away from Ravensgate Manor, Jake felt a closeness, an intimacy here, like he had discovered a long-lost room in his home.

"How long do you think we have to stay in here?" Kady finally asked with her usual ring of exaggerated impatience.

Jake turned to the door. The commotion had died down out in the courtyard, but voices still murmured, too low to make out words. Thunder still rumbled. Unlike his sister, Jake was in no hurry to leave. A twinge of possessiveness fired through him. He didn't want anyone else in here. It would be like someone trespassing into his heart. In fact, he barely tolerated his sister's presence.

He needed to see the exhibit's centerpiece.

Free of any glass case, it rested open on a pedestal: a two-foot-tall pyramid made of solid gold. It climbed in nine steps to a flat summit, where a dragon with outstretched wings crouched atop it. The dragon had been carved from a large chunk of jade. Its eyes, two fiery opals, seemed to stare straight into Jake's heart.

"Kukulkan," he mumbled, naming the feathered dragon god of the Maya.

Jake recognized this object, too. According to his father's field log, the priceless relic had been found atop the lid of a limestone sarcophagus. Jake tucked away his father's logbook and opened his mother's sketchbook. Flipping through the sketches, he searched for the match to the pyramid.

From halfway across the room, Kady finally spotted what he held in his hands. She stalked over to him. "Jake! What are you doing with that here?"

She hadn't known he had brought their parents' books to London.

No one did.

Ignoring his sister, Jake found the right page. He compared the sketch of the pyramid to the original. He studied his mother's precise pencil drawings, the eraser marks, the corrections, the tiny notes scrawled in the margins. They were pieces of his mother. And here was her inspiration.

Jake's sight blurred with tears, and his hands shook.

Before he could drop the book, Kady snatched it out of his hands. "Why did you bring it here?" she scolded. "You could have lost it or had it stolen."

"Like you would have cared." He moved closer to the pyramid.

She pushed next to him and grabbed his elbow. "What do you mean by that?"

He tugged his elbow loose and glared at her. "You didn't even want to come here!" Jake found his voice choking and that only made him even madder. "The only reason you came was to pose for some stupid cameras!"

Kady's face flushed angrily. "You don't know—"

Jake reached and yanked the sketchbook back out of her hands. "So what if I lost Mom's book? You haven't looked at it for years."

Kady grabbed for him, but he danced back and kept out of reach.

Jake circled to the far side of the pyramid. "Don't you even care about Mom and Dad anymore?"

Kady stood on her side of the pyramid. Her shoulders trembled, and her face had turned crimson. "Of course I care!" she shouted and waved her arm around the room. "Do you think all of this—*any* of this—is going to bring Mom and Dad back?"

The raw pain in her voice silenced him. He had never heard that tone in her voice. It scared him.

She continued, "All this! Mom's sketchbook, these treasures—to see them, to be near them—all it does is *hurt*." She turned her back on the pyramid. "So why look? What good does it do?"

Jake's eyes widened.

She shook her head. "I can't stand it. Even you!"

"What about me?" Jake asked, wounded.

She swung toward him again. "Why don't you cut your hair like everyone else?"

Jake fingered the hair from his eyes, confused.

"You look *so* much like Dad that I can hardly stand to look at you."

He remembered her earlier words. *All it does is hurt.*

She sniffed and turned her back on him. "Some-times . . . sometimes I wish you were never—"

A sudden flash filled the room accompanied by a cracking *boom.*

The floor jumped underfoot, and frightened screams echoed from the courtyard. Jake and Kady both turned toward the courtyard and stepped closer to one another. The overhead lights flickered and died.

Blackness swallowed the room.

"What happened?" Kady whispered in the darkness a moment later.

Jake offered a guess. "Lightning strike. Must have hit the museum."

As their eyes adjusted to the sudden darkness, Jake noted a soft glow—coming from behind them. He turned and let out a surprised squeak.

"What is it?" Kady gasped.

Jake fumbled, grabbed Kady's elbow, and turned her around. "Look!"

A soft blue fire now bathed the pyramid. The flames

danced at the feet of the dragon and spilled down the nine steps. Jake stared with his mouth hanging open. It took him a full breath to realize he had seen a similar display at a science museum.

"Saint Elmo's fire," he said with awe. "Sailing ships used to see such ghostly flames along their masts during thunderstorms."

"But what's causing it?"

Jake stepped closer.

"Be careful," Kady warned, but still she followed him.

Jake felt the hairs on his neck stand on end. "Don't worry. It looks like it's already dying down."

Like an ebbing tide, the fire receded, swimming and swirling away. Jake circled the pyramid and noted something strange.

"Come see this," he said, and pointed.

The flames weren't so much going out as they seemed to be draining down a round hole in the pyramid's side. Curious, Jake bent closer. A curl of the stone dragon's tail circled the hole. But the hole wasn't really a hole. It was more of a shallow indentation in the gold surface— as if some jewel might have rested there but was now missing.

The flames vanished away just as the red emergency lights kicked in and cast the room in a ruby glow.

Jake straightened.

Strange . . .

Curious, he flipped open his mother's sketchbook and

found the page with the pyramid's sketch. In the weak light, he spotted the same hole portrayed on the drawing. It was just as blank.

"Nothing's here," he mumbled, and tapped the spot.

Kady leaned over him. "At least not any longer." She reached out and felt the paper. "Look at how it's smeared. I can still feel a faint impression in the paper. Something was once drawn here."

"You think it was erased?"

Kady nodded. "Whoever did it, they did it in a hurry."

"Mom?"

"I don't know."

Jake lowered the sketchbook and stared at the gold pyramid. *Why would their mother draw something, then erase it?*

He cocked his head and studied the hole.

It was perfectly round, about the size of a—

Jake slapped himself on the forehead.

"Of course . . ." he mumbled.

"What?"

Jake didn't answer. He closed the sketchbook and tucked it back away. He remembered another of his father's lessons.

Never assume something—that's bad science—always test, then retest.

Jake reached to his neck, slipped the braided cord over his head, and pulled free his half of the gold Mayan coin.

He held it up toward the pyramid. It seemed the same size as the hole.

Always test . . .

Jake stepped closer and reached out with his coin.

"What are you doing?" Kady whined in fear.

Ignoring her, he placed his coin in the hole. It seemed to be a perfect fit—but he had to be sure.

. . . then retest.

Still holding his half in place, he turned to Kady. "Try yours."

Jake knew she had her coin, but she shook her head.

"Kady! Mom and Dad must've sent us the broken coin for a reason. Don't you want to know why? This might be the first clue."

She hesitated. Jake saw the fear in her eyes . . . and maybe pain.

Still, she slowly reached under her hair at the back of her neck. She unclasped the fine gold chain that bore her half of the coin. She shifted next to Jake, shoulder to shoulder.

She shook her coin off its chain and held it up.

"If I get a shock from this . . ." Kady warned, but her voice also held a hint of excitement.

"Just see if it fits."

She lifted her coin, but as she reached for the pyramid, a shout boomed across the marble hall like a blast from an elephant gun. Jake turned and spotted Drummond running straight at them.

"DON'T TOUCH—"

Jake couldn't explain why he did what he did next. It was some instinct buried deep in his heart. Ignoring Drummond, Jake turned and grabbed Kady's hand. She had frozen in place with the sudden shout. Jake shoved her half of the Mayan coin toward the pyramid's hole. It snugged neatly in place next to his.

A perfect fit.

The re-formed coin suddenly glowed brightly, highlighting the joined Mayan glyphs in the center.

Jake mouthed the words represented by the two symbols: "*sak be.*"

They translated to "white road."

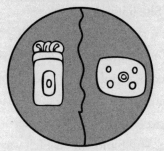

"NO!" Drummond shouted. The man tried to yell something else. It sounded like a warning, but his words were drowned in another shattering crack of thunder.

Blinding and booming, the explosion blew away the emergency lights.

Before Jake could react, the world fell out from under him. Blood rushed to his head as if he were plummeting down a well. Stars danced across his vision. A roaring filled his ears. Then even the stars vanished, and darkness somehow got *darker* again.

Still, he held Kady's hand. It seemed his only connection to anything solid and real. His fingers tightened on hers. The moment stretched.

Though still blind, Jake sensed they weren't alone in the blackness. The tiny hairs on the back of his neck stood on end. He knew something was staring at him out of that darkness.

Then it began to move toward them.

He saw nothing, but he sensed it like a pressure building in his head as it got closer. Kady's fingers squeezed harder on his. She felt it, too.

A few words scraped into his mind, like fingernails digging at the lid of a stone coffin. *"Come to me . . ."*

Jake pictured skeletal fingers reaching through the darkness. Before those fingers could reach him, something dove between Jake and the lurker in the dark, as if protecting him. Still blind, all Jake felt was a rush of wind, as if something with wings had swept between them.

As it passed, Jake tumbled, and the blackness shredded to scraps around him. The world returned in a kaleidoscope of color and sound. He caught a flash of emerald green, heard the screech of a strange bird. Then the world righted itself. With a heavy sinking in his gut, Jake's knees caught his weight though he hadn't truly fallen anywhere.

Or maybe he had.

Jake crouched next to Kady in deep grass. The two halves of the gold coin clinked together as they dropped to his toes. He snatched them up. His other hand still held tight to his sister. Something he hadn't done since he was six years old.

The world had indeed returned—but not the same world of a moment ago.

PART TWO

5

LAND OF THE LOST

Jake straightened next to Kady. He sucked air deep into his chest. With the one breath he knew something was dreadfully wrong. The air was too thick, too steamy to be London. And it smelled of mud and rotting plants.

He pocketed the two halves of the gold coin and stared around him. Leafy ferns the size of beach umbrellas spread all around. Towering trees rose from massive tangles of roots, like the knobby knees of giants. Overhead, branches wove a dense emerald canopy.

Jake shook his head, trying to clear the illusion.

It didn't go away.

Had he and Kady been knocked out? Gassed? Kidnapped and dragged off to some jungle?

Insects whirred in a rasping chorus.

"What did you do?" Kady asked.

He glanced hard at her. "*What did I do?* What are you talking about? I didn't—"

She cut him off, deaf to his words. "What happened? Where are we?"

From the fear in her voice, Jake knew she was struggling to understand as much as he was.

He craned upward. Sunlight poured through the occasional cracks in the dense canopy. A wider gap overhead revealed the sun. The moon rested next to it, like the sun's dark shadow. As Jake stared, the moon slipped clear of the sun's face. An eclipse was ending. But was it the same eclipse that had started in London? It had to be. Another was not due for seven years.

But if this was the same eclipse, then no time had passed.

Is that possible?

As he stared at the sun and moon, something glided across the gap in the canopy. It stretched wide with leathery wings—then vanished before Jake could get a good look at it.

Despite the heat, Jake felt his blood go cold.

Something brushed his cheek. A flying beetle had landed on a frond of a fern in front of him. It was as large as his palm and was fronted by a wicked pair of pincing hooks. It clacked at him, then spread its iridescent green shell with a blur of flapping wings and took flight.

Jake ducked and stumbled back a step in shock. His foot sank into the muck of a small creek flowing through the meadow. He stared down as something scurried away from his toe. It was flat like a crab, but its oval body was segmented into ridged plates.

No way . . .

Dropping to a knee at the bank of the creek, Jake shrugged off his pack and picked open a pocket. He reached for an object he had stashed there.

"What are you doing?" Kady asked sharply.

Jake pulled free the trilobite fossil he had dug out of the rock quarry behind the house. He held it over the creature in the creek. It was an exact match—only the one in the water wasn't stone. The creature scuttled away and disappeared under a rock.

Jake stood up. "It's . . . it's . . ." He had to force the words past his disbelief. "It's a *living* trilobite!"

Kady was not impressed. She waved his response away as if it smelled bad. "What is going on?" she asked again with more force. She even stamped her foot. She wanted an answer. Now.

She got one.

A trumpeting roar.

Jake and Kady bumped against one another in shock. A second roar shook the leaves and sprinkled Jake with dew-drops. Off to the left, trees and saplings began to snap and fall. Underfoot, the ground trembled. Something massive pounded their way.

Jake squeezed Kady's hand.

Before they could take another breath, a boy and a girl

burst out of the underbrush. They raced straight toward Jake and Kady. The girl, her dark hair flying behind her like a pair of raven's wings, was in the lead. She half dragged a taller boy along with her. He struggled with a long spear that kept getting snagged in the bushes and branches.

"Oh, just drop it!" she yelled.

"My father's spear? I would rather die!"

"More like your father would kill you if he ever found out you lost it!"

A louder bellow roared out of the jungle. The ground trembled.

The pair raced faster.

It was only when they were a couple yards away that one of them finally noted Jake and Kady. The girl stumbled aside in surprise, then leaped past them like a fleet-footed deer. She wore a loose embroidered shirt and a long skirt tied at the waist and slit to mid thigh. Her eyes flashed a brilliant emerald, matching a jade necklace that bounced around her neck.

"Run!" she shouted back at them.

The boy pounded after her, eyeing Jake up and down with a stern frown as he passed. Gangly and long-necked, he was dressed in a grass-stained white toga with a leather belt, along with leather sandals strapped to mid calf. Another strap of corded leather tied back his curly, mud brown hair. He held his spear over his head as he ran.

Frozen in place, Jake stared after the strange pair.

Kady shoved Jake. "Do what she said! Run!"

Jake didn't argue. Together, they fled after the other two kids.

An earth-shattering crack erupted behind them, accompanied by a screech of rage. Jake glanced over his shoulder. A thick branch from one of the giant trees broke away and crashed to the ground.

A giant head shoved a hole in the canopy. It was the size of a refrigerator. Its scaly skin steamed, its shark black eyes rolled, and its muzzle split wide with a roar. Razor-sharp teeth, like rows of yellowed daggers, gnashed and tore at the smaller branches.

Jake recognized the beast.

It was a carnivore that sat at the top of the food chain.

Millions of years ago.

Impossible . . .

"A tyrannosaurus," Jake gasped out.

Looking back, he tripped on a root and went down on one knee.

Kady yanked him back up.

Behind them, the creature shook its thick head and bulldozed between two of the giant trees. More branches snapped. It was almost free.

"Hurry!" the strange girl shouted.

How could he understand her? Was this all a dream?

Ahead, the far side of the glade rose up into a jungle-shrouded cliff. It blocked the way. They would never be able to climb the cliff fast enough to escape the T-rex.

The girl seemed to read his thoughts. "We'll never make it! Need to hide! This way!"

She veered off to the left and they followed. At the foot of a cliff was a tumbled nest of massive boulders. The girl aimed for them.

Another bellow chased them, followed by a shattering of branches. Jake risked another glance—maybe he shouldn't have.

The T-rex heaved into the open glade. It shook its muscled frame. A thick tail whipped out and axed through some saplings and beheaded giant ferns. Scaly nostrils huffed, scenting the air. It cocked its head from one side to the other, like a bird searching for prey.

Despite his terror, Jake remembered an article he'd read about how birds were modern-day descendants of dinosaurs. But this T-rex was no clucking chicken. The beast was twenty feet tall.

Those black eyes found Jake. It froze, head still cocked, one eye fixed to its escaping prey.

"Run faster!" Jake yelled.

The T-rex leaped after them. It pounded, seven tons of muscle shaking the ground, gaining speed.

The girl reached the piled boulders first. She searched for a gap in them, some way to crawl to safety. Jake and

Kady reached her, along with the other boy.

"Over here!" the girl called out.

She dropped to her hands and knees and crawled into a gap between two of the boulders. "It widens!" she echoed back with relief.

Jake nudged Kady toward the hole. "Go."

He made her head in first, but he kept tight to her heels. The boy in the toga followed last. He climbed in backward and kept his spear pointed toward the opening.

Jake discovered the girl was right. Behind the boulder, a small cave was formed by slabs of broken rock. Though it was a cramped squeeze, it held the four of them.

Just as Jake started to sit, their temporary shelter shook. The T-rex had slammed into the rock pile. Dust drifted down along with a scatter of pebbles. Jake stared up. He pictured the stack of stones overhead and cringed lower.

A huffing breath washed over them. It smelled like rotten eggs. The T-rex snuffled after its prey. Jake leaned down to stare out the tunnel.

"Stay back," Kady warned.

All Jake could see was a pair of tree-trunk-sized legs. Massive claws clenched and sank deep into the ground. One leg kicked back and threw aside a thick clot of mud and rock, leaving a deep gouge in the forest floor.

Jake lay shoulder to shoulder with the other boy. His companion kept a grip on his spear, but the weapon wasn't long enough to reach the tunnel's end. Their eyes met. They sized each other up. The boy seemed about his age.

"My name's Jake," he offered as introduction, not knowing if he'd be understood. He didn't know what else to say. What was proper etiquette when hiding in a hole with a stranger while a T-rex outside wanted to eat you?

"Pindor," the boy replied. "Pindor Tiberius, second son to Elder Marcellus Tiberius." Jake heard a note of shame in his voice. "And that's Mari." Pindor pointed a thumb behind him.

"Marika," the girl corrected.

"Who cares who you all are!" Kady blurted out. "What the heck is going on?" Her exasperation and anger made her move too quickly. Her head hit the rocky roof of their cave. "Ow."

Before anyone could answer, the T-rex began to kick and claw again. It ripped more gouges, like a chicken digging for worms. But the four of them were the worms. The T-rex slashed at the entrance to the tunnel.

If it didn't stop, the beast could bring the whole place crashing down on them. Jake glanced around. There was no other exit. They were trapped.

He stared out again. Why was the T-rex so determined? There had to be easier prey.

The explanation came from Marika.

"You shouldn't have tried to steal her egg," she accused her friend.

Pindor twisted around. "I would've gotten it if *you* hadn't stepped on that broken shell and made so much noise."

Jake sighed. So the T-rex was a female, a mother guarding her nest. *No wonder . . .*

The beast suddenly slammed again into the rock face and rattled their shelter. Somewhere overhead, a boulder crashed. They all held their breaths—but their shelter held.

Only for how much longer?

From behind, Kady poked Pindor in the back of his leg. "You have a spear. Go out there and drive it away."

The boy's face blanched. He turned aside and mumbled under his breath. "It wouldn't do any good."

"He's right," Marika said. "One spear is not enough. Not against such a creature."

Still, Jake noted how Pindor's fingers tightened on his spear—to stop the trembling in his hands.

"We'll have to hope she goes away on her own," Marika said with little conviction.

Kady swung around, as if putting her back to the matter would make it all go away. It was how she faced anything beyond her control. By denying it existed. Out of sight, out of mind.

He remembered her heated words back at the museum. About their mother and father. She seemed to find it easier to bottle the hurt away, to deny it, to turn her back on it all.

Jake refused to do that.

What would his parents do in this situation?

He struggled for a long breath and came to one firm conclusion.

He had no idea.

The T-rex struck the rocks again with its shoulder. Another boulder came crashing down outside and bounced across the forest floor. Startled, the T-rex grumbled at the stray boulder—then returned its attention to its buried prey.

Claws began to dig.

Jake backed away and bumped into Kady. She pulled him closer. "This has gotta be a dream, right?" she asked.

He had wondered the same thing. But from the fear in her eyes, she didn't believe it. Neither did Jake. This was all real.

"What are we going to do?" she asked.

With his eyes accustomed to the dimness, Jake spotted movement at Kady's shoulder. Dangling from her vest pocket were the earbuds from her iPod. As the buds bobbled and swayed, Jake stared for a second, half hypnotized. An idea struggled through his panic.

Something . . .

Hadn't he read . . .

High ranges of pitch . . .

"Watson!" he suddenly yelled out.

Kady jumped and struck the crown of her head on the rooftop again. "Ow . . . Jake, you idiot . . ."

Jake twisted around to his new backpack, khaki colored to match his clothes, and fumbled it open. He searched inside. Back at the hotel, he had simply dumped all the stuff from his old backpack into the new one. He should have spent more time organizing it.

The T-rex roared.

At last, Jake's fingers blindly found what he was searching for. He pulled it out and scooted next to Pindor by the entrance.

"What are you planning?" the boy asked. "Do you have a weapon?"

Jake lifted the dog whistle up. "I hope so."

The T-rex filled the world outside the cave. One claw lifted to attack the boulder pile again.

Jake took a deep breath and brought the whistle to his lips. With all the strength in his chest, he blew as hard as he could. No noise came out, but Jake knew the effect the whistle had on his basset hound at home. Watson could hear it from a mile away.

As he blew, the T-rex lowered its raised claw and backed a step away—then another. It shook its head, plainly bothered.

Out of breath, Jake had to stop and suck in more air.

The T-rex lowered its muzzle and bellowed.

Jake's hair blew back from his forehead. The T-rex's

breath reeked worse than a gym locker.

"What are you doing?" Kady said, and tried to pull Jake away. "You're just making it more angry."

Jake shook her off. "That's the point!"

Turning back to the entrance, Jake blew the whistle again. The T-rex shook its head and began to wobble on its feet.

"What's happening?" Kady asked.

"The skulls of T-rexes," Jake explained, sucking in another breath. "At least, their fossils . . . show they have giant tympanic cavities."

Kady frowned at him. "In English, Einstein."

"They have big ears!" he gasped out. "So high pitches are magnified to them. Dog whistles should be excruciating."

Bringing the steel whistle to his lips, Jake blew with all the strength he could muster. It felt like his head was going to explode.

At last, the giant carnivore swung around with a heavy sweep of its tail. It pounded away with a final roar over its shoulder—then dove back into the jungle.

They waited to be sure.

Marika finally spoke. "I think she'll head back to her nest now!"

Just in case she was wrong, Jake kept the whistle in his hand.

"Is it safe to leave?" Kady asked Marika.

The girl shrugged and stared at Jake's hand. "A silent flute that scares away thunder lizards. You bear powerful alchemies."

With the immediate danger over, questions flooded Jake's mind. They jumbled together. What was this place? How were humans and dinosaurs living together? How did Jake and Kady get here?

Before he could settle on a single question to ask, Marika said, "We should go now. All the noise might attract other creatures."

Pindor shoved forward with his spear. "Let me go first," he said glumly. "In case there are more beasts about."

But the boy's look betrayed him. He would not meet Jake's eye. After the demonstration here, Pindor plainly wanted some distance from these strangers. Suspicion pinched his face.

Pindor's companion was not as wary. After they climbed out of the cave, Marika's gaze locked on Jake for a moment. Sunlight flashed from her eyes with an emerald fire, revealing a mix of curiosity and amusement.

She pointed an arm up toward the neighboring cliff. "There's a path up that way. We must get past the Broken Gate. Then we'll be safe."

Safe?

Jake glanced back toward the dark jungle as it resumed its squawking and buzzing chorus. Just as he suspected, no place was truly safe in this new world. A saurian bellow echoed out of the deep jungle.

Jake shivered, suddenly remembering the darkness that had brought them here. And the words that had scratched out of the blackness between their world and this one.

Come to me...

6

BROKEN GATE

Jake climbed the narrow trail that headed up the cliff in a series of steep switchbacks. Marika led the way. Pindor guarded their rear and urged them to move silently so they wouldn't attract other monsters. They hiked quickly. The pace had left little time for questions.

Still, Jake managed to get a closer look at Marika's jade necklace. It was carved with a symbol.

There was no mistaking it. It was definitely Mayan. The glyph's name, *balam*, meant "jaguar." The symbol even looked like the jungle cat. Marika also wore an embroidered Mayan blouse, like one Jake's mother once brought home from Central America. Even the girl's skin was the same shade as his mother's morning tea, mixed with a generous dollop of cream.

Could she truly be Maya?

And what about Pindor? Jake managed a closer look at the cut of his sandals and the bronze work of his spearhead. It was all of Roman design, possibly second century B.C. Even his hair, tied long in back, had bangs cut straight across the front like some caesar out of time.

Maya, Romans, and T-rexes.

What was going on?

After another two turns in the trail, the top of the cliff appeared high overhead. A narrow pass cut through two massive guard towers built out of dark stones, each ten stories high. An archway once bridged the two towers, but it had fallen away, leaving only stumped ends. The spires appeared long deserted.

"The Broken Gate," Marika said.

As they climbed toward the pass, Jake noted the pocked and blood-dark color of the gate's bricks. *Volcanic stone.*

Marika stopped ahead of him, so suddenly that Jake bumped into her. An eerie screech split the continual droning whir of insects. It came from the sky, sounding like a rabbit being strangled. Marika twisted around, her eyes wide with raw terror, more terror than she'd showed with T-rex.

Jake turned, too, and Pindor and Kady halted. High in

the sky, a large creature drifted on leathery wings. At first glance, Jake thought it might be a pterodactyl, another saurian hunter like the tyrannosaurus. But as he squinted, he recognized his mistake. The wings were attached to a gaunt creature that appeared to be just leather over bone. As it swept past, Jake spotted arms and legs and a bald domed head ridged by a hard crest.

Jake's whole body shuddered, sensing the unnaturalness of this creature. Yet, at the same time, it reminded him of something—something he'd seen before.

"A grakyl!" Marika's voice rang with disbelief and horror. Her gaze ripped from the skies and fixed on Jake. For the first time, he read suspicion in her open face. Then it was gone, hardening into concern. "Make for the gate! It's our only chance!"

Marika set off as another screech split the sky.

Jake followed, but he kept watch. Overhead, the creature turned on a wing tip. Jake sensed its cold gaze upon them. With another cry, its wings tucked and it tilted into a dive. They'd been spotted.

Marika sprinted up the rocky trail toward the pass. The stone towers waited. Jake chased after her, followed at his heels by Pindor and Kady.

As they neared the towers, Jake's skin began to prickle, as if a thousand spiders were dancing over his flesh. With each new step, the feeling grew more intense. The prickling began to burn. Confused, Jake stumbled on a loose rock.

"Mari!" Pindor called ahead.

The Mayan girl glanced back and saw Jake stumble. She reached and grabbed his wrist. The burning sensation snuffed out with her touch, though Jake still felt a strange electricity and pressure in the air.

He allowed himself to be dragged up to the Broken Gate and into the shadow of the towers. Marika hauled him another few steps, and the pressure popped away. He turned and saw Pindor had a grip on his sister's elbow as they dove together through the gate.

The winged creature swooped down with a shriek, diving under the broken archway. Jake ducked, but the creature slammed to a halt. It writhed in midair, fixed in the archway like a living insect pinned to a board. Spatters of lightning coursed over its body. Some kind of field seemed to restrain it.

Jake fell back, getting a good look at the creature. Thrashing limbs ended in claws. Razored spurs decorated knee and elbow. But its face was the worst of all—not because it was monstrous with its porcine nose and fanged maw, but because it was *too* human. Jake read the intelligence in its agonized eyes. That gaze focused on him, intently, as if recognizing him.

Then with a final screeching cry, the grakyl battered back against the force that held it trapped. It twisted away from the Broken Gate, wings beating desperately. Once well enough away, it finally seemed to catch a bit of wind and flew a crooked path back into the forest.

At his side, Marika let out a long rattling sigh. Her eyes tracked the creature, making sure it had truly departed. Finally she turned away. "A grakyl," she mumbled again. The fear in her voice was still there, but now it was threaded with elation and a trace of amazement. "I never saw one before . . . only drawings . . . from stories."

"But what the heck *was* it?" Kady asked, pushing forward.

Marika finally seemed to notice that she still held Jake's wrist. She pulled her fingers away.

Pindor answered Kady's question. His voice dropped to a whisper, his eyes on the sky. "A grakyl. They're the cursed beasts of Kalverum Rex. The Skull King. His slaves. They—"

Marika cut him off. "We should be going. The sun's already dropping low."

Jake rubbed his wrist where Marika had gripped him.

He remembered the pricking burn as he neared the far side of the Broken Gate. Jake sensed that if Marika hadn't grabbed him, he might have ended the same as the creature. Unable to pass.

Had it been some form of invisible wall? A defense to keep anything from passing over the ridge? Jake studied the towers. While the stones did seem to be volcanic, no mortar glued them together. Instead they were fitted together in a complex pattern, a jigsaw puzzle made of stone. Jake also noted faint writing in bands along the tower on the left.

It wasn't like any writing he'd ever seen.

Before he could study it further, Marika headed down the trail away from the gate.

Jake had no choice but to follow.

Past the towers, a huge valley opened. Steep cliffs surrounded the valley in a continuous circular ridge. The valley looked like a meteor crater, but Jake noted vents dotting the edges, steaming with sulfurous gases.

No, it wasn't a meteor crater.

The valley was the cone of a massive volcano.

And it wasn't empty.

* * *

"What is that place down there?" Kady finally asked.

Jake had the same question as he tried to make sense of what he was seeing. Far below, a good section of the valley floor had been cleared of trees and spread outward in a patchwork of tilled fields and orchards. The open lands all surrounded a sprawling city of stone buildings and timbered lodges.

From the distance, there seemed no rhyme or reason to the place's layout. To one side rose what appeared to be a medieval castle. But beyond that, carved into the far ridge, were tiers of cliff-dwelling homes, similar to ones Jake had visited in the deserts of New Mexico. And was that an Egyptian obelisk rising out of a town square? It looked like a miniature Washington Monument but was topped by a scarab beetle, the ancient Egyptian symbol for the rising sun.

It made no sense.

"Calypsos," Marika said proudly. "Our home."

She began to head down the gentler slope on a narrow road of crushed gravel.

"Hold on," Jake said, struggling to find words to voice the sheer volume of his confusion. "How . . . Where . . . ?"

Pindor headed after Marika. "You'll get your answers in Calypsos." His words almost sounded like a threat.

"Wait," Jake continued, needing something, anything.

"You're Roman, aren't you?"

The boy straightened his toga. "Of course. Are you calling my heritage into doubt?"

"No, no . . ." In a hurry, Jake turned to the girl. "And Marika, you're Maya, yes?"

A nod. "Going back fifteen generations to the first of my tribe to arrive here. Pindor traces his family to sixteen. But other Lost Tribes have been here longer. Much longer."

She headed down again.

Jake stared after her.

Lost Tribes?

He studied Calypsos again. Could that grass-roofed structure be a Viking longhouse? And what about that pile of homes raised on stilts? It looked African. But he wasn't sure. Either way, it seemed all of history had been gathered down below, ancient peoples from every age and land.

But how . . . and why?

Jake itched for a closer look.

Unlike his sister.

Kady still hung back. Her eyes were narrow with worry and suspicion. "Maybe we shouldn't go too far." She glanced back to the stone towers. "If there's a way out of this Jurassic Park wannabe, maybe we should stay close to where we landed."

Jake barely heard her. One last structure drew his gaze. It lay beyond the strange town and rose on the right from the wild region of the valley, surrounded by forest. In fact, most of it remained hidden within the jungle. That was why Jake hadn't spotted the structure right away.

"We need to find some way back home," Kady continued.

Jake lifted his arm and pointed to the half-hidden structure. "How's that for a place to start looking?"

Kady studied where he pointed.

Only the top two tiers of the pyramid rose above the jungle, enough for Jake to see the massive sculpture on top. It was a stone dragon, lit with fire by the glancing rays of the sun. The dragon crouched there, its neck stretched high, its wings unfurled wide, as if readying to take flight. Its shape was a match to the one atop the gold pyramid at the museum, the same one sketched in his mother's book and described in his father's log.

Jake's hand drifted to his khaki vest. His palm rested over the books in the inner pocket. There was no mistaking the structure out there.

It was the *same* pyramid.

Only full size!

Amazement kept Jake rooted in place.

"Are you coming or not?" Marika called back anxiously.

Jake glanced to Kady. He needed her to understand. His fingers tightened over the hidden books. If the small pyramid back at the museum had somehow transported them here, surely the larger one out in the valley could hold the key to a way back home. But more than that, Jake pictured his mother and father working inside the tomb in Mexico, discovering the smaller gold pyramid in the first place.

Had they suspected the truth? Had they died to keep its secret?

More than a way home, the pyramid might offer an answer to that bigger mystery in Jake's life—in both their lives.

What had truly happened to their parents?

A new noise intruded: a creak of wheels and a rattling jangle, along with the clip-clop of something large. Pindor scooted ahead to scout the bend in the road.

The noises grew louder. Jake could make out a few mumbled voices. Below, Pindor lifted his spear in a sign of greeting, then backed to the side to allow room.

Two creatures clopped into view, tethered and drawing a two-wheeled chariot. Jake swallowed in disbelief. The gray-green creatures that pulled the chariot were the size of draft horses—but they weren't horses. Each looked to weigh a half ton, trundling on four legs.

"*Europasaurus*," Jake named them. "Pygmy dinosaurs."

Three men crowded the chariot: one held the reins and the two others bore spears and swords. One hopped off and crossed toward them. He was dressed like Pindor, but he also wore bronze armor and a helmet.

"Heronidus," Marika said. The girl crossed her arms and said sourly, "Pindor's older brother."

The newcomer spoke loudly. "Father is furious, Pin! What are you doing up here by the Broken Gate?"

"We were . . . I wanted to show . . ."

Heronidus pointed. "By Jove, is that Father's spear?"

Pindor shifted the weapon behind him. He glanced up the path toward Marika for some salvation.

Heronidus stiffened in surprise as he saw Jake and Kady. His hand dropped to his sheathed sword. He waved the second Roman soldier out of the chariot.

"Trespassers . . ."

The second soldier drew his sword.

"Who . . . ?" Heronidus asked boldly, having to clear his throat to achieve the right rich baritone of command. "Who are you?"

Pindor stepped forward and planted his spear more firmly. "I think . . ." His voice cracked. He glanced to Jake, then down to his toes. His voice hardened to match his brother's. "They are spies. Spies sent by the Kalverum Rex, the Skull King."

7

CALYPSOS

As the day grew hotter, the road down into the valley proved to be longer than it appeared from the Broken Gate. It was made even longer by the tense stretches of silence and suspicious glances from the two older boys in the chariot. The pair of pygmy dinosaurs tugged at their leads, as if sensing the anxiety. The driver kept hauling back on the reins, to keep pace with those on foot.

They were marched quickly through the farmlands that covered the valley floor. Jake tramped behind the chariot with Kady on one side and Marika on the other. Pindor and Heronidus followed, one with the spear, the other with his sword.

No one was taking any chances with *spies* in their midst.

Eyeing the sword and spear, Jake considered ways to escape, but where would he and Kady go? Back out into the surrounding wild jungle? They would not survive long on their own.

And besides . . .

Jake's attention turned forward.

Marika must have noticed his sudden focus on the dragon pyramid. Pointing, she said, "That is the great temple of Kukulkan. It protects this valley and—"

Heronidus cut her off with a bark. "Mari! You'll not speak to the spies."

"I'll speak to whoever I want! And they're not spies," she said for the tenth time, as if declaring it enough would make it so. "They are *newcomers*."

Heronidus scoffed. "Newcomers? There have not been strangers to these lands in a score of lifetimes. And if they truly are newcomers, I wager it was the dark alchemies of Kalverum Rex that brought them here. To plant spies in our midst."

On Jake's other side, Kady exhaled loudly with disgust. She eyed Heronidus up and down with disdain. It was a look she had perfected at school, capable of withering a freshman with a glance.

The older boy tried to ignore her, but Jake noted he grew a little red around his tunic's collar and shifted his sword nervously for a better grip.

A muffle of movement drew Jake's eye to the left. From out of the meadow, a snaking head rose. It stretched higher and higher, twenty feet into the air, then tilted over to spy on the small band of travelers on the road below.

Jake stared upward, holding his breath. The creature's

skin was purplish, its eyes large and moist above blubbery lips. It blew a short bleat from its trumpet-shaped nose at them, then sank away and returned to its grazing.

Kady grabbed Jake's elbow. "What was that?"

He shook his head, too awed speak. It looked like some type of duckbill dinosaur.

"We call it a blow horn," Marika said. "They're very good at pulling plows."

As the dinosaur vanished, Pindor rubbed his belly. "Shouldn't we stop to eat?"

Heronidus scowled at his younger brother. "We're not stopping. Not when we have prisoners with us." He looked hard at Jake, then back to Pindor. "You'll be lucky to get water and dry bread after Father finds out you went to the Broken Gate by yourself . . . *and* took his spear."

"Father doesn't have to know about the spear, does he?" Pindor pleaded.

Heronidus shrugged and continued down the road. "We shall see."

A half mile ahead spread the city of Calypsos. Built on a small hill, it rose from the valley floor. But as much as the place intrigued him, Jake's attention was drawn beyond its borders. Deep within wild woodlands that ran up against the city walls on the right, the massive stone dragon hovered over the treetops, its wings spread wide. It seemed to be staring straight at Jake. Only the dragon was visible from this angle. The pyramid was buried in the forest.

Jake shared a hopeful glance with Kady. Even this close, the dragon appeared an exact match to the artifact at the British Museum. The pyramid had to offer some clue as to a way home.

Marika must have read the desire in Jake's face. She shook her head warningly. "It is forbidden to trespass there. Only the three Magisters of Alchemy are allowed to enter and gaze upon the crystal heart of Kukulkan."

Jake heard the longing in the girl's voice, which further set fire to his own curiosity.

The crystal heart of Kukulkan? What was that?

Heronidus grunted his displeasure. "Enough, Marika. I've already told you. No speaking to the spies."

"They're not spies!" she insisted yet again.

Kady cleared her throat. Loudly. All eyes immediately turned to her. Even the chariot's two pygmy dinosaurs swung their long necks in her direction.

Jake frowned. How did she do that?

Kady planted a fist on one hip. Her initial shock had grown into irritation. She fanned her face with her khaki hat, then waved it at the group. "I don't understand. All you weird people. How come you all speak English?"

Heronidus cocked his head, appraising her. "*Ang-lash?* It this the tongue of your land?"

She nodded. "Of course. It's what you're speaking, too."

"No. Here we speak All-World. As you are doing now."

Kady touched her fingers to her lips, looking concerned.

"All-World?" Jake asked.

"It is a gift of the temple gods," Heronidus said, and pointed his sword toward the pyramid, violating his own order not to talk to them.

Marika explained in more detail. "The same shield that rises from Kukulkan and protects our valley also grants a common tongue to all the Lost Tribes. So one neighbor can understand another. To unite all in peace and harmony."

Jake stared toward the stone dragon. It sounded like some universal translator.

"But we have not forgotten our own tribe's language," Heronidus said, and puffed out his breastplate. "It can be spoken, but it takes concentration."

Demonstrating this, Heronidus spat out something in Latin, aimed at Pindor. It sounded like an insult.

Pindor blushed, while Marika bristled. She must have understood the Latin. "Pindor is not a coward! He's a thousand times braver than you!"

This only earned a dismissive chuckle from Heronidus.

The Mayan girl pointed back the way they'd come. "I'll have you know that we were not just *at* the Broken Gate. Pindor and I went *outside* them."

Pindor stiffened. "Mari!"

"We went off into the jungles to snatch an egg of a thunder lizard!"

Heronidus's eyes grew huge as he turned his full attention back upon his younger brother. "You went *beyond* the Broken Gate?"

"Heron . . ." Pindor blustered for a bit, searching for words. "I had to try . . . because . . ."

Heronidus cut away any further explanation with a swipe of his sword. "When Father hears about this, you'll be locked up in your room until the next full moon. And rightfully so!"

Pindor gave Marika a sad shake of his head.

Marika winced and mouthed, *I'm sorry*.

Marched even faster, they quickly reached the gate to the city. The walls climbed two stories tall. The heavy iron gate stood open.

Heronidus ran forward and spoke to a guard leaning on a spear. Jake could not make out what was said, but Heronidus pointed an arm toward him and Kady.

The guard leaned out. His eyes grew huge upon seeing the strangers. He finally nodded, stepped back, and waved. A moment later, two huge beasts stamped into view.

Jake recognized the species.

Othneilia.

Standing on two legs, each beast bore a rider in light

armor, burnished and shining in the sun. One rider leaned from his saddle and spoke to Heronidus, who nodded and came running back.

"Let's go!" he ordered, his face flushed with the excitement of it all.

With the monstrous escort, the group headed through the gate and into the city proper. Jake didn't know what to expect, but Calypsos proved as chaotic as it was colorful.

Inside, the streets were paved with cobblestones, and the homes stacked close together. A woman in an apron leaned out a second-story window and called down to a thin man dragging a wagon. "I'll take two bloodmelons and one pail of mushberries! But they better be ripe this time, Emmul!"

"Ripe and mushy as they come!"

Jake had expected the place to smell bad with so many people and animals in one place, but the city was crisscrossed with flowing canals, along with raised aqueducts and roadside drains. It was amazing engineering. Even the main street formed a spiraling corkscrew that wound around and around. It led toward the crown of the hill where a stone castle, flanked by two towers, waited behind tall walls.

"Kalakryss," Heronidus said, naming the place. "Home of the Council of Elders."

It was plainly their destination.

As they continued, Jake stared down alleys and narrow

avenues. Everywhere he looked he spotted bits of other cultures from every continent and age: a Native American sweat lodge, a Sumerian temple, a large wooden Buddha. In one square stood the slender Egyptian obelisk carved with hieroglyphics.

Marika must have noted the wonder in his eyes. "The tribes are many. We number over two score."

"How did you all get here?" he asked.

It was a question that had plagued Jake through the march. The weight of the coin around his neck grew heavier the more he pondered the miracle of their own arrival. There had to be some sort of portal. The coins must have acted like keys. But that could not be the only path here, not with all these people.

Marika shook her head. "We don't know. Centuries ago, the Lost Tribes were drawn to this savage world, pulled from their own homelands. We all arrived within a few generations of each other and made our homes here in this valley. Where Kukulkan protects us."

Jake stared between Marika and Pindor. How could tribes from so many different eras of human history arrive in this place at relatively the same time? If what Marika said was true, the Tribes hadn't just been pulled from their homelands, but also from their *time lines*.

"There are rumors of other towns like Calypsos," Marika continued. "In other valleys far out in the jungle. But here we live as best we can, in peace and cooperation with each other and the land. Or at least we used to. . . ."

Jake heard a trace of worry behind her last words. He could guess the root of it. "The Skull King you mentioned? Who is—"

"You two shouldn't be talking!" Pindor urged, stepping between them. "We're all in enough trouble already."

Heronidus glared back. "Hurry up!"

Marika sighed, but she obeyed.

With his mind awhirl, Jake continued through the town. *Lost Tribes.* Jake had heard of matching tales throughout history, of villages that suddenly disappeared, of Roman legions that vanished without a trace, of entire civilizations that were simply swallowed up by time.

Was this where they all ended up?

He sensed there was much more to learn.

"Ugh!" Kady danced a step away from Jake's side. She scraped vigorously at the bottom of her left boot on one of the cobblestones.

Jake glanced over a shoulder and saw her boot print in a pile of dark, earthy-looking material along the edge of the street. Only it wasn't *earth.* The ripe smell made that clear. Dinosaur dropping.

Jake tried not to smile—especially after she came back to his side, her face pale and slightly green.

"We don't belong here," she said. "We have to get home."

"We'll get home," Jake assured her with more certainty than he felt.

Kady took a deep breath and nodded.

"It just might take some time to figure out a way," Jake added under his breath.

He looked around at the mix of cultures here, his worry growing. A new worry took root. If these people—after so many centuries—hadn't figured out a way to open a portal back home, how could he hope to do so on his own? He kept this fear to himself and reached over to take Kady's hand.

She squeezed back.

Until then, at least they had each other.

By now, their parade had begun to draw more and more eyes. People pointed, and children ran up and tugged at Jake's backpack and plucked curiously at Kady's clothes. Heronidus or one of the mounted guards continually waved them off.

An Egyptian girl, no older than five, with a shaved head and painted eyes, ignored Heronidus and rushed forward to Kady. She held up a flower with crimson petals. "You're pretty."

Kady accepted both the gift and the compliment. "Thank you."

Jake noted a ring of relief in his sister's voice at the simple act of welcome. Kady let go of Jake's palm and clutched the flower with both hands. A ghost of a smile played over her lips. With this small gesture, maybe Kady now had something to grasp onto, something from which she could gain her bearings.

Was this how Calypsos's community had first been founded?

By a simple welcome from one to another.

Jake watched at they rounded the next curve in the road. Directly ahead rose the castle of Kalakryss. He noted guards walking the walls. He wondered what sort of welcome they could expect.

He glanced to Marika.

Her face was pinched with worry.

Not a good sign.

8

STRANGERS IN A STRANGE LAND

With a spear at his back, Jake marched into the castle's open courtyard. In the center, under a tree the size of a giant redwood, more soldiers lounged and laughed. To the left, backed against the castle wall, rose a set of stone stables and wooden corrals.

A soft chuffing noise came from their escorts' mounts, sensing home and food nearby. The *Othneilia* threw their heads a bit, but the soldiers in the saddles tapped the beasts' flanks with small sticks like batons, guiding them and calling out in soothing voices. Elephant riders in India controlled their mounts in the same manner.

As they passed through the gate, a group of soldiers approached. They came from exercise fields on the opposite side of the courtyard, where practice skirmishes with swords and spears were under way. Two-story barracks lined the fields. A tall man wearing a helmet that sprouted a crimson plume led the soldiers.

"The Saddleback Guard," Marika whispered at Jake's side. "Heronidus is in training to join their ranks."

Heronidus stepped forward and saluted the soldier in the plumed helmet by raising his right fist to his chest. "Centurion Gaius, we have strangers to our lands to present to the Council of Elders."

The centurion glanced to Jake and Kady. His only reaction was a slight widening of his eyes.

"We believe they may be spies sent by Kalverum Rex," Heronidus added, and stiffened his back to the point Jake thought something might snap.

The centurion studied Jake and Kady. The hardness in his face softened with amusement. Crinkles around the corners of his eyes deepened, indicating the man laughed often. Jake found himself liking Gaius though he hadn't spoken a word.

"If these are spies," the centurion said, "then the Skull King certainly starts with them young."

Heronidus shifted his stance. His face was beet red at the doubt in the centurion's voice. He glanced quickly over to Pindor, as if blaming his younger brother. To save face, Heronidus turned back to the centurion and sputtered, "But shouldn't the Council of Elders decide such matters and rule—"

Centurion Gaius clapped Heronidus on the shoulder, silencing him. "You are correct, young Heronidus. These two should be brought before the Council. Strange tidings mark their arrival here. Especially with rumors of late from our scouts sent into the deep jungle—at least those few who have returned. . . ."

His face darkened, and he nodded to the two mounted riders. "I will take your charges to the Council. You two return to your posts at the gates."

Gaius turned back to Jake and Kady after speaking to a young boy in a belted toga. The boy took off on foot, running toward the castle. Probably a courier, sent ahead to announce their arrival. "I am Marcus Gaius, first centurion of the Saddleback Guard."

"Jake . . . Jacob Ransom. This is my sister. Kady."

"*Katherine* Ransom," his sister corrected, standing a little taller, though she blushed a bit at the man's attention.

Gaius nodded. "Names as peculiar as your dress. If you'll both follow me, we shall seek an audience with the Council." He turned his gaze upon Heronidus, along with Pindor and Marika. "You shall all come and give a full report to the Council."

To Jake's right, Pindor groaned under his breath. He plainly was not happy that he would have to explain where he had been with Marika. On the other hand, Marika nodded sharply, fully ready to cooperate, to prove she was right about the strangers.

As a group, they set off toward the castle's main entrance. Passing into the shadow under the tree, Jake heard a rustling overhead and stared up. Among the lower branches hung small creatures with scaly wings and pointed heads.

Tiny pterodactyls.

"Any word from the hunters in the field?" Gaius asked one of the lounging soldiers, who snapped to attention.

"No, Centurion Gaius. Not a single dartwing has returned from the jungle in a fortnight. We're preparing to send one out now." The man pointed to where another soldier sat on a stool. The soldier had one of the pygmy pterosaurs secured between his knees and set about tying a small silvery tube to its back, like a little saddle.

"We've been sending out two dartwings a day as ordered," the soldier walking stiffly next to Gaius said, "but not one has returned."

The seated soldier finished his work, stood, and tossed the tiny pterosaur into the air. Its wings snapped out, and it caught the wind. The creature sailed across the yard, and with a fluttering beat of its wings, cleared the castle wall and headed away.

Jake watched its flight, then stared up at the branches full of pterosaurs. They must be used as messengers. Like homing pigeons.

Distracted, Jake banged his knee into a box on the ground. A spitting hiss drove him back. The box was a wooden crate with bars across one side. A creature hunched at the back of the cage. Jake couldn't make out what it was, only that it was angry at being disturbed. All he saw was a pair of golden eyes, reflecting the shine of the setting sun.

He stepped nearer, curious—then it suddenly lunged against the bars. Startled, Jake dropped back and landed on his rear. The caged creature was no larger than his dog, Watson. But this beast was all black fur with ripples of fiery orange. Hackles were raised and a short mane framed a muzzled face that sprouted fangs as long as Jake's outstretched hand. The creature spit and hissed. Its curled lips revealed the full length of those fangs.

Like a saber-toothed tiger but smaller, Jake thought. Perhaps an early ancestor of the larger saber-toothed cats. Something like *Rhabdofelix*.

"Get back from there, boy!" a guard warned.

The commotion drew the centurion's attention. The soldier at his side explained. "A patrol trapped it in the Sacred Woods. Thought maybe we could train it. Can't be more than a year old. Maybe as young as nine moons."

Gaius hunched down. "Nine? She's going to be big."

The soldier next to Gaius sighed. "But she's too wild, too dangerous. Almost took a chunk out of Huntmaster Rullus. So we're saving it to use as bait during a practice hunt."

Jake tensed. During the discussion, he had moved closer to the crate again and stared inside. They planned to kill her.

Jake couldn't say why he did what he did next. With a

glance over his shoulder, he reached toward the latch that secured the cage. Kady noticed him and mouthed, *No.*

He stared hard at her with his eyebrows high. Kady might sometimes be a self-centered, stuck-up brat, but she had a soft spot for animals in need. Last year, she even got her cheering squad to sponsor a walkathon for the local animal shelter.

Kady rolled her eyes and turned her back on Jake. She pointed off across the yard and yelled quite sharply, striking a pose of terror. "What's that over there?"

As usual with Kady, everyone turned and stared.

Using her distraction, Jake flipped open the latch, then hurried a few steps away. He checked around. No one saw what he did. Not even the cat. It remained crouched in the back of the cage.

Jake risked a hushed *"Go,"* willing it to move.

The *Rhabdofelix* finally slinked toward the bars and creaked the door wider with a nose. As it swung open, she slipped out, low to the ground, her long tail curled into a question mark, her posture all suspicion and wariness. Her eyes were fixed on Jake. Her nostrils flared, taking in his scent. Her ears, high and alert, swiveled like radar dishes.

"Run," he urged under his breath, and waved toward the open castle gates.

With a surge of muscle, she suddenly shot away. The only mark of her passage was a panicked burst of wings as the flock of the dartwings took off in fright from the tree branches.

Their squawking drew the attention of the soldiers upward—then down to the cage with its open door. A flurry of commotion and yelling erupted, but it was too late.

The cat swept out the gate and vanished into the tangle and tumble of the city. Soldiers took off on foot, but Jake suspected the cat would never be caught.

Trying his best, Jake kept his face innocent. He caught a spark in Marika's eyes. She stared at him a few seconds before she turned away. If she suspected anything, she stayed quiet.

Centurion Gaius spoke sharply and pointed toward the castle. "Enough. We should not keep the Elders waiting."

The castle of Kalakryss filled the back half of the courtyard. Jake studied the fortification as they approached the main gateway. As he craned his neck, he spotted something shining atop the right tower. The slanting sunlight sparked brightly off a domed structure made of beaten bronze. It looked like an observatory used to study stars.

Before he could examine it further, they passed under the archway and through a set of huge doors. Jake had expected the inside of the castle to be dark and gloomy. Instead he found the entryway warmed by colorful tapestries on the walls and rugs underfoot. The air was refreshingly cooler, well insulated against the heat of the sun. A massive bronze chandelier lit the space— but not with flickering candle flames. The light shone steadily.

Jake thought there were lightbulbs up there, but the shape of each bulb was jagged and angular. They looked like chunks of raw crystal—only each shone with a brilliance that stung the eye.

Jake looked away with a frown. *What was powering the crystals?*

Gaius led them down the center aisle of a long and narrow hall. Wooden benches, like church pews, lined both sides, all facing toward the hall's far end. The walls were hung with banners, a dozen to a side. Each was emblazoned with symbols, like a collection of knights' coats of arms.

Flags.

Marika saw his interest and said, "The banners represent each of the Lost Tribes."

They stopped at the front of the hall under a set of high, narrow windows, flanked by archways. Beneath the windows stood an upper and lower set of judicial benches with three tall chairs on each level.

Three people marched out of the left archway, each wearing matching expressions of concern. But they couldn't have been more different. One wore clothes like Pindor and Heronidus, but a crown of laurel leaves marked his brow.

He was flanked by an old man with Asian features, bald except for a long white mustache that draped below his chin and a thin beard. On his other side strode a long-limbed middle-aged woman with braided red hair, dressed in a green tunic and pants. A helmet with two curled horns sat atop her head.

"Calypsos's high Council," Marika whispered.

Pindor hung back with the spear, trying to hide behind Gaius.

Under the heavy gaze of the Council, Kady moved closer to Jake.

Before anyone could speak, a sharp voice rang out from the right archway. "Newcomers! Surely that isn't possible. But if true . . . can you imagine?"

The speaker appeared. He was short, and his gray hair stuck out a bit, like he had just woken up. He was clearly Mayan from the square of cloth tied around his shoulders, called a *pati*, adorned with feathers at the sleeves.

Another man waddled alongside him. He was as wide as he was tall. This rotund man wore a long robe with a hood, though the hood was down, revealing a head of bushy brown hair that was shaved on top. He looked like an English monk out of the Middle Ages. The monk pointed toward their group, and the Mayan man turned. His eyes widened, and he took a step toward them.

"Mari?" he said. "What are you doing here, my dear?

Why aren't you at school?"

"Papa, it was Pindor and I who—"

Papa? Jake glanced over to her.

She was cut off by a deep voice booming from the upper bench. "Pindor?"

The man with the crown of laurel leaves stood up from his chair. His eyes searched the floor below. Pindor reluctantly showed himself.

"What is this all about? What mischief have you and your friend conjured up? If this is some hoax? . . . If you're wasting the Council's valuable time . . ."

"No, Father." Pindor spoke to the floor. "It is no hoax."

Before anyone could explain, a third man appeared in the archway behind the monk. He moved silently, as thin as the shadow of a sundial. He wore a solid black robe that brushed the floor. Shaved-headed, his skin was dark, and his manner darker. His black eyes were cold and stony. His gaze swept the group without any flicker of emotion. What made his appearance even more disturbing were the tattoos across his forehead, inked in blood red. They were Egyptian hieroglyphics.

The man joined the first two, and together they crossed to the lower level and took their seats. Jake noticed each man wore a small silver hammer on a chain around his neck.

Jake glanced at Marika. She whispered, as quiet as a breath. "Those three are the Magisters . . . the three masters of alchemy."

Pindor's father had remained standing on the upper level. "With the Council fully assembled, let us discover who these strangers are and what danger they pose to Calypsos."

Jake felt the weight of six pairs of eyes fall upon him and his sister.

9

THE COUNCIL OF ELDERS

". . . and that's how we came to bring them through the Broken Gate," Marika finished.

Silence settled over the Council. Marika and Pindor had already been questioned at length, and there had been some commentary from Heronidus. So far, Jake and Kady had been ignored.

Marika's father finally spoke up. "I would like to see a demonstration of this strange alchemy that drove away the thunder lizard."

The monk nodded beside him. "I agree with Magister Balam. I would like to witness it myself."

The third of the Magisters merely stared at Jake.

Pindor's father waved from the top bench for them to obey.

Jake reached into his pocket and pulled out the dog whistle. "I don't know if you're going to hear anything." He lifted the whistle to his mouth and blew into it.

Jake heard nothing more than a whispery keening note. The Elders at the bench seemed to hear even less. They shook their heads and shrugged shoulders.

"And *that* chased off a thunder lizard?" Pindor's father asked, the doubt evident in his voice.

"It did, Elder Tiberius," Marika declared. "It bears a strange silent alchemy."

Jake spoke to the bench and held up the steel whistle. "This did not come from alchemy. It came from what we call *alchemy*."

Jake frowned. He had been thinking *science*, but the word had come out of his lips as *alchemy*.

Confusion spread along the benches—all except for the Egyptian, who remained expressionless.

Jake touched his fingers to his throat and remembered what Marika had explained. Some mysterious force helped to translate his words into this All-Worlds language. Did the universal translator think *alchemy* and *science* were the same? And maybe in some ways they were. Didn't ancient alchemists dabble in chemistry and physics? Even Isaac Newton considered himself an alchemist.

Jake tried again, concentrating on his words. "The whistle came not from alchemy . . . but from *science*."

This time the word came out the way he wanted it to, but it took focus. His tongue fought forming the word. Sort of like trying to talk after the dentist had totally numbed his mouth.

"*Sy-enz?*" Marika's father echoed.

Jake sought some way of demonstrating. He swung to Kady and pointed to her vest pocket. "Show them your iPod."

"My iPod?"

"Let them listen to it."

She frowned but obeyed.

As she fished out her iPod, Jake explained. "Where we come from, we use a different sort of alchemy called *science.*"

Kady fixed one of the earpieces in place and switched on the music player. Her eyebrows shot up. "Ohh, this is 'Straightjacket Lover'!" she blurted out loudly. As all the eyes fixed on her, her voice turned meek. "It's . . . it's one of my favorites."

Jake waved her forward. "Let them hear."

Kady moved to the lower bench. The Elders and Magisters gathered and took turns listening though the earpieces. Eyes widened in surprise, but they didn't freak out as much as Jake had been expecting. Afterward, the three Magisters leaned together in discussion.

Jake overheard a few words from Marika's father: ". . . some type of farspeaker . . . an amalgam of green crystals perhaps . . ."

Jake lost the rest of the words as Pindor's father pounded a fist on his side of the bench. "Enough of this. I would know more about the grakyl that tried to attack you at the

Gate. Are you sure it was one of the Skull King's minions?"

"I am certain of it, Father," Pindor said.

The woman with the horned helmet—who had to be of Viking descent—spoke. "Kalverum Rex grows more bold with every passing season. If what the children say is true, he is scratching at our very gates."

"It is indeed worrisome, Astrid. What is the latest word from your huntresses?"

She shook her head. "We've still not heard from those sent deepest into the jungle. We pray to Odin with each moonrise for their safe return."

"We will add our own prayers," the Asian man assured her. He turned to Jake and Kady. "Before we judge these newcomers, I would know more about what land they have come from. How did they come to be here?"

Jake felt the weight of the half coin around his neck. He cleared his throat first, fearing Kady might explain about the coins. He didn't want that to happen. The coins might be their only way home. If they were taken away, it could leave them stranded here forever. But deeper down, Jake simply refused to be parted from them. They were the last gifts from his parents.

"We don't know how we came here," Jake said hesitatingly, cautiously. "One moment we were in a . . . in a great hall. During a big thunderstorm."

He turned to Kady, who nodded.

"And the next, a bolt of lightning cracked and—*bam*—the world went dark. It felt like we were falling, then—*wham*—we are standing in the jungle."

Nods from the Elders followed his words. He heard the word *lightning* repeated from the top level of the bench. It seemed such stories must be recorded from their own peoples' landfall here.

"We come from a town called North Hampshire," Jake continued. "In the land of America."

"Ah-Merika?" Pindor's father said with a crinkled brow. "This is an unknown tribe to us."

Jake raised his voice a little to make it stronger. "We don't know how or why we were brought here. But we know nothing of this Skull King, and we certainly are not spies for anyone. I swear." Jake held up his right hand like a Boy Scout—though he'd never been in the Scouts.

Elder Tiberius stared down at Jake for a long breath. Jake kept his hand up and matched the intense gaze. Finally the Roman waved to the centurion guard. "Take these two somewhere private while we talk about all we've learned here."

Gaius tapped his chest with a fist and motioned Jake and Kady to come.

Tiberius called out once more. "And have the boy leave his pack and the girl her strange musical tool. They will be examined by the Magisters for any sign of the Skull King's alchemies."

Their makeshift cell had no windows and was hardly larger than a walk-in closet. The floor was covered in dry hay. Shelves climbed the back wall and were stacked with green glass jars, sealed in thick wax, which hid murky contents. Wooden barrels and waist-high clay pots lined another wall. The place smelled musky and peppery.

Some sort of pantry, Jake thought, earning a growl of protest from his stomach. *How long has it been since I've eaten?* London seemed a million miles and a million years away. And maybe it was.

Kady paced back and forth in the small space, her arms folded over her chest.

Jake crossed to one wall and studied the single light in their cell. An iron torch was bolted in the stone and held aloft one of those brilliant-glowing crystals. It was too high up the wall to reach, but he searched for any wires or cords, some connection to power. He saw none, but he wanted a closer look.

Maybe if I dragged one of those barrels over here . . .

Kady kicked one of the clay pots and faced Jake. "How *did* we land in this insane place?"

Her eyes had grown a little wild. Jake shrugged, sensing she needed some answer, any answer. "Maybe we triggered some sort of . . . I don't know, maybe a quantum wormhole."

"A quantum *what?*"

"Some rift in time and space. A spatial anomaly."

Kady rolled her eyes. "In other words . . . you don't have a clue."

Jake frowned at her—but in fact, she was right. He pictured the glowing artifact. "Well, I *do* know that it must have something to do with the broken coin Mom and Dad gave us."

Kady lifted a hand to her throat. "Then why did they send us these stupid things to begin with?"

Jake retreated and sat on one of the barrels. "I think . . . just to keep them safe and hidden. But I don't know. . . ."

His voice cracked at the end. All he knew for sure was that he was growing more worried with every second. What if the Council banished him and his sister back into the jungle? They'd never survive.

Kady crossed and sat on a neighboring barrel. "Maybe you're right, Jake," she said softly. "Mom and Dad couldn't have known we'd end up sticking our coins in that pyramid thing."

She hugged her arms around her chest and looked worried.

Jake pictured the glowing artifact in the British Museum. He also remembered Morgan Drummond running toward them, warning them away. Had the man known something? Or was he merely worried about them messing with an ancient treasure under his charge? Jake shook his head and tried to settle the questions bouncing around his skull.

"What we know for sure is that we are not the *only* ones who landed here," Jake finally said, centering on what he knew to be true. "Someone or something has been collecting bits of Earth civilizations—from different times and different places—and stranding them in this world."

"Lucky those *tribes* didn't just kill each other off when they got here," Kady said.

"They must have banded together for survival. In this dangerous place, the enemy of your enemy is your friend." Jake touched his throat. "Plus that universal translator effect. Being able to talk must go a long way to keeping peace here. Wherever *here* might be."

"But where are we?"

Jake shook his head. "Maybe another world? Another dimension? If we can figure that out, we might be able to figure out how we got here."

Kady sighed loudly, as if it were all too much work. "Forget *how* we got here. How do we get home?"

Jake again noted a rising edge of hysteria. Before it could spread to him, he spoke out loud, keeping his head busy against the fear in his own heart. "The two mysteries are tangled together. *How* we got here, *how* we get home. We won't be able to solve one without solving the other."

Kady reached over and squeezed his fingers. "You studied all that archaeology and ancient history stuff. If anyone can figure this place out, it's you."

Jake shook his head, but at the same time, he pictured the stone dragon floating above the neighboring forest. The pyramid had to hold some answers. He had to find a way to get inside. But he remembered Marika's warning.

It is forbidden to trespass there. Only the three Magisters of Alchemy are allowed to enter and gaze upon the crystal heart of Kukulkan.

Jake stared up at the glowing fist-sized gem atop the iron torch and began to piece together a sketchy plan.

"What we need to do first . . ." he mumbled.

Kady leaned closer, listening.

Jake firmed his voice. "What we need to do first is gather *information*."

"Information?"

"Find out as much as we can. But in order to do that, we'll have to cooperate and lie low while we investigate this place"

Kady crinkled her brow. "So we have to do what we're accused of doing. We have to *spy* on these people."

Jake nodded and understood the danger. "As long as we stick together, we'll be fine. We should be able to—"

A loud knock made them both jump. With a creak, the pantry door swung open, and Gaius entered. His voice was hard and unforgiving.

"Come with me," he ordered. "The Council of Elders has decided your fate."

* * *

All eyes turned to them as they approached. No one spoke. The silence made the air feel heavier as Tiberius stepped forward to meet them. He wore a stern, unwelcoming expression.

Uh-oh.

The Roman's first words offered no relief. "You've come upon Calypsos in troubling times. Dark creatures haunt our borders. Rumors abound of even greater monstrosities deeper in the jungle, of forces building like a storm against us. So your arrival is not without suspicion."

Jake's stomach tightened.

"But from its founding, Calypsos has been a place of peace and welcome. And even in the face of darkness, we will not forsake all our principles. Additionally, through your strange alchemies, you saved not just one of our children—" Tiberius raised an arm toward Marika. "But you also saved my son."

Pindor's shoulders, already slumped, bowed even further.

Tiberius continued, "Magister Balam's daughter has also testified as to the terror on your faces upon seeing the grakyl, one of the Skull King's minions. She believed that fear was real."

Jake remembered the creature pinned between the towers, writhing in midair, trying to break through. His fear had been real all right. Jake glanced over to Marika, silently thanking her for supporting their story. She glanced shyly down to her toes.

Tiberius continued, drawing back Jake's attention, "While the decision was not unanimous among the Council, the majority voted to allow you to remain in Calypsos for now."

Jake let out the breath he'd been holding. It wasn't the warmest of welcomes to this strange land, but he'd take it.

Tiberius pointed to Marika's father. "Magister Balam has been gracious enough to open his home to you, young Jacob. He has expressed interest in learning more about your sy-enz."

Jake found his voice. "Th-Thank you. We'll be no trouble. We promise."

Tiberius held up his hand. "You mistake my words. Your sister will not be going with you.

"What?" Jake stammered. "Wait. I don't think—"

Tiberius silenced him with a frown. "Elder Astrid Ulfsdottir has petitioned for Katherine Ransom to join her at Bornholm Hall."

The tall woman nodded. "She is fit and strong of limb. I see the makings of a warrior in her."

Jake turned to his sister. Kady's face had paled.

Tiberius continued, "A final condition upon your dwelling here in Calypsos is that my sons will be assigned to the two of you as . . . as attendants. You are not to roam our streets without their company."

Jake understood the meaning behind his words. They were being assigned *guards*.

"Pindor will see to you." Tiberius nodded to Jake. "And Heronidus will attend to your sister. At least, for a period of time."

Until we can be fully trusted, Jake thought.

"For now, the day grows late," Tiberius finished. "Best we let you two retire to your new homes and get yourselves settled."

The Viking woman stepped to Kady's side and clamped a hand on her shoulder. Marika rushed over to Jake. The girl's expression was a mix of apology and excitement.

But Jake stared over at Kady. Their eyes met. He knew what she was thinking. She had placed her trust in him to figure out a way home. His earlier words of assurance echoed in his head.

As long as we stick together, we'll be fine.

As they were about to be pulled away, Jake realized his plan—only a few minutes old—was already falling apart.

How would they ever get home now?

THE WHITE ROAD

Jake hugged his sister before they were separated. It was awkward. He couldn't remember a time when he'd actually hugged her before. And everyone was watching them, making it doubly uncomfortable. He whispered in her ear, forcing his tongue to speak English versus All-Worlds. He didn't want to be overheard.

"Keep a watch on everything. Learn what you can."

"What am I supposed to—"

"Just play along. Make friends." It was a talent Kady had mastered and a skill Jake barely understood. But in terms of espionage, such an ability went a long way.

Tiberius cleared his throat behind them. "That will be enough. Night falls, and we all have much to do before we find our beds."

Jake stepped back. Kady, no longer hugging Jake, seemed at a loss as to what to do with her arms. She ended up folding them around her own chest, plainly nervous.

The Viking woman crossed to Kady and touched a hand to his sister's elbow. "It is not a long walk back to Bornholm. But we should set off now or we'll find only a cold supper awaiting us."

Kady gave Jake one last forlorn glance, then accompanied Astrid Ulfsdottir across the hall. Jake watched them leave.

"Fret not, *ah xi' paal*," Marika's father said to Jake, slipping into the Mayan tongue. "You'll see your sister at least once a day . . . if not every other day. Until then, let us show you where you'll be staying."

Marika pinched the edge of his safari jacket and tugged him toward the archway to the right of the upper bench.

"Papa and I live in the Tower of Enlightenment, as do all the Magisters of Calypsos." Shyness shone in her jade eyes. "Come, let me show you—"

"Mari, let your friend breathe," her father warned. "There'll be plenty of time to show him around, but I imagine something to fill his belly might interest him more at the moment."

Jake's stomach growled its agreement.

He was led to the archway, where he found a narrow spiraling staircase. As Jake entered the stairwell, he paused, not sure whether to go up or down.

Marika said, "Below lies the domain of Magister Zahur. He keeps to the roots of the tower, where he houses small jungle creatures in cages and baskets for his examinations into the alchemy of life."

Jake remembered the tattooed Egyptian. He also noted Marika's mouth crinkle with distaste, plainly not happy with the man's line of study.

Marika directed Jake up the stairs. "These first floors belong to Magister Oswin." She lowered her voice as they crossed through the levels of his domain and hid a small smile. "He doesn't like to climb any more stairs than he must—unless there's a meal to be had."

Climbing several more floors, they reached a landing, and Marika headed down a short entry hall that ended at a wooden door. She pulled out a long brass key from a pocket and inserted it into a lock. With a twist, she pulled the latch and opened the door.

"Our home," she said, and waved Jake inside ahead of her.

He stepped over the threshold into a large common room, circular in shape. Other doorways led off to neighboring rooms, and a narrow staircase climbed up to a second level. While there were no windows, the room was lit by jagged chunks of glowing amber crystals that hung from iron chains bolted to the rafters.

A round table in the center of the room had already been set with white pottery bowls that steamed around the edges of their lids, smelling of spices and simmering stew. To one side rose a stack of flatbread. On the other side, a pile of spiky-skinned fruit the size of cantaloupes filled a large bowl.

As Jake stepped toward the table, movement to the left caught his eye. He turned in time to see a narrow door, hardly wider than an ironing board, close without a sound.

"Who . . . ?" Jake asked as Marika and her father crowded in behind him. He stared at the door. "Is there anyone else living here with you?"

"Just the two of us . . . now," Magister Balam said with a trace of sadness. "Come. Let us eat while the food is still hot."

Jake craned a look over to the narrow door as he was ushered to the table. Maybe he'd imagined the movement. Turning back to the table, he dove into the meal, following Marika's example, using the flatbreads like tortillas to heap up some of the stewed meats from one of the pottery bowls.

The bread was chewy and warm, and the meat melted on the tongue. He ate quickly, not realizing how hungry he actually was. After a few bites, Jake's face grew hot, and he waved a hand in front of his mouth. The burning only grew worse.

Marika smiled at his distress. "Firepeppers."

The burn subsided enough for Jake to speak. "It's . . . it's good."

Marika's father patted him on the back while chewing around a mouthful himself. The old man's eyes watered.

"Could be hotter?" he gasped out.

Marika's smile widened, encouraging Jake to try everything on the table. She also poured a dark slurry out of a tiny ceramic teapot into a cup. Jake frowned at the warm muddy liquid, but he picked up the cup and sniffed at it. His eyes widened in surprise at the distinctive and familiar smell, like a bit of home.

"Chocolate!" But he shouldn't have been surprised. The Maya had invented chocolate drinks. He sipped his. It was more bitter and thicker than the hot chocolate he was used to. Maybe a few marshmallows to sweeten it . . .

"We call it *cacao*," Marika said.

Jake nodded and sipped at the drink, but he felt Marika's father studying him from the side. Jake did his best to look nonchalant. He did not want anyone to know how much he already knew about Mayan customs. They were already suspicious of him.

As the meal came to a close, Jake was so full that he had to lean back in his chair. To his right, Marika's father did the same and let out a platter-rattling belch.

Marika looked horrified at his outburst.

Seemingly blind to the offense, her father winked at Jake and stood up. "I have some reading to do in my study before I retire. Mari, why don't you show young Jacob to his room."

"Papa, before I do that, can I show him the Astromicon? He might like to see the view from up there."

When her father agreed, Marika sprang to her feet and practically dragged Jake out of his chair.

"But no touching anything, Mari."

"No, Papa."

"And don't be up there too long!" her father called back as he crossed to one of the doors and pulled it open. Past the man's shoulder, Jake caught a glimpse of a desk piled high with scrolls and sheaves of parchment, and shelves stacked with more books and papers.

Jake glanced longingly in the direction of the study. Perhaps somewhere in those piles of books was an answer to where he was, how he got here, and how he could get home.

Marika hauled him toward the door that led back out to the spiral staircase. Before he knew it, he was climbing up after her.

"Where are we going?" he asked, holding back a jaw-cracking yawn. With his belly full, his body felt twice as heavy.

"You'll see."

As they climbed, a question nagged Jake. Still tasting the hot chocolate on his lips, he asked, "Mari, how do you make *cacao* here in Calypsos? Don't you need your cocoa trees from home?"

She nodded. "While we've learned to harvest what grows in this world, we have not totally abandoned our old ways. Some of our people came here with seeds that we planted. It is a custom, going back to the founding of Calypsos. While we work together in harmony, each tribe honors where they came from. In the hopes that one day we will be allowed to return home."

Jake pictured the town, beginning to understand the place a bit better. The town wasn't so much a melting pot as a *stew* made up of chunks of different cultures—each preserving their unique individual identities and flavors.

Until they were allowed to return home.

Jake understood that wish all too well.

"Here we are," Marika said, and hurried up the last steps.

They'd reached the end of the spiral staircase. As Marika pushed open the door at the top, a fresh breeze washed over them. The stifling heat of the day had subsided to a balmy evening. The wind helped clear the cobwebs out of Jake's head after the big meal.

Jake stepped onto the tower roof, his eyes wide. The sky overhead was a vault of stars—more stars than Jake had ever seen. He attempted to spot any familiar constellations, but nothing looked quite right. Then again, his knowledge of astronomy was limited. Back at home, Jake spent much of his time looking *down*: searching for fossils, studying books, always looking for clues in the dust or dirt.

Still, one item in the night sky was unmistakable. A

swath of stars and shimmering light swept across the sky in a shining arc.

"The Milky Way," he whispered to himself. He felt something warm swell through him, a welcome sense of familiarity, of home.

Marika stood at his shoulder and gazed up, too. She lifted an arm and traced the band of brightness. "*Sak be*," she said in Mayan.

Jake's heart pounded as understanding dawned. The same words were written as symbols on the two halves of his gold coin: *sak be*, which meant "white road."

He stared up into the sky.

The Milky Way—that was the Maya's *White Road*.

Marika continued, "It's believed among our people that the White Road is the path to this world. It's how we came here."

Jake studied the splash of brightness. What had seemed warmly familiar a moment before now took on a cold and mysterious cast. His fingers still clutched at the cord around his neck. At least for Jake and Kady, the White Road *had* led them here.

But could it somehow lead them back?

"Every night, Papa searches the skies, seeking answers about the world and the passing of time."

"And for a way home?"

Marika nodded. Her voice grew quieter. "He spends so much time up here. Especially the last few years."

Marika guided Jake's attention from the stars back down to the tower roof. Its edges were lined by a shoulder-high stone wall, but in the center of the open roof rested a giant bronze dome. Jake had spotted it from the ground. It was the size of a two-car garage.

The bronze had been beaten to a polished mirror. Starlight was reflected across its surface, only interrupted by small slits around its top, like the hour markings on a clock.

"The Astromicon," Marika said. "It is here my father works, mapping the movement of the sun, moon, and stars. He predicted the great eclipse that occurred yesterday."

Curiosity and desire drew Jake toward a hatchway in the dome. He had to see inside.

As he stepped closer, something dark swept over the reflection of the stars. Marika saw it, too, and gasped in fear.

Jake's mind snapped back to the monstrous winged grakyl. Had it somehow found them?

He pulled Marika toward the stairwell door. Both stared up as a large shape circled the tower top and tilted on a wing. Illuminated by the moonlight, it was clearly not a grakyl. It was too big—and darkly feathered. Its wings folded and the creature dove downward and landed heavily with a braking rush of its wings. It perched on the raised parapet wall that lined the tower.

Marika stopped retreating. "It's one of Calypso's scouts."

The creature's head lowered and revealed a man seated on its back, strapped into a saddle. With a skill born of experience, the scout ripped away the bindings and scooped up a passenger from behind. He then slid out of the saddle and landed on the tower roof.

The scout took two wobbling steps toward them, but exhaustion drove him to his knees. He sprawled his passenger out across the stone floor.

"Get help . . ." the scout eked out hoarsely.

Marika turned to the stairwell door. Shouts echoed up to them. Someone had spotted the arrival and help was already on its way. Marika turned to Jake. "Stay here."

She took off like a frightened rabbit and headed down the stairs.

Jake stayed, in case he could help.

The winged creature remained perched on the wall, its beak agape and panting, clearly as worn as its rider. The massive bird looked powerful enough to nab a cow out of a field.

The scout moved closer to the figure sprawled across the stones. Jake did the same and saw the passenger was a woman. She was dressed like the Viking elder who took Kady, with green leggings and a tunic, and boots that rose to her knees. From her blond hair, she had to be one of Astrid Ulfsdottir's people. Jake remembered the talk of the missing huntresses.

It seemed one had been found.

"Come here, boy," the scout ordered, his voice iron and uncompromising. "Stay with her."

Jake hurried forward and dropped down, kneeling on the edge of the woman's cloak. The scout stood and stepped over to his mount. He reached a hand to settle it, then crossed to where a bucket rested under a hand pump. His head was crowned by feathers, the same color as his mount. From the hard planes of his tan face, he appeared to be Native American.

The man offered the bucket of water to his giant bird, then reached out an arm to soothe it.

Jake returned his attention to the woman. Her eyes were open, but Jake suspected she saw nothing. Her chest rose and fell, but she gave no other movement. No blinking, no twitch of muscles. Even when Jake reached a hand to hers and squeezed, thinking to let her know someone was there with her, she gave no response.

A feathered shaft protruded from her shoulder. The tunic around it had darkened with her blood. He reached toward the shaft, and—

"*Do not touch that!*" A shout burst out and froze Jake in place.

It had come from the stairwell. Jake turned as Magister Zahur swept toward him like a black raven, cape billowing out behind him. In the starlight, his red tattoos blazed on his forehead.

Zahur dropped to the stone floor and waved Jake away as if he were a bothersome gnat. Just then Marika returned with her father. Magister Balam joined his colleague on the woman's other side. Zahur had already begun an examination. He touched the woman's throat and lips, then leaned to stare deeply into her eyes.

The scout joined them. "I found her with two of her sisters just beyond the Bony Pinnacle. They had been carrying her on a litter. The two were barely on their feet themselves. My scoutmaster took the two to Bornholm but ordered me to bring the huntress here. To see if there is any hope."

"It's Huntress Livia," Magister Balam said in dour tones.

Marika joined Jake. Worry etched her face. "That's Elder Ulfsdottir's bloodsister. She and my mother were once very close. She used to read me stories."

"We have to get her to my rooms down below," Zahur said, his words rising like steam from a fury deep inside him. "All my healing salves are down there. But first the head of the arrow remains buried in her flesh. We must get it out. Now."

Balam turned to Jake and Marika. "Help us."

The Magisters rolled the woman on her side. Jake cradled her head, while Mari straddled her hips to help hold her steady.

Zahur gripped the feathered shaft. "I must push the head of the arrow the rest of the way through her shoulder—then we can snap off the arrowhead." Zahur stared at Jake. "No one touch it!"

Balam braced the woman's other side as Zahur clenched his fingers. "Now!" he gasped out, and shoved against the shaft.

From the woman's back, the point of the arrow burst out. For just a moment, Jake thought it looked like the fanged head of a serpent, ready to strike, but then he blinked and saw it was only an arrowhead, like a glassy shard of obsidian as black as the darkest shadow.

"Hurry now!" Zahur warned.

Balam slipped a short stick from his pocket. It looked like its tip was on fire, but Jake saw its point was actually a fine shard of crystal.

Reaching out, Balam touched his crystal to the arrowhead. A scream pierced the night and sailed toward the sky. The woman's body wracked in their grip, but the scream had not come from her throat. Jake was sure of it because he was still cradling the huntress's head. The cry had come from the arrowhead.

As Balam leaned back, Jake saw the point was no longer black but a pure translucent crystal. Balam quickly reached forward with a fistful of leather and broke the head from the shaft.

Zahur allowed the woman to be rolled back. She had gone limp again. Her eyes were closed, but her breathing was more steady.

"Will she live?" the scout asked.

"It's too soon to say," Balam answered. "The bloodstone has poisoned her. And there may be tiny shards still inside, pieces that splintered off the arrowhead."

They were interrupted by the huffing arrival of the English Magister. He dragged his heavy frame through the door. "I heard . . . what can I do?"

"Calm yourself, Oswin." Balam crossed and showed the rotund Magister the arrowhead wrapped in leather. "We have it out."

Oswin's face blanched, but he still reached for the arrowhead. "We must examine it before whatever alchemy completely fades."

Zahur closed in on them like a storm. "Are you mad? It must be destroyed."

"But it could answer questions about what the bloodstone . . ."

Further words dropped to an urgent whisper among

the Magisters. Jake could not make out what they were saying. Instead, as he held the woman, he noted her lips were moving. Very slightly. He leaned closer, bringing his ear to her lips. With each fading breath, Jake heard two words repeated over and over.

"*He comes . . . he comes . . . he comes . . .*"

Suddenly her eyes fluttered open. Her gaze locked onto Jake's. A hand clutched his wrist. "Help me. . . ."

Before Jake could respond, she collapsed back into herself, eyes closing, lips going silent, lost again to the world.

Not noticing what had happened, Zahur broke away and stepped back to the woman's side. "Enough." He pointed to the scout. "Help me carry her below! I must do my best with my salves to save her life."

Jake stood up. "But she—"

Zahur elbowed him aside. The scout and the three Magisters used the woman's own cloak like a stretcher to lift her away.

Marika's father called, "Mari, take Jacob and show him to his bed. I think we've all had enough excitement for one night."

Marika nodded. Stepping aside, Jake waited for the group to head downstairs. He crossed over to the parapet and stared out across Calypsos. He could make out the spiral of the main street as it wound away from the castle and out toward the main gate. So peaceful and quiet. Yet

Jake only had to turn and see the fresh blood on the stones to know that such tranquility was an illusion.

He comes . . . he comes . . . he comes . . .

Jake also pictured the bright blue of the huntress's eyes. In that brief flash, her eyes reminded Jake of his mother's—always laughing and bright and so full of love. Eyes he would never see again.

Help me . . .

Jake shivered. He had not been able to save his mother, but he made a silent vow now to do what he could for the woman here. *But how?* He knew nothing of this world. As he despaired, his gaze settled upon one last sight, one last hope.

Lit silver by moonlight, a stone dragon hovered over the neighboring dark woods. It stared out toward the ridges of the valley, like a watchdog vigilant against intruders.

Jake sensed answers hidden there.

But could he unlock them in time?

THE ALCHEMIST'S
APPRENTICE

Jake woke with his blankets knotted around his body. It took him a frantic moment to remember where he was. He'd been dreaming of his parents. He sat up and rubbed his eyes. His heart still pounded like a racehorse's after a sprint around the track. The dream remained vivid—and still terrified him.

He had been down in the rock quarry at home, rooting around for fossils, when his mother and father started calling down to him. The panic in their voices had him scrambling for a way up out of the rock pit, but its walls had grown to twice their normal height with no path out. And all the while, his parents yelled for him to hurry, but he couldn't see them. As he searched for a way up out of the quarry, a speck in the sky caught his attention. Jake knew it was the source of his parents' fear. As he stared, it grew larger and larger, revealing a winged creature, as black as the deepest pit, with a serpentine neck and spear-like head. It plunged toward him, and still its wingspan spread wider and wider, blocking the sun. Its shadow swept over Jake and swallowed up the quarry. The temperature instantly dropped to a wintry cold.

Then a voice called down to him, as if the winged creature bore a rider on its back, hidden out of sight.

"Come to me . . ."

The words—the same he'd heard when falling through the darkness to this strange land—had shocked him straight out of the nightmare.

Jake sat a moment longer, waiting for his heart to slow. His entire body was damp with sweat, as if he'd had a fever that suddenly broke. He could still hear that voice, scratching like something trying to claw itself out of a grave. Finally he kicked away the sheets and quilted blanket and crossed to the window in his boxer shorts.

He pulled open the shutters and morning sunlight flooded into the room. One of the tiny saurian birds swept past his window, what the people here called dartwings. It cawed out a piercing note and was gone.

Jake took deep breaths, steadying himself.

Far below, the town of Calypsos was already bustling. Wagons rolled, people crowded the streets, and lumbering beasts stalked the wider avenues. Jake felt a pull to get outside and explore this new world.

He turned from the window and crossed to where he'd climbed out of his clothes and dropped them to the floor last night. After the long day, the strange introduction to Calypsos, and the excitement atop the tower, he'd barely made it to his bed.

His room was little bigger than a stone closet, but it was cozy. It held a bed and bedside table with a lamp, a chair, and a wooden wardrobe carved with Mayan glyphs.

As he stepped across the room, Jake noticed two things immediately. His clothes, which he'd left on the floor, were now neatly folded on the chair. They looked freshly laundered. He picked up his safari jacket. It still felt warm, as if it had just come out of a clothes dryer.

But that was crazy, wasn't it?

Second, he noted that the wardrobe door was cracked open. He nudged it wider and saw that someone had returned his pack. He tugged open the zipper and checked inside. All his stuff seemed to be there, but he searched the pack to be sure. Near the bottom, his finger poked into something strange.

What is this?

His finger probed an inner pocket. During all the tussling of the past day, it must have torn open. Inside, he discovered a silver metal button about the size of a dime. Jake flipped it around. With a fingernail, he teased out a tiny antenna.

"A bug of some sort . . ." he said aloud, shocked.

His brow crinkled. The Bledsworth corporation had given him the pack, along with his new clothes. Apparently they'd also given him something extra.

Anger boiled through him at the violation. He crossed the room and whipped the device out the window. As it flashed across the sky, a dartwing dove down, snatched it out of the air like it was a real bug, and flew off.

Jake shook his head.

Why would the corporation—the same ones who had financed his parent's dig—plant a bug on him?

He frowned as he quickly dressed. He had no answer, and any investigation would have to wait. Right now he had a more pressing concern.

Jake searched around his room. The bedroom door was closed, but clearly someone had been in his room while he'd slept.

His fingers suddenly clenched with worry. Last night, he'd taken one extra precaution. Jake hurried across the room and slid on his knees to the edge of the bed. He reached under the frame and found his parents' journals. He'd hidden them there for safekeeping.

He gathered the books, suddenly feeling like unseen eyes were spying on him, ears listening to him. He tucked the journals back into his jacket and patted them in place, feeling more secure again. He also shrugged his pack over one shoulder.

Once ready, he crossed to the door and opened it. His room was on the second level of the Balams' home. The stairs to the common room were just down a short hall. He heard voices mumbling, too low to make out. He crossed to the top of the stairs when he heard one voice say a bit loudly, "Just go wake him, Mari!"

"No, Papa said to let him sleep."

Jake spied below and spotted Marika sitting at the table with an open book in front of her. One finger rested on a page. A boy in a Roman toga and sandals stalked around the table. It was Pindor. Jake remembered that the boy had been assigned by Elder Tiberius to act as his guard. Apparently Pindor had already reported for duty.

Marika must have sensed Jake's presence. She glanced up at him. Jake straightened, blushing a bit, embarrassed to be caught eavesdropping. He lifted a hand, acknowledging her, and headed down the stairs.

Marika stood. "There's some porridge," she said, and pointed to a covered bowl. "It's still warm."

Pindor rolled his eyes. "We don't have time—"

Marika silenced him with a glare. "Just because you ate three bowls already."

"I was hungry!" He rubbed his stomach. "I got sent to bed without any dinner last night." This last earned another frown at Jake, as if it were his fault.

Marika sighed and faced Jake. Her eyes were shadowed and tired. It looked like she'd gotten little sleep. "Papa asked that we speak with him before we leave."

Jake glanced at the closed study door.

"No," Marika said. "He's up in the Astromicon. With

Magister Oswin. The two have been up there all night."

"Studying that arrowhead?" Jake asked.

"I think so."

Pindor drew closer. "Did you actually see the blood-stone?"

Jake crinkled his brow. "The what?"

"The arrowhead that struck down Huntress Livia and poisoned her."

Jake remembered the deadly shard of crystal, how its blackness looked like a solid splinter of shadow. Coldness crept over him at the memory of it.

"We both saw the arrowhead," Marika said. She caught Jake's eye. "Father doused it quickly, quenching its power."

"I wish I could have seen it," Pindor said.

"No," Marika and Jake both said at the same time, causing Pindor to step back.

"Don't ever wish that," Marika finished. She waved again to the table, changing the subject. "Jacob, would you like something to eat? The porridge has twistberries this morning. It's very good."

He shook his head. Remembering last night's blood-shed killed his appetite. "No, thanks . . . and you can just call me Jake," he added.

This concession drew a small smile from her before she turned and headed toward the stairs. "Then we'll say good-bye to my father and be on our way."

"To where?" Jake asked.

"Papa thought you'd like to visit your sister. To know she is safe and settled. Like you."

Jake slowly nodded. Though he was far from *settled*, he didn't say anything. He also felt a twinge of guilt. He'd barely considered how Kady might be faring. She was probably hiding under her bed.

Back up on the tower rooftop, the sunlight blazed off the bronze dome of the Astromicon. Jake squinted against the glare and hurried after Marika as she headed to the hatch.

She knocked, and after a moment, the door cracked open with an oily creak of its hinges. Magister Balam popped his head out. His gray hair was in even more disarray than last night, and his eyes looked haunted. But he worked up a grin when he saw who was at his door.

"Ah, good. I wanted a word with young Jacob before he departed." He backed to the side and waved Jake through the door. "Come inside. Magister Oswin has left to find his bed . . . and a bit of porridge, I suspect. And a good thing or there'd be hardly enough room in here."

Jake climbed through the low door. Marika and Pindor attempted to follow, but Jake had frozen in midstep, looking up at the curved dome.

The entire space overhead was filled with a maze of copper tubes and spiraling curls of amber-hued glass. Fluids bubbled through the pipes, and occasional tiny spats of steam hissed out of copper valves. Even more disconcerting, the entire contrivance slowly turned around a central axis. Tinier sections whirled faster. It was like staring up into the open heart of a giant clock. Only this mechanism continued to gently hiss and sigh, burble and creak, like something alive.

Adding to the marvel, the entire contraption was decorated with chunks of crystals, every hue of the rainbow. They hung like Christmas ornaments on a metal tree. Were the crystals some sort of balance for the device or were they actually powering it?

Probably both, Jake decided.

Whatever their purpose, this was far more than a crude observatory.

Marika's father urged Jake to come farther inside. Jake's gaze dropped to the lower section of the dome. It was empty save for a bronze workbench that circled the entire wall. The curved table was crowded with all manner of bizarre tools and devices: tangles of tubing, pails of scrap metal, wooden racks holding shards of crystals. Scattered everywhere were leather-bound books, fragile-looking scrolls, and loose-leaf stacks of parchments. One section of the workbench propped up a stone tablet as tall as Jake. Every inch of its surface was etched with tiny lines of writing. It looked like the same odd script he'd seen carved on the Broken Gate.

Magister Balam directed Jake over to something he recognized. Kady's iPod had been taken meticulously apart.

Kady would pull her hair out if she saw this.

"We Magisters talked yesterday," Balam said, and waved an arm over the gutted electronics. "We find this sy-enz of yours most intriguing. We could find no crystals inside your box, no explanation for this farspeaking alchemy of yours. It seems you have much to teach us, to share . . . as we will do the same for you."

Balam turned with his arms folded. "So it has been decided that I will take you under my tutelage. As my apprentice. Alongside my daughter."

Marika squeaked behind Jake, sounding both excited and happy.

"Apprentice?" Jake asked.

"To begin your own training in alchemy."

Jake didn't know what to say, but he remembered Marika's warning about the dragon pyramid, how it was forbidden to trespass there unless you were a Magister, a true master of alchemy. Perhaps here was a way of achieving that! His hope was quickly dashed.

"If we start with you now, who knows?" Balam continued. "You may be a Magister when you're as young as thirty years."

Thirty years?

"Would that not be wonderful? You'd be the youngest Magister in the history of Calypsos." Balam grinned broadly.

Jake swallowed back a groan. But he could not refuse.

"How . . . where do we start?"

Balam straightened. "On the morrow will be soon enough. I know you want to see how your sister fares. But I wanted to give you this first. A symbol of your apprenticeship."

Balam reached inside a pocket and removed a flat silver square about the size of Jake's thumb. The old man stepped forward and pinned it to the front of Jake's jacket like a badge. Jake stared down at it. Four tiny shards of crystals were imbedded in the silver. In the center was a white crystal as bright as a diamond. Only this diamond glowed with its own inner light. Jake recognized it as the same stone that shone in the lamps and sconces of Kalakryss. Around the diamond, three other stones formed a triangle: a ruby, an emerald, and an icy blue sapphire.

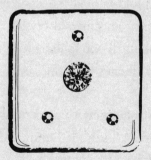

"The four principal crystals of alchemy," Balam said, noting his attention. "The four cornerstones that support our world."

Marika's father turned to the bench and lifted an

egg-sized chunk of ruby crystal. He rubbed it between his hands, and it began to glow with an inner fire. He held it out toward Jake.

Curious, Jake took it and quickly began bobbling it between his palms. It was hot—and growing hotter.

Balam snatched it back with a grin. He tapped the crystal with a silver hammer, like the one he wore around his neck as a Magister. The crystal chimed like a bell, and the fire inside it died.

"Such crystals grant us heat, while stones of blue . . ." Balam lifted another chunk of crystal, this one a pale sapphire. Puckering his lips, he blew across its surface. A frosty glow inside the stone's heart grew.

Jake could guess its purpose. He held a hand over the crystal. "It's cold."

Balam nodded and tapped the stone and set it aside. He reached next for an emerald crystal. "We use these stones for farspeaking. If one splits a green crystal into two pieces, each half vibrates the same, even when far from the other. Like—"

He was cut off by a new voice coming from another section of the bench. It sounded tinny. "Magister Balam, I must speak with you. It is urgent."

"Excuse me." Balam crossed and lifted what looked like a wooden Ping-Pong paddle, but it was hollow in the center with a green chunk of crystal suspended in the center by a fine mesh, like a spider in a web.

Jake saw the web gently vibrate as a voice emanated from the center. "Magister Balam . . ."

Balam touched the stone with a finger, silencing it, then spoke with his lips almost touching the stone, like using a walkie-talkie. "I'm here, Zahur. What is it?"

Jake recognized the strain in Balam's voice. The calm casualness had hardened with worry.

"It's Livia." There was a long moment of silence. "She continues to decline. My salves and unguents should be helping by now. I fear I will need your help to search for poisoning splinters still in her flesh."

Jake pictured the huntress. A stab of worry shot through him. He remembered the vow he made last night, to help her in any way he could.

Balam sighed and closed his eyes. There was a hopelessness to his posture, as if the prognosis were grim. He leaned to the crystal. "I will join you in your cellars."

With a touch of his finger, he ended the conversation and turned to Jake and the others. Balam tried to force his face into something that resembled encouragement, but it came out false. "We'll have to continue our talk later. See to your sister, Jacob."

Marika's father waved them out with a tired gesture. But Jake held his ground. Maybe there was one small way he could help the huntress.

"Magister Balam," Jake said. "Last night. After you removed the arrow from Huntress Livia, I heard her mumble. I don't know if it's important, but if they end up being her last words . . ." Jake's voice caught in his throat. He swallowed hard, but it was the least he could do for the woman, to share her last words.

Balam's bushy eyebrows pulled together. "You heard her speak?"

"Yes. But she seemed delirious . . . unaware of what was going on . . ."

"What did she say?"

"She asked for help, but also two words. She kept whispering them. *He comes.* Then she went silent."

"*'He comes.'*" Balam repeated. His gray eyes went flinty with worry. "Thank you, Jacob. But say not a word of this to anyone else. For now, go see to your sister. We'll talk more on the morrow."

They were quickly ushered toward the door.

Once outside in the morning sunlight, Marika and Pindor both stared at Jake. Pindor's eyes were huge, while Marika's had narrowed with concern. Jake didn't need any magical crystal to read their minds. He knew what they were thinking.

He comes.

There could only be one person who triggered that much fear.

The Skull King.

BORNHOLM HALL

"Who the heck is this Skull King?" Jake asked as they crossed the castle courtyard. He'd been wanting to ask that question, but it was only in the bright sunshine of the day that he felt comfortable enough to bring it up.

Pindor grimaced and bit his thumb. He glanced to Marika.

She lowered her voice to a whisper and edged closer to Jake. Pindor leaned tighter, too. "His full name is Kalverum Rex. He was a Magister in Calypsos over half a century ago. My father was one of his apprentices." Marika pointed to Jake's new silver badge. "Back then, Kalverum was Calypsos's most skilled alchemist, outshining the other two Magisters. But like Magister Zahur, he took to the cellars and forbade anyone to trespass. He also kept creatures of the jungle down there."

Marika shuddered.

Pindor continued. "It's said he committed all manner

of horrors down there, dabbling with a new type of crystal—the bloodstone—a black crystal that poisoned and twisted flesh."

"And maybe that poison twisted him, too," Marika continued. "He became more and more reclusive, sometimes not coming up into the sun for months at a time. Then children began to disappear . . ."

Jake felt his stomach churn.

"My father would never say exactly what was found in those cellars. One Magister was killed. A fire came close to burning the tower down. But Kalverum escaped. He fled beyond the Broken Gate and out into the jungle. A handful of people went with him. It was a hard time for our people. We were left with only one Magister, and even he was ancient and doddering . . . and the three apprentices at the time."

"Your father," Jake said, "along with Zahur and Oswin?"

She nodded. "We lost much knowledge, but at least we were rid of the monster."

"Or so we thought," Pindor added.

Marika continued. "Twenty years later, rumors began to come out of the deep jungle of twisted beasts—like the grakyl you saw. One was caught and brought here. The Magisters examined it and recognized the evil alchemy of Kalverum Rex. They believed he'd built a stronghold among the crags of the Spine, the mountains that lie beyond Fireweed Swamp. Over the years, hunters and scouts have vanished, while others who come back from the edge of the swamp tell stories of great columns of foul smoke rising from the snowy crags of the Spine."

"So he's still out there," Jake said.

"And growing stronger," Marika finished. "For the past few years, his horrid beasts have been ranging farther afield. All the way to our very borders."

Jake pictured the grakyl pinned at the Gate, held back by whatever force protected this valley.

"And this bloodstone?" he asked, thinking of the arrowhead. "What exactly is it?"

"No one truly knows. After the fire at the tower, it was forbidden to dabble into that dark alchemy. You'd best ask my father—"

A shout cut her off. "*Ho!* Look, it's Heron's little brother!"

Jake turned and spotted a group of older boys across the courtyard. They were sitting on a corral fence. Behind them, some *Othneilia* mounts were being saddled.

"Still afraid of lizards, are you, Pin?" one of them called out.

Another leaned toward his companion. "Hard to believe that's Heron's brother. Too scared to even fit a sandal in a stirrup."

Pindor's face turned a deep scarlet. Marika touched her friend on the elbow, but he roughly pulled away. Pindor stalked toward the castle gates, leaving Jake and Marika to follow.

"What was that all about?" Jake asked softly.

"Pindor wanted to join the Saddlebacks who patrol the city, like his brother and father before him." Marika shook her head sadly. "It didn't go well. He panicked while trying to climb onto a mount. Everyone was there. Even his father. Now he'll have to wait until next year."

"What happened?"

"Pin . . . well, he can be skittish around the bigger beasts. See that limp in his left leg? His father's old mount—a real ornery fleetback—broke Pin's shinbone when he was five years old. He had wandered into its stall to offer it a handful of sweetstalk. No one was paying attention."

Jake stared at Pindor's back. He walked stiffly, but looked like he wanted to break into a run toward the gates, to get out of sight of the young riders in the practice yard.

"Word of his humiliation spread . . . and grew larger with each telling," Marika said. "If Pin hadn't been Elder Tiberius's son, it might not have been so ripe a story. People can be so cruel. It was one of the reasons we went beyond the Broken Gate—when we found you and your sister."

"What do you mean?"

"If we could have returned with a piece of a thunder lizard's shell—or even better an egg!— it would've proven Pin's bravery and stopped the stories. Perhaps even allowed him a second chance to become a Saddleback."

They reached the gates and followed Pindor out into the main street. He finally slowed and allowed them to catch up. He stared down at his toes as he continued sullenly through the streets.

Jake strode next to him. He didn't know what to say, but he certainly knew how Pindor felt.

The Roman sniffed and kept his voice low. "Back yesterday, with that thunder lizard—you chased the beast off with that flute of yours."

"It's a whistle actually." Jake reached and pulled the steel tube out of his pocket. He offered it for Pindor to examine. The boy took the whistle with a longing look in his eye.

"It blows a note that we can't hear," Jake explained, "but some animals can. Why don't you keep it for a while?"

Pindor stared down at the whistle. "Truly?"

"Sure." Jake shrugged, figuring Pindor could use something to cheer him up.

Pindor's fingers closed over the gift. "And this can be used to control beasts of the fields?"

"I don't know about that, but it definitely gets their attention. And with practice, it can certainly be a good training tool."

Pindor nodded. The pain in his eyes had softened to wonder. "Thanks," he mumbled, and continued down the road with a lighter step.

Marika stepped next to Jake and smiled over at him.

"What?" Jake asked.

She turned away, then glanced back out of the corner of her eye at Jake. Her lips danced with a grin.

"What?" he asked again.

"Nothing," she said. "Nothing at all."

The Viking hall of Bornholm rose ahead, like a warship forging across the rooftops of Calypsos. The top half of the building had clearly once been the bow of an ancient ship. A prominent wooden prow, carved into the shape of fanged sea monster, jutted out over the street. Below it were doors built of heavy timber, perhaps salvaged from the ship itself.

Pindor grabbed an iron knocker shaped like a wolf's head and pounded it firmly.

A tiny barred grate opened in the door. "Who wishes entry to Bornholm?"

"I . . ." Pindor cleared his throat because his voice had come out like a scared squeak. He tried again, deepening his voice. "I come upon the orders of Magister Balam. With the newcomer Jacob Ransom. To visit his sister."

A moment later, one half of the double door was pulled open. A tall blond woman stepped into view and sized up Bornholm's new guests. From the deep crinkle between her brows, she must not have liked what she saw. "Come in," she said brusquely.

Past the doors, a raftered hall spread all the way to the back of the building, where another set of double doors led out to a sunny courtyard. As Jake entered, he was surprised by the cavernous space. Iron chandeliers shaped like deer antlers glowed with chunks of white crystals. They helped illuminate a painted mural on the wall opposite the fireplace. A ship rode the whitecapped waves of a stormy sea, with its square sails puffed out and oars poking from its sides.

Their guide noted Jake's attention. "The *Valkyrie*," she said, kissing her fingertips and touching the ship as she passed.

It was plainly the name of the boat. But Jake also recognized the name from Norse mythology. "The *Valkyrie*? Weren't they female warriors? The shieldmaidens of Odin?"

Their guide turned to Jake, a fist on her hip. "You know our stories."

Jake stared up into those ice blue eyes. "Some of them."

She nodded, satisfied. "I am Brunhildr, hearthmistress of Bornholm. Be welcome," she said a touch more warmly. "Your sister is outside. Follow me."

But as she turned, a clatter of boots sounded from a stairwell ahead. Two girls leaped out, both black-haired with matching tanned faces. Twins. They had to be no older than Kady.

Brunhildr stopped before them. "How does the Elder fare?" she asked.

One of the girls shook her head. "Elder Ulfsdottir spent all last night at Kalakryss, at her sister's bedside. Even now, she ignores her bed and spends the morning praying to Odin."

"And she refuses all meals," added the second. "But we saw who came to the door and hoped that there was further word about Livia."

All eyes turned to Jake and the others.

"This is Hrist and her sister, Mist," Brunhildr said. "They were the ones who carried Huntress Livia all the way back from the shores of Fireweed Swamp."

Marika stepped forward and spoke softly. "I'm afraid we don't have glad tidings. My father and Magister Zahur continue to care for Livia with all their skill, but they fear splinters of bloodstone may still remain in her flesh, holding her trapped between this world and the next."

Hrist and Mist shared a worried look. The one named Mist looked close to tears. Hrist spoke to her sister. "We did all we could." She then turned to Jake and the others. "Huntress Livia went alone across the swamp in a small raft, leaving us on shore while she spied closer upon the lair of the Skull King. She was gone five nights and returned half dead with a fresh arrow wound and collapsed as soon as she set foot on shore. She said not a word."

Marika glanced to Jake and shook her head very slightly.

Her father had warned them about repeating what he'd heard on the rooftop.

Mist wrung her hands. "She must live."

"The Magisters are doing their very best," Marika promised.

Hrist sighed. "We will relate this news to Elder Ulfsdottir." She collected her sister by the elbow, and the pair ran back up the stairs.

Brunhildr continued across the hall and headed for the sunny courtyard. "These are dire times," she said through clenched jaws. "I'm sorry your sister comes to Bornholm under such a heavy cloud."

Jake grew worried. He wondered how Kady was faring with these hard women. As he stepped out into the sunlight, he spotted his sister in the center of the yard—with a pair of swords in her hands!

"No, like this," Kady said, speaking to the handful of women around her. She wore a green tunic and a pair of knee-high boots.

Kady danced back from the women and swung the short swords in a deadly dance around her body.

What was she doing?

Jake gasped as she tossed one of the swords into the air. It spun, catching the sunlight and sparking brightly— then fell. Kady caught it cleanly by the hilt and swept it out with a flourish and half bow.

Jake suddenly realized where he'd seen this routine

before. It was during baton practice with Kady's cheer squad. His sister had rehearsed the routine so often she could probably do it in her sleep—and apparently with swords.

Claps followed her demonstration.

A bench along the back wall was crowded with men in Viking helmets and cloaks. They laughed and whispered to each other. At the end of the bench, Jake spotted a familiar older boy in a tunic. It seemed Heronidus was enjoying his guard duty. He sat transfixed by Kady, following her every movement. He was certainly keeping a close watch.

"Kady!" Jake called, drawing her attention.

She spotted him and broke into a wider smile. "Jake, there you are! I heard you were coming!"

Kady handed off her swords to another woman, then crossed over to join him. Jake saw she had also braided her hair, as was custom among the huntresses, but she had done hers up in a fancy French braid.

Kady noted his attention and patted her hair. "How does it look? I didn't want to do that ponytail thing. Too *Heidi* for me."

But that wasn't all. Jake noticed two of the Viking women had their hair French-braided also. He squinted closer. And was one of them wearing eye shadow?

Oh, brother.

And here he'd thought she'd be curled in a ball crying.

"How did you . . . what are you . . . ?" Jake stammered.

"I'm fine, if that's what you're asking. They've been taking good care of me. Are you okay?"

Jake didn't know where to start. His night had involved pain, bloodshed, and rumors of a foul army building out in the jungle. And what had Kady been doing? Braiding her friends' hair and sharing cosmetic secrets. Did nothing ever change?

Kady laughed. "What? You told me to make friends."

That was certainly true.

Her voice dropped lower. "What about you? Did you learn anything?"

Jake glanced around at the others. Everyone was staring at them. He dropped his voice to a whisper. "I'll tell you more later. But for now, I'm still trying to find some way of getting over to that pyramid. There must be some power source over there."

He touched the silver badge on his safari jacket. "Something to do with the crystals."

Kady leaned and stared at his pin. "It's pretty."

Jake's cheeks heated up. "It's not *pretty* . . . it . . . it's important."

She straightened and shrugged. "So then if the pyramid is so *important*, what are you doing here?" Her tone was basically *Why are you bothering me?*

"Because I wanted to find out how you were doing."

Kady frowned at his concern, apparently reading

between the lines. "I'm not totally helpless, Jake."

"I never said you were."

Okay, maybe he had actually thought it. . . .

Still, the conversation was not going the way Jake had hoped. Trying one last time, he waved toward the front of Bornholm. "And I thought maybe you'd want to go check out more of the town with us?"

"With you?" A familiar thread of disdain entered her voice. "Heron was going to take me out to their gaming fields."

Heron? Since when were Kady and Heronidus so chummy?

Kady continued. "Apparently there's some sort of big contest in another couple days. A championship between the Romans and some . . ." She crinkled her nose. "I think Sumo wrestlers, or something like that."

Sumo wrestlers? Jake ran other possibilities through his head, going over the other cultures he'd seen here. "Do you mean *Sumerians?*"

"I guess. Whatever. Heron tried to tell me about the game. Sounds sort of like polo. Anyway, he's going to take me to one of his practices." She waved to her guard, who waved back, wearing a goofy smile.

Jake finally backed away, giving up. "Then if you're okay, I'll just head out with Marika and Pindor myself."

She shrugged, but an edge entered her voice. She stared hard at him. "Just make sure you know what you're doing.

Don't get too distracted."

He understood what she was implying. In other words, *Don't fool around . . . find a way home.* And while he worked at doing that, Kady could continue to play Valkyrie-warrior Barbie.

As his sister returned to the others, Jake frowned at her back. Kady was leaving everything up to him, to figure out what was going on and how to get home.

But could he do that?

Dark words echoed in his head, reminding him he was running out of time.

He comes, he comes. . . .

THE FIRST TRIBE

Back out on the street, Jake stood under the prow of the Viking warship. He faced Marika and Pindor. "What next?"

Jake had thought he would need the entire day just to pry Kady from underneath her bed. But that wasn't the case. As usual, she was the center of attention. This both irritated and relieved him. He stood at the edge of the street, unsure what to do, where to begin his own investigations.

"We could show you more of Calypsos," Marika answered.

"I say we go to the market," Pindor said. He stared up at the sun and held a palm over his stomach. "I'm starving."

"You just ate," Marika said.

"That was forever ago."

Marika rolled her eyes. "First, we'll see as much of the city as we can."

With Marika leading, they headed back out to the streets. Everywhere there seemed an excitement in the air, an electricity generated by all the bustle of the people and crackle of their shouts and laughter. Outside a Chinese pagoda, very young children were practicing with cymbals and horns.

"The Spring Equinox approaches swiftly," Marika explained. "It comes in two days. The entire town celebrates with a great feast and party."

"And it's the day of the Olympiad!" Pindor added with a rare note of enthusiasm. "The final battle to decide which tribe will win the Eternal Torch for this year. See over here!"

Pindor hurried forward. A few families were picnicking in a small park outside the castle walls. Pindor ran past them toward a ledge that stuck out and offered a wide view. He pointed toward the north end of town.

A large stone stadium, like a miniature Roman coliseum, extended to the volcanic rim of the valley, one side carved into the steep ridge.

"We hold plays and shows over there, too," Marika added. "It's not all brawl and tussle."

Movement to the right of the coliseum drew Jake's attention. Cliff-dwelling homes had been dug into the ridgeline neighboring the stadium. From the highest level of the dwellings, a team of giant birds took flight and coursed out over the city in a strict V-shaped pattern.

"People of the Wind," Marika said, watching alongside Jake. Her voice was full of wonder. "They're the only ones who know how to tame the great winged raz. They raise them from hatchlings, bonding them to their youngest children. It is said they grow up closer than brothers and sisters."

As the team flew past, Jake pictured the scout who had landed atop the tower, dressed all in leather with a crown of feathers. Of course, his tribe wouldn't call themselves Indians or even Native Americans. Those were names placed upon them by outsiders.

Jake stared upward as the birds swept past, rising high on heated air from one of the volcanic vents. People of the Wind. The name was certainly fitting.

The three of them tracked the birds across the sky and over the castle. As they finally disappeared, Marika sagged. "It's getting late. We should be getting home."

Jake glanced back over to the cliffs, but a slide of shadows along the edge of the bushes caught his eye. A slow dark shape dashed across the rocky lookout, grabbed a bone left behind by one of the picnickers, and dove back toward the bushes. Then it suddenly froze at the edge and stared straight back at Jake.

Large feline eyes flashed golden in the slanting sunlight.

A *Rhabdofelix*! The same one Jake had set free. So she had escaped and found a place to hunt for scraps.

"Hey, look at—" Jake turned to show Marika, but the cat had vanished.

"What?" Pindor asked.

Jake shook his head and waved them onward. "Never mind."

They circled the castle wall to the main gates. Pindor said his good-byes, leaving Marika and Jake to cross the courtyard and enter the castle keep.

Marika had gone silent, deep in her own thoughts, so Jake kept quiet while they climbed the tower. As they reached the landing, Marika keyed open the door to her home and finally spoke. "I wonder how Huntress Livia is—"

Jake gasped out loud, silencing her. As he stepped inside, he saw the room was not empty. A small boy, maybe a year younger than Jake, was setting a bowl of fruit on the table. Jake stared at the stranger. The other stared back—then quickly retreated to the narrow side door. He vanished through it, closing the door behind him. Jake caught a glimpse of tiny stairs beyond the door before it shut, like a secret servant's stair.

Marika frowned at Jake's stunned reaction. "That was Bach'uuk. He helps keep our home."

Jake still pictured the stranger's face. The boy had wide cheekbones and a prominent brow that stuck out from a sloped forehead, half hidden under lanky black hair. His blue eyes had locked upon Jake, almost as if in recognition, before he darted away.

But Jake had definitely recognized him . . . or at least he knew what *tribe* that boy belonged to. Jake was certain of it.

Bach'uuk was a *Neanderthal*.

"They call themselves the Ur," Marika explained after guiding Jake to the table.

She urged him to sit down and showed him how to peel one of the fruits on the table. It looked like a banana, only it was shaped like a corkscrew. It took some care to peel it. She called it a kwarmabean, but it didn't taste like a banana or a bean, more like an overripe peach.

Marika still wore a frown at Jake's startled reaction and misunderstood it. "Fear not, the Ur may look strange, but they're harmless and peaceful."

Jake nodded, his mind awhirl. So it wasn't just human tribes—*Homo sapiens*—that had been drawn to this world. Earlier tribes of mankind had been snatched from their homelands and become trapped here, too.

"They are a simple people," Marika continued. "Even aided by the alchemy that grants a common tongue to all, the Ur seldom speak, and when they do, it is slow and very basic. Papa believes there is a dullness to their thoughts, but they are strong and obey simple directions."

Trying to hide his reaction, Jake peeled another of the kwarmabeans. He didn't contradict Marika, but he remembered that archaeologists like his parents now considered Neanderthals to be as intelligent as modern humans.

Marika continued, pondering her own words. "Still, a group of Sumerian scribes went out to their caves in the ridge walls last summer and came back to describe elaborate wall paintings."

"Done by the Ur?"

Marika nodded. "Someday I'd like to see those caves. The scribes tell of beasts painted on the walls that no one has ever seen before. But then again, the Ur were the first ones to come to this valley and must have witnessed many amazing sights."

Jake focused his attention back. "They were the first?"

She rubbed at her lower lip in thought. "It is said that they were here long before any of the Lost Tribes. The earliest stories of Calypsos say that the Ur were found living in the shadow of the great Temple of Kukulkan and were the first to welcome strangers to these harsh lands, laying the foundation for the Calypsos to come. And still they help us, serving at Kalakryss and mining the cliffs for the raw crystals used in our alchemy."

Jake stared at the narrow door, recalling how the table had been set last night and how his clothes had been cleaned and returned. Had the Neanderthals become mere servants here—or worse yet, were they slave labor? This last thought took more of the shine off Jake's image of the peaceful and harmonious Calypsos residents.

Marika sighed. "But mostly the Ur keep to their caves. They are very private and shy. Their homes are on the other side of the ridge walls, facing the dark jungle beyond. You have nothing to fear from Bach'uuk. He and his father have served our family for many years. When my mother became ill . . . when she . . ."

Marika's voice suddenly trailed off. She shook her head and became intensely focused on her own kwarmabean. She was saved from continuing by a rasp at the front door.

A key turned, and the door swung open. Voices carried inside, while the speakers remained outside on the doorstep.

"There's nothing more we can do, Oswin." It was Marika's father, sounding bone tired and deeply worried.

"But we know there must be bloodstone splinters in her shoulder wound or she would've woken by now. If we could collect a few splinters and study them, we might better understand the threat against us."

"The risk is too great. Both to Livia and Calypsos. Bloodstones taint everything . . . and everyone around them."

"But we can't live in the dark forever, not when a shadow threatens to fall over our valley. Zahur moves too cautiously. Maybe deliberately so."

There was a long pause, then Balam spoke firmly. "Now

you don't truly believe that, do you, Oswin?"

A great rumbling sigh followed. Marika and Jake shared a glance. They shouldn't be eavesdropping, but neither of them moved.

"I suppose not. But I can't forget that Zahur was once Kalverum's apprentice."

"Yes, but we all studied under him at one time or another."

Jake glanced at Marika.

"And what of Zahur's experiments?" the English monk pressed, lowering his voice. "He uses Kalverum's cellars. He works with caged beasts and treads a path similar to that monster."

"That's because he studies the art of healing. An important discipline requires such work. You know how much of the healing arts were lost after Kalverum was expelled."

"Yes, yes, yes, I know you're right," Oswin admitted. "I guess too little sleep has me jumping at shadows. I just wish Zahur would move more quickly. I sense time weighing upon us. Those words that the boy overheard. *He comes.* We cannot sit wringing our hands forever."

"I understand, Oswin. And I honor your methods of study. Your bold experiments have discovered many practical alchemies that have bettered our lives. But here I agree with Zahur. Even if it means the death of Huntress Livia, we must move with caution when it comes to the bloodstones, even mere splinters."

"I hope you're right, my good friend," Oswin said. "I see dark times ahead."

"And in the dark," Balam said solemnly, "we must trust the light."

A small tired laugh broke the tension. "That was not fair. Quoting my own father."

"He was a wise man."

Another sigh. "Wiser than his son, it seems."

A few mumbled good-byes followed—then the door swung wider. Marika twisted in her chair and pretended exceptional interest in picking out a kwarmabean from the bowl.

Balam stepped into the room. His eyebrows rose in surprise at the sight of them. "Ah, you're back already." He glanced toward the door, then over to the table again. He combed his fingers through his hair but only succeeded in making it more rumpled. "So you heard all that."

"I'm sorry, Papa," Marika said, and stared up into his face. "But is it true? Is Huntress Livia truly going to die?"

Balam cupped his daughter's cheek tenderly, then moved to the table. Jake saw his face fall as he passed behind her, unsure whether to tell the truth or not. Finally, he turned and stared into his daughter's eyes.

"Yes," he finally said. "It is only a matter of time. We can do no more."

Marika's face paled, but she nodded and stood up. She

hugged her father. He put his arms around her, too.

Jake felt a sharp pang in his own chest, suddenly missing his own mother and father so badly that he could hardly breathe.

Father and daughter broke their embrace. Marika kept a hold of her father's sleeve. "Papa, you've not slept at all. You need a bath and some rest."

He glanced at the door to his library. "But I've more work—"

"It will keep until after you've had a short nap." She tugged him, like a mother with an unruly child. "Let me draw you a bath. I'll wake you in time for dinner."

Balam allowed his daughter to drag him toward the stairs.

As the two headed away, Jake remained seated at the table—but his attention shifted to the study door. He remembered the stacks of papers, scrolls, and books inside. What might he learn?

Before he knew it, he was on his feet. He didn't have much time. Rushing to the door, he tried the latch. It was unlocked and opened with a small squeak that made him wince. Telling himself it wasn't too loud, he slipped through the crack in the door and entered the library.

The room was pie shaped, stretching wider toward a pair of windows that overlooked the city. A desk stood under the windows. To either side, bookshelves rose to the rafters, crammed with dusty tomes and rolled parchments.

One section was stuffed with strange odds and ends: a bony skeleton of some creature held together by bronze wire, a neat row of polished rocks, a collection of small wooden blocks carved with Mayan glyphs. Walking into the library was like stepping inside one of the Cabinets of Curiosity back at his family home in North Hampshire.

But Jake didn't have time for sightseeing.

He crossed to the desk and searched without touching anything. Books were stacked as high as Jake's shoulders, and he was afraid of toppling them over. Instead his attention was drawn to an open book in the center of the desk. It had a cover made out of wood and pages that were coarse and thick.

The book was a rare Mayan codex, one of their great books of ancient knowledge. The invading Spanish conquistadors had burned most of them centuries ago. Only a few still existed in the world.

Jake leaned over the open codex. The page showed a map of the valley. A jagged circle marked the volcanic cone, and in its center had been drawn a crude representation of the pyramid. From the tip of the temple a stylized spiral wound outward and brushed the valley rim at four points.

North, south, east, and west.

Jake leaned closer.

The western point had an arch drawn over it. Despite the sketchiness of it, Jake recognized the Broken Gate, or rather how it might look if it wasn't *broken*. The picture at the point of the eastern gate looked familiar. It was a two-headed snake tied up into the shape of a figure eight.

Jake tensed, recognizing it though it was crudely drawn. He hurriedly reached into his pocket and removed his father's field logbook. He flipped open the page he had read in the British Museum.

> *Clearly from the intricate curling of the serpent into a figure eight, the relic must represent the Mayan belief in the eternal nature of the cosmos. . . .*

Jake heard his father's voice as he read, while at the same time picturing the museum artifact, a golden snake with ruby eyes, a Mayan treasure recovered from his parents' dig.

Jake swallowed and stared at the map. Here was a drawing of that same artifact, marking the eastern gateway into the valley. How could that be? Jake's mind whirled. He could come up with only one explanation: *Someone must have seen that gateway and gone back to their own time to tell about it.*

Jake felt a surge of hope. He stared at the pyramid in the center of the crude map. He guessed the spiraling line represented the field that protected the valley.

He had to know more.

A scrape behind him made him jump. He'd been so focused on what he'd found that he forgot about being here too long. If Marika discovered him trespassing . . .

Jake whipped around to find a figure standing in the doorway. But it wasn't Marika. The small Neanderthal boy—Bach'uuk—stood at the entrance to the library. His face showed no shock or emotion at Jake's trespass. He merely stared. Then the boy turned and returned to the table outside. He had been bringing in plates for dinner.

Jake followed him out and closed the library door. "I was just looking," he mumbled.

Bach'uuk ignored him.

A few seconds later, a shout echoed from upstairs. "Papa, I'll call you when supper is ready." Marika was heading down. "Ah, Bach'uuk. Let me help you with that." Marika took the last of his armload of plates.

The Neanderthal bowed his head and backed toward the servant's door. As Marika turned away, Bach'uuk stared at Jake and lifted a finger to his lips in the universal gesture to remain silent. Then he vanished, closing the door behind him.

A MIDNIGHT INTRUDER

It was hard to say what woke him.

One moment Jake was in a deep sleep, and the next he was wide awake in his small bedroom. The room was pitch-black. The window was tightly shuttered, and the door firmly closed. He heard no noises.

But something had woken him.

Wrapped in his bedsheets, Jake strained to figure out why he was instantly tense. Every fiber and nerve in him felt stretched taut. He searched the room, holding his breath. Beyond the foot of his bed, he could make out the bulk of the wardrobe. But nothing else. No shadows stirred, nothing rustled.

Still, Jake knew he was not alone. He couldn't say how he knew this with certainty, but he did. The hairs on his arms stood on end. Someone—or some*thing*—was in the room with him. He felt eyes studying him out of the dark.

Then he heard it—a low buzzing, like a thousand bees. It started, then immediately stopped. Jake could not tell where it came from, but it froze his blood. It was an alien sound. And it was in his room.

His eyes ached from trying to see into the dark corners. His heart pounded. Then he heard a quiet, furtive noise.

. . . *scritch, scritch, scritch* . . .

It sounded like fingernails scratching on wood. He didn't know what was making that noise, but he knew it was getting closer to him. His fingers bunched the blanket tighter to his chin. He slid his legs away from the foot of the bed, pulling tight to himself.

There was a lamp on a small table next to his bed. Marika had shown him how to turn its crystal on and off. But he was afraid to reach out from under the blanket.

. . . *scritch, scritch, scritch* . . .

The sound was definitely closer. Then the strange buzzing rose again.

What was it?

Jake's eyes strained. Dark shadows shifted and rose from the foot of his bed. He could stand it no longer. He shot an arm out toward the bedside lamp and flicked a fingernail against the crystal bulb. It chimed and light flared brightly. He closed his eyes for a blink against the glare, then stared at what crouched atop the footboard.

It was a huge black insect, the size of a small dog, with

crablike claws in the front. Wings like those of a dragonfly stretched to either side. As Jake cringed back, the wings fluttered up into a whirring buzz. The insect rose into the air like a helicopter taking off.

Suddenly, from behind its back, a curved scorpion's tail arched up, ending in a vicious barb as long as Jake's index finger. In the lamplight, the barb looked wet with poison, and giant claws snapped in the air.

Jake wanted to scream but his chest was too tight with terror.

The giant scorpion tilted further and suddenly dove straight at Jake. He reacted on instinct, drawing upon a lesson his mother had taught him about how cannibals in Papua New Guinea trapped their victims in snares.

As the monstrous beast dive-bombed toward him, Jake bunched his legs and arms, then shoved and kicked his blanket straight into the air like a net. The blanket fell over the scorpion, tangled around it, and knocked it to the floor. Jake rolled out of bed in his bare feet, dressed only in his boxers. He had no weapon.

The creature fell between him and the door. It thrashed and writhed under the blanket. He would have to jump over it. Then one black claw cut through and waved wildly. It was almost free. Jake backed up a step and bumped the bedside table, causing the lamp to bobble.

The lamp!

He reached behind him and grabbed it up.

The scorpion wiggled through the hole in the blanket. Jake jumped forward with the lamp over his head and swung it down hard. Something crunched, and liquid shot out and sprayed his bare foot.

Disgust froze him for a fraction of a second too long.

The blanket ripped, and the barbed tail struck out, lancing straight for Jake's calf. He swung the lamp and knocked it aside. The barb only grazed his right leg and struck the stone floor. Poison splattered from its tip.

Still, a line of fiery pain ignited where the barb had scratched him.

The tail lifted again.

Jake did not hesitate and hammered the lamp into the blanket, again and again, as if trying to drive a tent stake into frozen ground. Black liquid oozed from under the blanket. He kept pounding until nothing moved.

Then he dropped the lamp and stumbled back.

His right leg burned like a flaming torch, but he hobbled to the door, opened it, and yelled. "Help!" It came out more as a gasp. But his pounding must have already woken Marika and her father.

Both of their doors flew open. Marika wore a long sleeping gown. Her father came out in an ankle-length robe. Balam signaled Marika to stay back and rushed over to Jake's side.

Jake tried to explain, but he was still shell-shocked. He

pointed an arm into the bedroom, toward the ruin on the floor.

Balam peeked under the blanket. "A stingtail!" He swung to Jake and grabbed him by the shoulders. He stared up and down his body. "Did it bite you?"

"Nicked me." Jake pointed to his right calf.

Only a trickle of blood flowed, but already the skin around the scratch had turned bright red. He felt woozy. If Balam hadn't been holding his shoulders, he might have fallen over.

Balam called over to Marika. "Grab a blanket! Then help me get him downstairs."

Jake waved for them not to bother. He could walk on his own. Then the world went all tilt-awhirl, and he fell into darkness.

"He's waking up," a voice whispered, sounding faint and far away, like a radio station that wasn't quite dialed in.

Jake groaned as darkness fell away and brightness swirled around him. He took a couple deep shuddering breaths, fighting off motion sickness. Then his vision settled.

"Help me get him up," a voice said in his ear. It was Marika's father. He had an arm under Jake's shoulder.

As Jake steadied himself, he was lifted up into a sitting position. He saw that he was in the common room, on the table, wrapped in a blanket. Marika stood a few steps away. One hand covered her mouth with worry. Magisters

Oswin and Zahur were also here. The round-bellied Magister wore a striped nightshirt that reached to his toes and a matching peaked hat. He looked like a blown-up version of one of Snow White's dwarfs. Plainly he had come here straight from his bed.

Zahur had grown dark circles under his eyes. He crouched at the edge of the table and had a grip on Jake's ankle.

Balam kept hold of Jake's shoulder. "How are you feeling?"

Jake's mouth was dry. He could hardly nod.

Fingers squeezed his shoulder reassuringly. "You are a lucky boy, Jacob Ransom. Few survive the bite of a sting-tail. If that cut had been any deeper . . ."

Jake knew the man was trying to comfort him, but he was not doing a very good job of it.

Zahur still held his ankle. Around his calf was wrapped a thick brown bandage that looked damp. Maybe some sort of poultice to draw off any poison from the scrape.

Then the bandage *moved*. Jake felt it squeeze a little tighter to his calf, then loosen again.

"The mud leech grows restless," Zahur said. "A sure sign that the blood is clear of poison."

He reached and peeled the meaty body from around Jake's calf. A large sucker at one end required a tug. It came off with a wet pop. Jake shivered as the leech writhed in Zahur's hand. The Magister dropped it into a jar of murky water. The leech continued to churn and wiggle.

Jake's stomach did the same.

But Jake's leg looked fine, except for the large sucker mark near the scratch. The redness was gone, and Jake felt no stinging burn.

"He should be fine," Zahur said. "Let him rest into the morning, and all will be well."

Magister Oswin shifted his trunklike feet. "Which only leaves the question of how the stingtail ended up in the boy's room."

Balam helped Jake off the table and into a chair. Marika came over and put a mug of hot chocolate in his hands. Jake's fingers wrapped around it, appreciating the warmth. He sipped it—and had never tasted anything better.

Oswin crossed his arms. "I checked his room upstairs. The shutters were tightly closed."

"But it could have gotten through the window earlier in the day," Balam said. "Perhaps it sought to escape the heat of the day for the cool shadows of the room . . . and once night fell, it came out of hiding. From under the bed, behind the wardrobe."

Jake tightened his fingers on his mug. He would make certain he checked every corner of the room in the future.

Balam turned to Jake. "Did you leave your windows open during the day?"

Jake thought back for a moment. He remembered opening them in the morning, after his bad dream. He slowly nodded. "I think I did."

Balam nodded, as if that settled the matter.

Oswin's eyes narrowed, plainly not satisfied. "It's still strange to find a stingtail so far from the jungle."

"They do sometimes fly into town," Balam said.

Zahur spoke up as he stood. "I fear I may be to blame. When I heard of what attacked the boy, I checked my cages. I keep six stingtails down there to aid in my study of their poisons. I found one of the cages empty, the door hanging open. I don't know how long it might have been gone. I've been very busy with the care of Huntress Livia."

The Egyptian's countenance grew grimmer. "And I should return to her bedside even now. She grows more fragile with every passing hour." He collected his leech jar and headed toward the door.

"Thank you for your care," Balam called over to him.

"Yes . . . thank you," Jake said.

Zahur said not a word and vanished through the door.

Oswin made a dismissive sound. "I don't care what you say. Something still stinks like a pile of skunktoad about all this. Maybe the stingtail flew in there . . . and maybe someone *planted* it in there."

"Planted?" Balam scoffed.

"To kill the boy."

Balam frowned at Oswin and gave him a slight shake of the head, as if to say *Not in front of the kids*.

But Jake sat straighter. "Who would want to kill me?"

Oswin shrugged. "Perhaps one of the Skull King's spies. Maybe he fears your sy-enz. Either way, you are an unknown piece in whatever game Kalverum is playing. Maybe he wants to take you off the board."

"Oswin, that's enough," Balam said. "You'll have the poor boy jumping at every shadow."

Oswin sighed. "Maybe it's time we were all jumping a bit more at shadows." He shook his head and lumbered toward the door. "Or maybe I'm just too tired. Everything looks the darkest in the middle of the night."

After he departed, Balam touched Jake's shoulder. "Don't listen to him. It was just an unfortunate set of circumstances. An accident."

But the fat Magister's words stayed with Jake. His father had once said, *Words are like bullets; once shot, they can't be taken back*. And those bullets had struck deep into Jake.

If it wasn't an accident, who could have planted the scorpion in his bed? Jake pictured the Egyptian Magister, who by his own word admitted that the stingtail had come from his cellar laboratories. But Jake also stared at the narrow door at the back wall of the common room. He remembered how he'd found his clothes laundered and folded. Bach'uuk had come and gone during the night without waking Jake before. And who else knew about the servant stairs that wormed secretly through the tower? The assassin could be anyone.

Jake set his mug on the tabletop, losing all interest in the hot chocolate as a new fear struck through him. If it wasn't an accident . . . if someone truly sought to kill him . . .

Balam must have read the distress in his face. "What's wrong?"

"Kady . . . my sister . . ."

Jake didn't have to say more. Balam's eyes widened. He immediately knew what worried Jake, and that scared Jake even more. Despite Balam's attempt to dismiss the attack as an accident, the Magister must have had some unspoken suspicions.

"I will go up to the Astromicon and call upon Bornholm. Make sure she is safe." He headed toward the door in his robe. Jake stood up to follow, but he swayed a bit on his feet. Balam pointed to him. "Stay here. Mari, make sure he rests. Warm up his cacao."

"Yes, Papa."

After he left, Marika pushed a chair closer to Jake and sat down next to him. A moment of uncomfortable silence stretched, maybe because he was half naked under his blanket. But then she turned to him and spoke firmly.

"I saw what you did to that stingtail," she said. "Bach'uuk helped me clean it up while you were being leeched of the poison."

She reached into a pocket and placed something on the table. It was the barb of the scorpion. "The Ur believe that what is killed should be honored, a piece kept for the hunter."

Jake refused to touch it.

"I've boiled it clean of any poison," she said upon seeing his expression. "It's safe."

He carefully snaked out an arm from his blanket and touched the barb. It had almost killed him. He picked up the barb and examined it. He could see himself one day placing it into his own Cabinet of Curiosity. The idea helped push back the edge of terror. It even made him a little less worried about Kady. She had to be fine.

"Thanks, Mari."

She glanced away a bit too quickly, blushing just a bit. "Bach'uuk suggested I give it to you. It was his idea. He seems really fascinated by you."

Jake remembered the Neanderthal boy touching a finger to his lips.

Marika suddenly stood up. "Would you like me to warm your cacao?" Before he could even answer, she had grabbed his mug and crossed to a sideboard against the wall. A stone pitcher rested on a trivet supported by four glowing ruby crystals. A gentle steam rose from the pitcher. Marika lifted the pitcher and carefully topped off his mug.

She came back. The blush was gone from her face, replaced with worry. She glanced to the home's door, then back to Jake. As Jake warmed his hands on the hot mug, Marika settled next to him again. Her brow was furrowed in thought.

"What?" Jake asked.

She shook her head.

"No, tell me."

She thought for an extra moment, then spoke. "I didn't tell my father this, and maybe I imagined it. I don't know. But I remember waking earlier in the night. I thought I heard someone out in the hall, but when I listened harder, all seemed quiet. At the time, I didn't think anything of it and went back to sleep. And maybe it was nothing."

Or maybe it wasn't.

Before they could talk further, the door swung open and Marika's father stumbled into the room, wheezing, out of breath. He must have run all the way there.

Jake stood up, fear for his sister drawing him to his feet.

Balam waved Jake back down. "She . . . she's fine," he gasped out. "I got Bornholm all stirred up like a nest of ants, but there's been no trouble there." Balam reached the table and leaned an arm on it. "See, it was probably all an accident, like I said."

Jake felt a surge of relief that Kady was safe, but it failed to completely wash away the suspicion in his heart. Magister Oswin's earlier words stayed with him.

And words are like bullets . . .

Jake clutched the scorpion's barb. He stared over to Marika and read the same doubt in her eyes. No matter what anyone said, Jake knew the attack had been no accident.

But who wanted him dead?

THE CRYSTAL HEART OF KUKULKAN

The next morning, Jake sat in the Astromicon, starting his apprenticeship. He felt 1,000 percent better.

Balam gave him a wooden tray that was sectioned into little boxes. The boxes held shards of crystals across a rainbow of colors. There had to be more than a hundred different shades.

"Each colored crystal serves a unique purpose," Balam explained, standing next to Jake. "Some we know what they do, like this one."

He plucked a crystal from the tray and held it up into a shaft of sunlight that beamed through one of the twelve holes in the dome. The crystal was the color of dark red wine.

Balam turned to Marika, who sat on a stool next to Jake. He raised an eyebrow toward her. "And what's the name of this crystal?"

She scrunched up her brow in thought. "Ironshine?"

"Very good," he said with a proud flash of a smile. "This stone, when wet, draws iron to its heart."

Balam licked the crystal and placed it near a small metal nail. The nail leaped off the table and stuck to the shard.

Jake leaned in closer, fascinated. The crystal had somehow become magnetized.

Balam smiled at his reaction, pleased with his demonstration, then tapped the crystal with a silver hammer. The iron nail clattered back to the tabletop.

"Other crystals remain a mystery, and it is such mysteries that I spend my days studying." Balam placed a hand on Jake's shoulder. "Most of the time, alchemy is one part wisdom and nine parts chance. And more often than not, *dangerous*." Balam touched the silver badge on Jake's jacket. "These are the four cornerstones of alchemy. And you must learn them well."

Jake stared down at embedded crystals on his badge. The ruby, the emerald, the sapphire formed a triangle around the diamond. Balam tapped each one.

"From these stones all others rise." Balam waved a hand over the box. "*'From the four flows all the power of Kukulkan.'*"

As Jake studied the badge, something began to trickle through his brain, something he'd learned long ago. But what was it? Something to do with the three colored stones that formed the triangle: *red, green, blue* . . .

Then he suddenly remembered. It was like a starburst going off in his head. Something his father had shown him when they were out camping. Jake twisted in his chair and bent down to his backpack on the floor. He searched through its content and found what he was seeking buried near the bottom of the pack.

His franticness had drawn Balam's interest.

Jake pulled free a chunk of quartz cut into a triangular prism. "Red, green, blue," he said. "They're the three *primary* colors of light!"

His father had explained how televisions and computers used red, blue, and green phosphors to produce the millions of colors on the screen. Jake's father had also shown him something else.

Before anyone could respond, Jake lifted the quartz prism into the shaft of sunlight. As the sun's ray shot through it, the light shattered into a small rainbow that splashed against the wall.

"This is advanced alchemy," Balam explained. "Few understand how hidden in the heart of sunlight are all the colors of the world. In fact, all alchemy starts with the sun." He pointed to the open slits across the roof of the dome, then turned his focus back to Jake. "Where did you learn this?"

"From my parents," he answered. "They taught me how if you mix different colored lights together, you can make a new color." Jake pointed to the rainbow on the wall, to where the red and green bands of light blended together to form a yellow streak. "Red light and green light make yellow. While red and blue blend into purple. And the more you mix, the more colors you can make."

Jake lowered his prism and the rainbow vanished.

Balam still stared at the wall, as if the rainbow still shone there. He slowly shook his head. "Such knowledge is reserved for journeymen of the third degree," he said. "Not for first-year apprentices. Such knowledge lies at the heart of how we forge new crystals, how we make the new colored stones."

He nodded to the box of multicolored crystals.

"Wait," Jake said. "Are you saying you *made* all these crystals? How?"

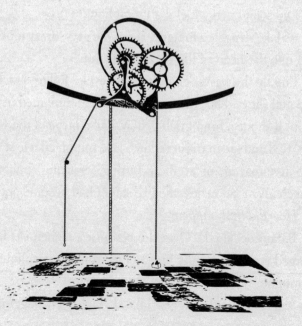

Balam reached over Jake. "Let me show you." He removed an emerald green shard and a sliver of ruby from the box. He crossed to the center of the room and lifted the two stones into a tiny bronze basket that hung by a chain from the clockwork mechanism that filled the dome overhead. Balam pulled another chain that sent the basket up into the mechanism.

Jake quickly lost track of it as it spun and whirled through the complicated mechanical maze. Fluid flowed through glass tubes, and sunlight refracted through the device from the twelve slits in the roof.

Jake remembered Balam's words: *All alchemy starts with the sun.*

Did solar energy fuel it all somehow?

As Jake struggled to figure it out, he grew dizzy looking up into the heart of the twirling machinery.

Finally the basket completed its cycle. Balam reached up and showed Jake that only *one* crystal remained in the pan. It shone a bright rich yellow, like a piece of the sun.

"Red and green make yellow," Jake mumbled. He stared up in amazement at the whirring, creaking, bubbling mechanism. Somehow the two stones had become one.

How did that happen?

Balam declared, "Over the centuries, alchemists have forged crystals of every hue, colors from every splinter of sunlight."

A question still bugged Jake. It had been nagging at

him since he first saw the crystal chandelier in the main hall of the castle keep.

"But what makes the crystals *glow*?" he asked. "What powers them?"

Balam smiled more warmly. "Such a curious mind, Jacob. No wonder you have grown so quickly in knowledge." Balam turned to his daughter. "But perhaps Mari could enlighten you on your question."

Jake glanced over to the girl.

Marika glanced shyly toward her toes. "All power rises from the crystal heart of Kukulkan."

Balam nodded. "Jacob, have you ever tossed a stone into the center of a pond and watched the ripples cast outward toward the shore in all directions?"

Jake nodded. Of course he had.

"It is the same with the crystal heart in the center of the great temple. Its heartbeat is like a stone dropped into a still pond. It casts out ripples over the valley that ignite our hearthlights and set fire to all our stones. It allows the tribes to speak with one tongue and washes up against the ridges that surround our valley, where it protects us."

Jake pictured the energy flowing outward from the temple, powering the crystals and protecting the valley.

Marika spoke, "But beyond the valley, the ripples fade quickly. More than a league from the valley, one tribe cannot understand another, and the green crystals lose their ability to farspeak. It is why we need dartwings to send messages out into the deep jungle, and why hunters or scouts travel with members of their own tribe."

Jake understood. The protective field only reached a certain distance. No wonder the Lost Tribes had remained in this valley.

With a worried sigh, Balam stared at the sun through one of the slits in the roof. "I must meet Magister Zahur and see how Huntress Livia is faring."

Jake twisted in his seat. He was curious about *one* crystal that Marika's father had failed to mention. "The stone that poisoned Huntress Livia. The bloodstone—"

A cloud fell over Balam's face. "We do not speak of such wickedness. It is forbidden to forge such stones."

Jake glanced up at the whirling mechanism.

Balam must have read his thoughts. "Such a curse was not born here in the Astromicon. The purity of sunlight did not give birth to that stone. It was cast from a much darker flame."

With those hard words, Balam strode toward the door. He paused with his hand on the latch and glanced back. "Mari, perhaps any further study for today should be limited to the naming of the stones. We don't want to tax Jacob too heavily after last night."

Balam opened the door and ducked out into the bright sunshine.

Marika took a deep breath as the door swung back shut. She had an apologetic look on her face. "Papa does not like even using the word bloodstone."

"But I don't understand. It's at the heart of the Skull King's power. Shouldn't you know more about it?"

Marika shifted in her chair and moved the box of crystal shards between them. "Maybe we should know more about these *first*."

Despite her hesitation, Jake had seen curiosity spark in Marika's eyes. It matched his own. He stared at the brightly glowing white crystal in the box. White light contained all the colors of the spectrum, while black was the *absence* of all light. Jake shivered, remembering how the bloodstone seemed to suck up the moonlight.

Balam's warning echoed in his head. Bloodstone was not forged in the purity of sunlight, but *was cast from a much darker flame.*

Jake hunched on his stool. What did it matter about bloodstones anyway? It wasn't his problem. All he wanted to do was find a way back home. And the only way to do that was to discover as much as he could about the pyramid—which meant learning more about these strange crystals.

And there was only one way to do that.

Jake nodded toward the wooden tray. "Maybe we'd better begin."

Hours later, Jake rested outside. He sat cross-legged atop the tower on a blanket. Sunlight blazed down. Though it was hot, the brightness helped melt the tension that had been building inside him.

A few steps away, Pindor sat on the edge of the parapet wall. For someone scared of saurians, he seemed fearless of the fall behind him. He rocked back and forth on the edge, while gnawing on what looked like a chicken wing. He had sauce all over his mouth.

"Not many people survive a stingtail bite," Pindor said, pointing the wing at Jake. "Apollo must be watching over you."

"I don't think it was the god Apollo," Marika said. She knelt on the blanket with Jake and searched through the reed basket that Pindor had hauled up to them. She fished through bread rolls and dried pieces of meat that looked like beef jerky. She found a kwarmabean and sat back with it. "Magister Zahur had more to do with keeping Jake alive than any god of Mount Olympus."

Pindor shrugged and slid off the wall. "And you think someone put the stingtail in your room?"

Marika looked at Jake. He nodded.

"Who would do that?" Pindor asked. "I heard my father talking with Magister Oswin. Everyone's saying it was an accident. That one of Zahur's beasties escaped its cage and ended up in Jake's room."

Marika shook her head. "I'm pretty sure I heard someone out in the hall earlier in the night. But I can't prove it."

"Why would they want to kill him?" Pindor asked.

Marika peeled her kwarmabean slowly. "Maybe because someone's scared of him. Of what he knows. Of his sy-enz?"

Pindor didn't look convinced, but he changed the subject. "So what else does this sy-enz do?" He leaned back and stared at Jake. "Show us some more."

"Pindor, he's not a trained rollywort who dances for a handful of nuts."

Still, Jake saw how Marika tried to hide her own interest. He also noted how her green eyes reflected the light like emeralds.

"I can show you a couple things," Jake offered.

"You don't have to," Marika said, but her expression brightened.

Feeling oddly warm inside, Jake scooted back to his feet. He had left his pack in the Astromicon. "C'mon."

He led the others back through the hatch and into the dome. His backpack was under the table near his stool. He pulled it out and fished through it. His fingers pulled out a penlight. It was about the size of a small screwdriver. "We call this a flashlight."

He flicked the switch, pointed it at the wall, and danced a spot of light over the curved bronze surface of the dome.

He glanced over at the other two.

Pindor stood with his arms crossed. "So we have hearth-lights, too. They're all over the place, lighting up Calypsos."

But Marika's eyes had narrowed with interest. "May I see it?"

"Sure." Jake passed it over.

She turned it over in her fingers then tapped the flash-light's lens. "Is this some shard of flat crystal? Is this what casts such a strong light?"

"No, it's run on . . ." Jake had to concentrate to get the English word out of his lips. ". . . *batteries.*"

"Bat trees," Pindor said. "What are those?"

Jake slipped the penlight from Marika and twisted it open. He dumped two AAA batteries out into his palm. "These make power and cause the bulb in the flashlight to glow. Using *electricity.*" Again he had to force his tongue to form the last word.

He passed one battery to Marika and one to Pindor. Marika examined hers with the intensity of a scientist studying a strange new beetle. Pindor sniffed at his, as if wondering what it tasted like. He ended up pointing the battery at Jake.

"Do something else with it."

"Pindor . . ." Marika scolded.

"I just want to see what else it does. Like what do these bat trees do to our crystals?"

Before anyone could stop him, he turned to the box of crystals and stabbed the battery into the piles of shards. Jake tensed. Marika knocked Pindor's arm away. But nothing happened.

Still, it gave Jake an idea. Maybe Pindor was on to something. Could his science and their alchemy be used together somehow? What if they were combined?

"Red and green make yellow," he mumbled, remembering the demonstration by Marika's father.

Jake took the battery from Pindor and bent down to pick up a sliver of blue crystal that had fallen to the floor.

Taking a step away, he tipped up on his toes and placed the battery and the blue crystal in the bronze basket.

"Jake," Marika said. "We're not supposed to touch that."

Jake glanced over to her. Her words of warning had sounded unsure.

Pindor was less reluctant. "Nothing's going to happen."

Jake kept his gaze on Marika. If she said no, he would obey her. But her curiosity only seemed to grow. She was like her father in that regard.

"'Alchemy is . . . nine parts chance,'" Jake said, quoting him.

Marika took a deep breath and crossed to the door. Jake feared she was leaving, but she only closed the door they'd left open. She turned to Jake and nodded.

With a smile, he reached and pulled the chain. The basket rose into the air.

Jake took a step back. Sunlight flashed and sparked as it refracted through the hundreds of crystals embedded in the gearwork overhead. At first nothing seemed to happen—then the mechanism began to turn a little faster. It scattered sunlight into rainbows on the walls.

"Jake . . ." Marika warned.

And it began to spin even faster. Steam escaped tiny valves and began to whistle. Gears spun into blurs.

"We have to stop it!" Marika yelled.

"How?" Jake asked.

They all ducked down as the mechanism churned into a whirling mass of glass and bronze. It heaved and groaned and rumbled and sighed. There was no stopping it.

As the mechanism sped faster, the entire room began to shake. Tools and crystals rattled on the table. A stack of books toppled over. And still it spun even more furiously.

Jake backed to the table. *What have I done?*

"Jake!" Marika cried out. She lifted up the second battery, still in her hand. Sparks shot out one end, snapped through the air, and were sucked into the churning mechanism.

Jake hurried to her side and grabbed the battery. It shocked him, stinging like a snapped rubber band. He tossed it to the tabletop, where it rolled and knocked into a chunk of red crystal the size of a goose egg. Sparks shot from the battery and struck the gem.

It immediately ignited, blazing like a crimson sun.

Before Jake could move, the red crystal melted straight through the tabletop. It wasn't just as bright as the sun—it was as hot!

The crystal dropped through the bottom of the table and hit the stone floor. Jake sighed with relief—until the granite began to bubble at the edges of the crystal. It was trying to burn through the stone floor!

Jake pictured the crystal burning from one floor to the next. When would it stop? Would it stop?

Marika stood frozen in shock.

Jake rushed over and grabbed one of the silver hammers. If he could strike the crystal, turn it off like Marika's father had done before . . .

He turned Marika. She nodded, immediately understanding his plan.

Together they dashed over and dropped to their knees. Jake shielded his face—against both the brightness and the heat. Through his squinted eyes, he saw the stone. It had shrunk to the size of a robin's egg. It now floated in a pool of molten rock.

As Jake reached forward with the hammer, the crystal shrank faster and faster, as if consumed by its own inner fire, like a dying star collapsing in on itself. Jake paused. In a matter of two seconds, the crystal had burned down to the size of a piercingly bright pinhead. Then it blinked out of existence.

"It's gone. . . ." Marika said, and shifted back. Her expression was a mix of horror and curiosity.

The molten pool of granite quickly hardened, as if it knew its very nature was wrong and sought to quickly reverse itself. Soon all that was left was a blackened spot on the floor.

The same couldn't be said for the table.

On his knees, Jake stared at the underside of a perfectly round hole in the bronze tabletop. He could see straight through it. The metal was no longer hot, but the damage was done.

"Look!" Pindor said.

During all the commotion, they'd failed to notice that the mechanism over their heads had slowed. It no longer raced and whined. It merely spun. Jake stared up at the delicate mechanism. Did it sound extra creaky? Was it wheezing a bit more loudly? Had he wrecked it?

From its heart, the bronze basket slowly lowered out of the mechanism. All their eyes were upon it.

Pindor pointed to Jake. "It's your sy-enz. You look!"

He was right.

Jake reached up and tipped the basket over and caught the battery in his palm. It looked unchanged—but there was nothing else! He searched the tray. The sliver of blue crystal was gone.

Jake glanced over to the smoky spot on the granite. Had the crystal vanished the same way? Had it been burned up by the mechanism, perhaps fueling its wild spinning?

Marika asked, "What happened?"

Jake could only shake his head. This was beyond him.

Marika's brow crinkled. She picked up the other battery from the table and handed it over to Jake. Her expression said she was sick with worry. She was done fooling with his science. Guilt shadowed her eyes and caused her to chew at her lower lip as she glanced back to the table.

Jake felt a stab of pain at her distress. It made his own guilt all that much worse. He remembered the words he'd said to her, quoting her father—that alchemy was nine parts chance. But he failed to take to heart what her father had said after that. *And more often than not, dangerous.*

Jake stared at the two batteries in his palm. He could've burned the entire tower to the ground. He gathered up his penlight, inserted the batteries, and screwed the top back on. Out of habit, he thumbed the switch. Light shone out. He clicked it back off. The penlight still worked. He shoved it into one of the pockets of his safari pants.

"What are we going to do?" Pindor asked. He stared at the melted hole. "The Magisters will hang us by our thumbs."

"I'm sorry," Jake said.

"You should be!" Pindor snapped back.

Marika frowned at them both, planting her hands on her hips. "You told him to do it, Pin. None of us said *Stop.* We're *all* to blame."

Pindor didn't argue. His face merely sagged with the truth of her words. "And tomorrow's the Equinox. And the Olympiad! Everyone's going to be there! Once my father hears about all this, I'll be lucky to see the sun before the *next* Equinox!"

"There's no fixing this," Marika said with a heavy sigh.

"But maybe we can hold off anyone finding out what happened."

Pindor's face brightened. "What do you mean? Your father's up here all the time. He'll see it."

Marika crossed to a stack of books that had toppled over during the commotion. She picked up two books, stepped over to the ruined section of the table, and covered the hole with the books. She stacked one atop the other. "Get the rest," she ordered.

Jake and Pindor quickly collected the books. The pile rose again to a teetering tower. Jake shared a grin with Pindor. The hole was now hidden, and the scorch mark under the table was easy to miss.

Marika inspected their work. "Papa leaves stacks like these all around and forgets about them."

"So he might not find the hole for several moons!" Pindor said.

"No, he'll find out sooner than that," Marika said with a stern pinch of her brow.

"How?" Pindor asked.

"Because I will tell my father all about it. But I'll wait until the morning after the Equinox."

"Mari!"

"No, Pin. He must be told. Still, it's no reason to ruin the celebrations. It was my father and mother's favorite day. And now there's only the two of us. . . ." Her words died away, but she glared at Pindor. "I will not have the

Equinox ruined! But after the celebrations, I must tell Papa."

The boy grumbled under his breath. It sounded like he was far from agreeing with her. In this instance, Jake sided with his Roman friend. If anyone found out what they did, Jake feared, his career as an alchemist's apprentice would end.

"Well, at least I won't miss the game," Pin said.

The sun was already heading toward the horizon as they exited the Astromicon.

Pin glanced one more time through the door before Marika closed it. "No wonder someone tried to get rid of you," he said to Jake. "Your sy-enz is nothing but trouble."

"I didn't know." Jake looked over at Marika. "I wish I could do it all over again."

"My father always says, *Look twice and step once, because down some roads, there's no turning back.*" She pulled the latch on the door and sealed the Astromicon. They gathered the remains of their picnic lunch in silence, lost in private worries and regrets.

Look twice and step once . . .

Jake remembered pushing Kady's half of the coin into the golden pyramid back at the British Museum. Even back then, he had leaped without looking and dragged Kady along with him.

Down some roads, there's no turning back.

Did the same hold true here?

Jake straightened with the picnic blanket folded in his arms. Beyond the castle walls, he spied the stone dragon stationed in the woods, guarding the great temple. Jake refused to believe that there wasn't a way back home. Still, he felt the pressure of time like bands of steel squeezing his chest. Once the accident here was discovered, he would lose all hope of exploring the pyramid. He had one more day at best.

But that might just be enough.

Jake remembered Pindor's pained concern about missing the Olympiad. *Everyone's going to be there!* Jake's eyes narrowed as he stared over at the pyramid. With the whole town looking toward the stadium, who would be watching the other side of town?

This might be his one and only chance. He had to sneak over there and discover what secret lay within the crystal heart of Kukulkan.

Still, Marika's words echoed in his head.

Look twice and step once . . .

If he attempted this and failed, there would be no turning back. He would surely be imprisoned or banished. And what about Kady? She would likely share his fate.

"Are you ready?" Marika asked.

Jake nodded.

He'd better be ready.

PART THREE

GAME DAY

As Jake climbed down the stairs the next morning, he spotted Marika and her father already in the common room. They moved like a well-oiled machine: placing bowls on the tables, testing a pitcher of hot chocolate with a finger, cutting a pink melon into slices. Balam whispered in Marika's ear, drawing a silly grin. She giggled when her father found the chocolate too hot and sucked on his burned finger. They moved with the ease of years of love. It was an effortless and happy dance of the morning, shared by father and daughter.

Jake paused in the middle of the stairs, remembering similar mornings at Ravensgate Manor: of his mother helping Aunt Matilda fry eggs and bacon, of his father at the table in his socks and robe, buried in one of his journals. He remembered laughter and hugs and warm smiles.

"Looks like someone's finally come to join us!"

Jake shook himself and reluctantly pushed aside the ghosts of his parents. He lifted an arm in greeting to Marika's father and continued down the stairs.

During the night, Jake had put together a plan, plotting it all out in the dark. He steeled himself for the bit of acting necessary to put the first stage of his plan in action.

Jake limped off the last step and faked a pained wince and a gasp. He felt a real twinge at having to deceive Marika and her father, but he had no choice. He hobbled toward the table.

"What's wrong?" Marika asked.

Jake leaned down and rubbed his right leg. "After sleeping, my leg's cramped up. And . . . and . . ." He put a palm to his forehead. "And I don't think I'm feeling all that well."

Balam hurried to his side, tested his forehead, and urged Jake to sit down. "Let me see your leg. Stingtail venom is nothing to be taken lightly."

Jake hiked up his pant leg. Balam examined the healing scratch on Jake's calf. "No redness. No puffiness," the old man said with relief. "Looks fine. The muscles must've been bruised by the venom and tightened up."

Jake nodded. It sounded good to him—and fit his plan. He needed to be left behind when everyone headed over to the stadium for the big game. Once alone, he'd have his best chance of sneaking over to the temple.

"Maybe you'd better spend one more day here in the tower," Balam said. "It's a shame that you'll miss the Olympiad."

Jake forced his face into a mask of disappointment. "I'll just lie down. Maybe by the evening I'll feel well enough to go to the Equinox party."

Marika touched her father's arm. "Papa, I can stay with Jake. We can't leave him alone. What if he needs something . . . or becomes sicker."

Jake straightened in his seat. "No, I'll be fine. Really. If you missed the Olympiad, I'd be crushed. I would feel so guilty."

But her father's eyebrows had knit with concern. Before he could answer, the narrow servant door opened. A small shape stepped into the room. It was Bach'uuk, balancing a large bowl in his arms.

"Ah, the porridge . . ." Balam said. "Just place it on the table, Bach'uuk. Thank you."

Marika's father kept his worried attention on Jake.

As Bach'uuk set the bowl on the table, Marika suddenly brightened. "What if Bach'uuk stayed with you, Jake? He wasn't going to the game anyway. That way you won't have to be crushed."

Before Jake could respond, Marika said, "Bach'uuk, Jake is feeling a little weak. Would you mind watching over him until we return from the Olympiad?"

"I can do that," Bach'uuk answered. He stared with a

focused intensity toward Jake.

Jake stood up. He certainly did not need someone guarding him, especially not the heavy-browed boy. Jake remembered his earlier suspicions about who might have left the stingtail in his room. Bach'uuk could have easily snuck into his room.

Marika's father spoke. "And if there is any problem, Bach'uuk could run down to Magister Zahur's cellars. The Magister will be staying in the tower to care for Huntress Livia."

Jake's stomach went cold. He felt his plan unraveling before him. Not only would he be watched over by the strange boy, but the only other person in the tower would be the one who had let the stingtail escape. What if there was another attempt on his life?

He quickly recalculated. Maybe he'd have a better chance if he went with them to the stadium. With all the people and chaos, he could lose the others and still sneak off alone to the temple of Kukulkan. Maybe he could salvage his plans after all.

Jake stretched his right leg and took a few steps around the room. "Maybe none of that's necessary. Now that I'm up and moving around, my leg's feeling much better." He circled the table to prove it. "Maybe lying around is not such a good idea. I might be better if I were moving. Exercising it. And . . . and I'd hate to miss the game."

"Are you sure?" Marika's father asked doubtfully.

"It truly feels much better. It was just cramped up."

Balam brightened. "We'll leave early then. Go slow. But if you tire out or the cramping sets in again . . ."

Jake nodded vigorously. "I'll let you know. I promise."

"Then let's finish our porridge, grab our flags, and be off to the game!"

Marika happily complied and dished out heaping bowls of warm porridge swimming with chunks of dried fruit and swirls of cinnamon and honey.

Forgotten by the others, but plainly understanding his presence was no longer necessary, Bach'uuk retreated by the servant door.

Out of the corner of his eye, Jake watched him. He read the boy's expression. Disappointment . . . and a trace of anger.

Jake was glad when he left.

"Eat up!" Balam said cheerily. "We have an exciting day ahead of us!"

Beyond the gates of the castle wall, crowds filled the streets. Banners waved, people sang, and still others danced in small parades.

Marika pulled him aside as a gaggle of children ran past, pounding cymbals and tooting horns, chased by a Chinese dragon made out of silk carried by laughing adults. Jake recognized the young ones; he'd seen them practicing in front of their pagoda two days ago.

The farther they moved out, the more people pressed around them. Jake's need to reach the pyramid weighed on him. He had to find the right moment to escape. But the crowd was so tightly packed.

And one other thing.

Marika had taken his hand in hers as soon as they passed through the castle gates. Plainly she feared losing him or that he might suddenly weaken again. She glanced over at him frequently. Her cheeks had a flushed excitement to them, while sunlight danced in her eyes. In her other hand she waved a crimson flag with a Mayan glyph on it.

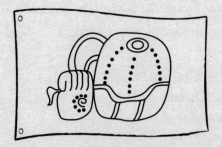

Marika caught him staring. "It's the flag for the Mayan team. We lost during one of the early rounds, but we have to show our pride."

Magister Oswin puffed and wheezed behind them, forcing them to go slowly. "I should have stayed with Zahur," the English monk complained to Balam. "If the huntress expires, I would like to attempt to collect one of the slivers of bloodstone."

"We removed all we could see that first night," Balam said softly. Jake had to slow down and slip closer to eavesdrop. "But she continued to fail. Whatever pieces remain are too small to pick out, and you'd only risk poisoning yourself if you should touch a sliver with your finger by mistake."

Balam patted a heavy pouch that hung from his belt. "I have Zahur's farspeaking crystal. If there are any problems, he will let us know. Until then, let's not cast shadows on this bright day."

"Fair enough." Oswin pressed a wide hand on his ample belly. "And I've already skipped my porridge to leave room for the dinner at the palace of Tiberius. The Romans do know how to put on the grandest of feasts!"

"They have to *win* first," Balam said with little hope in his voice. "The Sumerians defeated our team without losing a single point. They are fierce and determined to win the Eternal Torch for their tribe."

By now, their group had reached the exit to the town, and the river of people bunched up even tighter. Still holding Marika's hand, Jake was pulled by the riptide of the crowd flowing through the northern city gates.

From this vantage point, the enormous stadium definitely looked like a Roman coliseum. Plastered in white and painted in hues of gold, it shone blindingly bright in the midday sun.

Massive archways surrounded the stadium and housed

enormous stone giants. As he followed the crowd, Jake stared up at the statue of Zeus, who leaned on a lightning bolt. His shoulders seemed to be carrying the weight of the entire upper section of the stadium. Jake spotted another statue—Odin, the chief of the Norse gods. He guessed each of the Lost Tribes must have some symbol cast in stone here.

As they continued toward the stadium, someone called out to them.

"Hey! There you all are!"

Pindor waved and headed over. As he joined them, Marika finally slipped her hand out of Jake's. He rubbed his hand on his jacket, relieved at being free, but also a little disappointed. Marika's look said maybe she hadn't just been holding his hand to keep from losing him in the crowd.

At this thought, Jake suddenly felt a little lighter in his steps, but his parents' journals in his jacket reminded him of his duty. He could not lose focus. He had to get over to the temple today.

"We'd better hurry," Pindor said, his face aglow with the thrill of it all.

Jake looked back to the city, then glanced at the crowds around him. Perhaps he could escape as they entered the stadium. The press of people would offer a good chance to slip off.

"Your sister, Katherine, is already inside," Pindor said to

Jake, drawing back his attention.

Jake nodded. Maybe it would be best to wait until he spoke to Kady before he made his escape. She should know what he was going to attempt to do. Maybe she could even help.

Jake rolled his eyes at this last thought—yes, he had become *that* desperate.

FIRST SKIRMISH

Jake stepped out of a short dark tunnel and into the sunlit stadium. It already rang with the excited babble of the gathering crowd. Across all three levels of seating, banners and flags waved. They formed a patchwork of colors around the central field as tribes staked out their own areas. Even the rim of the stadium jostled with the giant winged raz and the People of the Wind.

"This way!" Pindor urged, and almost dragged Jake after him. Marika hurried to follow.

Pindor led them to the front of the Roman section, where a group of empty seats waited for them. Jake and Marika hurried into the first row. The two Magisters settled into the row behind them, sighing happily, content never to move again.

Pindor refused to sit and stood at the fence at the bottom of the stands. Jake and Marika joined him.

On either side of the field were two teams of *Othneilia,*

what the people here called fleetbacks. Each beast was saddled, while men and women bustled around, adjusting straps and checking each mount. The Roman team wore white sashes bearing the red lightning bolt of Zeus. On the far side of the field must be the Sumerians. They wore snug black scarves that covered the lower halves of their faces. They were already climbing into their saddles.

"It won't be long now," Pindor said.

Marika glanced to the sun in the sky and agreed. "It's almost the middle of the Equinox day."

Centurion Gaius suddenly appeared on the step next to them. He called to Jake. "I was ordered to fetch you to see your sister before the Olympiad begins."

Jake saw that the Viking party had taken up seats in a neighboring section. They waved flags that were sea blue with a silver eye in the center.

Jake followed the big man down a narrow set of stairs. Sand crunched underfoot as they skirted along the field. At the far side of the Viking section, he spotted a group of older girls in horned helmets, wearing green tunics and breeches.

As Gaius approached, a few of the girls straightened their tunics or leaned to whisper and point toward the tall, broad-shouldered guard. Jake searched for Kady.

Then the group of girls parted before the centurion, and Jake saw her. Kady leaned against the wall beside a gate. One of the Roman riders stood next to her, an arm on the wall. He leaned forward like he was about to kiss her.

"Heronidus!" Gaius barked.

Pindor's brother turned and snapped to attention. Gaius pointed toward the gate. "Shouldn't you be seeing to your mount rather than moon-eyeing a young woman?"

"No . . . I mean, yes, Centurion Gaius."

"Then I suggest you attend to it."

Heronidus snapped a fist to his chest, then turned and scrambled away. Kady straightened. She had a rolled flag in her hand, probably a gift from Heronidus. She at least had the decency to raise a blush to her cheeks as she crossed over to join them.

Jake shook his head. *Nothing changes.* Even in this strange land, Kady was already dating the captain of the football team.

"Jake," she said, and moved closer. "I heard you got stung by something. Are you all—"

He cut her off. "There's no time to explain. But I think someone tried to kill me. Left a giant scorpion on my bed."

Her eyes grew wider and more intense. "What?" She clutched the sleeve of his shirt. "What happened?"

He switched to English. "It's a long story . . . with lots of holes in it. But I need your help."

"How? Doing what?"

"With everyone here at the stadium, now's the best—

and possibly only—chance for me to sneak over to that pyramid and check it out. I'm just looking for some sort of distraction. A commotion or something. Anything so I can slip away without anyone really paying attention."

"Okay."

"Okay what?"

She nodded. "My team and I will come up with something."

"Your team?"

Jake stared over at the gaggle of Viking girls. Only now did he note that all of them had their hair up in a French braid, an exact match to Kady's. "What are you going to—"

She waved him away. "Not exactly sure yet. But just watch for my signal, then get moving."

Before he could ask more a gong sounded, followed by the heavy beat of a drum.

Centurion Gaius crossed over to them. "Best you return to your seats. The Olympiad begins."

Once back with Pindor and Marika, Jake watched the two teams form lines on opposite ends of the field. There were seven players on each team. The saurians huffed and tossed their long necks. The riders shouted last-minute instructions to one another. The crowd grew hushed in anticipation. Jake felt the beating of four massive drums— one at each corner of the stadium—in his chest.

Pindor leaned over the fence. Marika chewed her knuckle.

His friends had tried to explain the game rules to Jake, but he'd barely paid attention. All he knew was that the first part of the Olympiad was called the *skirmish*.

A horn blew a single long note, and from overhead, one of the mighty raz took flight from the highest perch along the stadium rim. A crimson ball, the size of a pumpkin, dropped to the sandy floor.

What followed seemed like pure chaos, a brawl of beast and rider for the ball, but there must have been some strategy.

"Oh, no," Pindor moaned. "They're going for the Dragged Foot Gambit—can't Heron see!"

A mighty cheer rose from the Sumerians and their supporters. Banners flew higher there, and flags waved like mad. The Romans yelled and groaned.

Pindor failed to lose his enthusiasm. "It's only the skirmish! So the Sumerians get the ball first. It's not the end of the game . . . only the beginning."

But the Romans fared no better on the next play.

"Watch the man on the left!" Pindor yelled. "He's slicing in for the pass."

Again Pindor proved he knew what he was talking about. Heronidus threw the ball, but it ended up in an opponent's grip. The Sumerian zigzagged between two more Romans, and using his arms like twin pistons, he shot the ball through the Roman goalpost. Groans spread through the Roman encampment.

Pindor fell back into his seat while the teams regrouped. "Why doesn't anyone listen to me?"

"Because they can't hear you," Marika answered as she and Jake sat down.

Pindor crossed his arms. He might be nervous around the big saurians because of his accident, but he clearly understood the flow and strategy of the game. Probably better than his brother. But that didn't get you into the saddle.

In the quiet of the dour mood, Jake sat and heard a squeaky, muffled voice: *"Magister Balam, can you hear me?"*

Jake twisted around in his seat. Marika's father fumbled with the pouch hanging from his belt. He tugged open the strings and pulled out the small frame that held a chunk of green crystal within a silk webbing.

"Magister Balam . . ." the crystal rang out a bit more urgently.

Balam hunched over the crystal with Oswin. Their crouched position brought the farspeaking device closer to Jake.

Jake straightened in his seat and pretended not to be listening, but Marika had reached over and gripped the back of Jake's hand. The call was from Magister Zahur. They both stiffened, trying not to miss a word.

"I hear you, Zahur. What's wrong?"

"It's Huntress Livia. In the last few moments, she's become wild, thrashing and moaning. She struggles fiercely. Between her moans, unintelligible words rise up like bubbles in an overheated bowl of porridge. She mumbles and clutches me, as if trying to communicate, but she cannot escape the shadows that hold her."

Oswin grumbled in his seat. "I told you we should have fought harder to get those last slivers out."

Not hearing him, Zahur continued, "It's as if the woman knows death is coming, but she struggles with her last breath to speak what she knows."

Jake felt a pang in his gut at these words. He pictured Livia's head cradled in his lap, her blue eyes, so like his own mother's. Jake couldn't help but still feel connected to her, bound by both bloodshed and the oath he had made.

Balam touched the crystal. "Zahur, is there nothing more you can do for her?"

"No. It is over. Her death now comes on swift wings."

Oswin stood up, bumping Jake in the back. "That's it. I'm going back to Kalakryss."

Balam nodded and spoke into the crystal. "Oswin and I will come join you, Zahur. I don't know what else we can do but offer our support and attend to her deathwatch. She won't live unless those fractured bits of bloodstone miraculously vanish from her flesh."

"I understand."

Balam ended the call and pushed the device back into his pouch. He leaned closer and placed a hand on Jake's and Marika's shoulders. "I must return to Kalakryss," he said.

"But, Papa—"

Her father stood up. "Stay and enjoy the Olympiad. I will do my best to join you at Tiberius's palace for the feast." He waved an arm to Gaius. "Centurion, would you be so kind as to keep an eye on my daughter and young Jake? And escort them after the game?"

"Of course, Magister. It would be my honor."

"Papa . . ." Marika attempted again to get his attention, but her father was already leaving with Oswin.

Centurion Gaius took one of the seats behind Jake and Marika.

A horn sounded from the field, and the riders climbed back into their saddles for the second quarter.

Pindor rose to his feet again. He was the only Roman who showed that much enthusiasm. Jake attempted to join Pindor at the fence, but Marika yanked on his arm and pulled him back down.

She leaned in close. "Did you hear what my father said?"

Jake pinched his brows, but nodded. "It doesn't sound good."

"No, not that. At the end. When my father mentioned

that Livia's only hope lay in a miracle. How if the blood-stone shards suddenly *vanished*, she might live?"

Her gaze bore into Jake, but he still didn't understand. She read the lack of comprehension in his face and sighed. "Your *bat trees* and its *elektra-city* powers. It consumed the ruby crystal back in the Astromicon."

Jake blinked, struggling to catch up with the swiftness of her thoughts. He pictured the red goose-egg-sized crystal shrinking and vanishing. But he also pictured the destruction it wreaked before that happened: the melted hole through the table, the scorched stone.

Marika leaned closer to Jake. "Can you cast your power into her flesh and make those shards vanish the same way?"

"Maybe." He thought quickly. What would happen if he shocked the huntress's wound? Jolted it with electricity? He still pictured the hole melted through the bronze. "It might also kill her."

"She's going to die anyway."

That might be true, but Jake didn't want to be the *cause* of her death. What if something went wrong?

"We could at least tell my father," she said. "Let him decide."

Jake hesitated. Once Magister Balam learned of the near catastrophe at the Astomicon, Jake could kiss good-bye any chance of visiting the pyramid. But could he let someone die to keep that secret? And he had made a vow. If there was even a slim chance of saving the huntress . . .

Marika read the determination that set in his face. "So we'll tell my father."

Jake nodded. The two stood up together and began to edge down their row, but something clamped onto his shoulder. He turned to find Centurion Gaius glowering down at them. He had a hold of Marika's shoulder, too.

"No one's going anywhere," Gaius said, and pushed Jake and Marika back into their seats.

Marika turned to Jake, the question plain on her face.

What are we going to do?

RACE ACROSS TOWN

Jake sensed the centurion's eyes on the back of his neck as he tried to think of some way to sneak off. Gaius would not be easily fooled. To make matters worse, the game was growing into a rout.

A chorus of voices suddenly shouted. "All right!" "Everyone on your feet!" "Now's not the time to accept defeat!"

Jake obeyed, not out of allegiance but out of a steely sense of horror. He joined Pindor at the fence and stared down at the edge of the field.

Oh, no . . .

A line of Viking women were arranged in a row. As Jake feared, Kady stood in the front. She was up on one leg, her arms out in a cheerleader position known as a High V. The women behind her matched her pose.

Kady waved her arms and pointed them at the crowd. "Let's go, Romans! Let's go!" She signaled for the row of Viking cheerleaders to continue the chant as she moved closer to the stands and sang out. "Let's hear your spirit!" She lifted her arms up and down, synchronized with the chant, urging the crowd to follow. "Let's go, Romans! Let's go!"

Kady's eyes found Jake and focused hard on him. He understood. Someone had to get this started. Jake cleared his throat, and on the next chorus, he joined in. "Let's go, Romans! Let's go!"

He elbowed Pindor, who awkwardly took up the chant. Marika joined in a moment later. It slowly spread through their group and beyond.

"Stamp your feet!" Kady yelled. "To the beat! Let's go, Romans! Let's go!" She and her team demonstrated by stamping their feet at the end of each refrain.

Jake didn't have to be first this time. In seconds, the stands rattled with the stamp of boots. People were on their feet, yelling along with her.

Kady encouraged them by clapping her hands over her head.

Her efforts were not wasted on the stands. Out in the field, the Roman team caught the excitement and fought more fiercely for the ball. Heronidus leaped headlong out of his saddle and caught a stray pass. He landed back in his saddle with the ball under his arm. His team closed in a tight formation around him, and together they slammed through a weak spot in the Sumerian line. Heronidus sent his ball flying. It arced high, skipped over the fingertips of a defender, and sailed cleanly through the rings of the goal.

The stands erupted in chaos around Jake. Already worked up by the cheering, the crowd surged closer to the fence line.

Down below, Kady pointed an arm to Jake, then to the sky. *Get ready to move,* she silently communicated.

She waved her other arm to her team. The team scattered wider and set up a line that stretched halfway down their side of the field.

"Right through the hoop!" Kady yelled. "Nothing but air! C'mon, Romans! Let's show them we care!"

At her signal, the women sank to a knee in succession along the line, then rose again. This went back and forth. Jake recognized they were performing the Wave. Off to the right, the Viking section took up the Wave, rising out of their seats with a shout, then back down again.

Kady egged Jake's section to follow suit. "C'mon, Romans! Show your spirit!" She pantomimed below, crouching and standing in time with her cheerleaders. "On your feet . . . or face defeat!"

With the next wave, the excited Romans caught the fiery spirit and extended the Wave. The chant continued, and the Wave flowed back and forth with bellows of support.

Jake glanced over his shoulder. Gaius was packed in by his fellow Romans, forced to rise and fall with the Wave.

Jake turned to Marika. "Be ready! On the next wave!"

"What?"

Jake grabbed Marika's elbow and dragged her low along their aisle as the Wave crested high around them. She snagged a fistful of Pindor's toga and forced him to follow.

He squeaked a protest.

"Be quiet! And run!" Marika urged.

Together, they flew up toward the exit tunnel, squeezing between people who continued to push toward the front of the stands.

They hit the tunnel at a run. Pindor kept up, but he continued to glance back. "Where are we going?" he yelled at Jake and Marika.

"Back to Kalakryss!" Marika answered.

"What? Why?"

They shot out of the stadium onto the cobblestone road that led back to town. Pindor slowed, hearing a mighty cheer for the Romans.

"Marika Balam! Jacob Ransom! Pindor Tiberius! Show yourselves now!" Gaius called, his commands booming out of the stadium tunnel.

Jake ran faster alongside Marika, but Pindor passed them with his long legs. They rounded a corner into an area where wagons and chariots had been parked.

"Over here!" Pindor called ahead. He reached a two-wheeled chariot tethered to a pygmy dinosaur. Leaping into the chariot, he waved Jake in and Marika toward the hitching post. "Um . . . can you free the lead rope?"

Marika quickly obeyed, then joined Jake and Pindor in the chariot.

Pindor tapped the dinosaur's hindquarters to get it moving. "Hie! Move it, thick thighs!"

He snapped the switch in the air, and the beast lumbered faster, its neck stretched low to the ground. As their speed picked up and the rattling of the chariot grew worse, Jake found an easy balance with his knees slightly bent and planted wide.

"Hie!"

The chariot sped even faster, flying now through the city gates. Pindor might be nervous in close quarters with the saurians, but he plainly knew how to drive a chariot.

Pindor continued at a reckless pace down the main thoroughfare. With the place mostly deserted, he didn't need to slow. Buildings flashed past.

"So why are we running from Centurion Gaius?" Pindor glanced over to Marika.

"To help Huntress Livia."

"What?"

Marika explained briefly what they wanted to do. She ended: "Borrowing this chariot was quick thinking, Pin. We might even be able to catch up with my father and Magister Oswin."

Even with the compliment at the end, Pindor had gone

pale. His steady hand on the reins faltered. They side-swiped an open-market fruit stand and sent a fountain of spiny-skinned melons into the air. Pindor waved an arm back toward the coliseum. "I thought we were in trouble back there! Running for our lives! But no! All this was on some soft-headed idea to use sy-enz to cure Huntress Livia. By Jupiter's knees, that's pure madness!"

Marika huffed. "We'll leave it to my father to decide, Pin! Just drive!" She pointed toward the castle.

An awkward tension settled over the chariot. Jake knew most of it was because they were all scared—both for what lay ahead and what lay behind them. They would get into a huge amount of trouble if Pindor was right and all of this was nonsense.

If they failed, Jake would lose any chance of getting to the pyramid. But he couldn't let Huntress Livia die for lack of trying. He knew his father and mother would've done the same. Kady, on the other hand, had gone to a lot of trouble to help him escape. She was going to be angry when she found out he'd never made it to the pyramid.

But he had no choice.

"Hurry!" Marika called as they ran into the tower to save the huntress. "Everyone must already be down in the cellars."

She clambered down the stairs, sometimes skipping two steps at a time. Jake knew her worry. What if they were too late? Marika wore a stricken, guilty expression—like she should have thought of this idea earlier.

The cellars lay deeper than Jake had expected. Marika passed two landings with doors, but she kept going. The grayish stone grew black around the spiral stairs, possibly scorched by the old fires that had rid the keep of the Skull King.

"Just up ahead," Marika said, breathless. She pointed to where the stairs finally ended at a slightly open door.

She reached it first, knocked loudly, and called, "Magister Zahur! Papa!"

Jake and Pindor joined her on the landing. The only light came from a pair of iron sconces on either side of the door. Marika's knocking had pushed the door open wider.

Jake leaned his head inside and saw that more stairs led down farther still. The glow from the landing's sconces extended far enough to reveal the common room below. He could make out the dark shapes of a table and chair.

"Magister Zahur?" Marika called again, sounding less sure.

Only silence answered her.

"Maybe they're back in his deeper cellars," Pindor said. "I've heard it's a maze down there."

Hearing him, Marika moved slowly, but her fear for Livia drove her onward.

Jake followed at her heels. "Maybe they've taken her somewhere else. Maybe up to your place or the Astromicon."

Or maybe Livia was already dead.

As they reached the common room, they heard a ghostly moan. Someone else *was* down here.

"Tap the lights," Marika said.

Pindor searched along one wall near the stairs. Jake did the same along the other. "Found one," Pindor said.

Jake heard a ringing *ting* as his friend flicked the crystal bulb with his fingernail. It remained dark. Jake's hand found another wall sconce on his side. He felt for the chunk of crystal, found it, and tapped the bulb.

Nothing.

. . . *ting, ting, ting* . . .

"It's not working," Pindor said.

The scuff of a boot drew Jake's attention around. The door at the top of the stairs slammed shut. The light from the hall was cut off, and a pitch-black darkness fell over them.

"Hey!" Pindor yelled, bumping into Jake. "We're down here!"

Jake grabbed Pindor's arm. "Be quiet!" A few steps away, Marika squeaked out in fear.

Pindor tried to shake free of Jake's grasp. "What're you—"

Jake squeezed harder, silencing him.

Then he heard it again. A faint buzzing—like a thousand bees. Jake recognized that sound. He'd heard it in

247

the middle of the night. A stingtail. One of the flying scorpions. Then over his head, Jake heard an equally familiar *scritch-scritch* of claws as something crawled along the ceiling. Another one!

"Marika," Jake whispered. "Get over here."

He pushed Pindor toward the stairs. "Try the door."

As Marika crept toward him, more buzzing rose out of the darkness. Jake remembered Zahur's comment about the missing stingtail that ended up in Jake's room—how it was one of *six*.

The buzzing grew louder and was answered by others in the dark, becoming a deadly chorus.

Jake jumped as Marika knocked into him.

"Stingtails," she whispered in his ear.

Someone had let all the scorpions loose.

Pindor called down from the top of the stairs in a frantic whisper. "It's locked."

Jake and Marika backed away from the scratching of claws and buzzing of wings. They had no weapons—and no way out.

DEATH TRAP

Marika and Jake backed from the common room and climbed three steps up the cellar stairs. Pindor stumbled down to join them from the locked door. There was no way out that way. Jake remained frozen on the step. He didn't want to be trapped in the stairwell when the rest of the deadly scorpions came flying out of the dark.

They needed weapons—and a light.

Then Jake remembered. He had stashed his penlight in his pants pocket after the disaster up in the Astromicon. He scrambled to unbutton the pocket and ended up ripping it in frustration. The button popped off and went flying across the room.

Jake pulled out the penlight and flicked the switch. A spear of brilliant light pierced the darkness. Pindor gasped in surprise and almost fell onto his backside.

Marika clutched Jake's other arm.

With the burst of light, all buzzing and scratching halted.

"We have to find somewhere to hole up," Jake said. "Somewhere where those stingtails can't get at us."

"Pindor was right about it being a maze down here." Marika pointed. "There are more rooms beyond this one. If we could make it over there . . ."

But that meant first crossing the common room.

Jake swallowed hard. The penlight only cast out a thin beam. The surrounding darkness looked even blacker now. As he shifted the beam around, shadows jumped and trembled. The light seemed to create more hiding places, not fewer.

But his light did reveal a closed door directly across from their position. They would have to make a run for it. It was their only chance. Still, what if it was locked? What if beyond it were worse horrors than stingtails? Who knew what else Zahur kept hidden in his cages down here?

A low moan answered him. Jake had forgotten about hearing the groaning earlier. The noise sounded like it came from behind that same door.

"Somebody's here," Marika whispered.

But was that good or bad?

Jake risked stepping off the stairs to the floor. He cast his light all around. He searched the floor, the tabletop, and the roof with its shadowy rafters. A flicker of motion drew his eye to the lights hanging from the ceiling. One of the chains swung and revealed a black mass latched onto it.

Jake speared the stingtail with his light. As the light struck it, the monster's wings snapped wide and blurred into motion with a furious buzzing. Its spiked tail curled high. Angered by the light, the stingtail flew off its perch and dove straight at Jake.

He leaped backward, bowling into Marika and Pindor. The scorpion hit where Jake had been standing—and shattered into a hundred pieces like a broken glass.

Its poisonous tail skittered and bounced to the foot of the stairs.

After a stunned moment, Pindor asked, "What happened?"

Jake reached out and poked the tail with a finger. It felt solid as a rock and *cold*. He tested it again. The thing was frozen solid, as if dipped in liquid nitrogen. What could've done that?

"Your lightstick!" Marika answered his silent question. Jake's penlight was shining on a crystal pitcher of flowers on the table. They had been blooming and green, but now they were blackened and covered in frost. The pitcher suddenly exploded and ice tinkled across the tabletop.

"It's your lightstick," Marika insisted. "The bat tree you put inside it! It came out of the Astromicon's device."

Jake remembered placing the battery in the bronze tray and sending it up into the machine—along with a shard of *blue* crystal, the same crystal that was known for its cooling ability. He'd thought the crystal had been consumed by the machine, but now he understood.

Red and green make yellow.

"The battery and the crystal fused into one!" The property of the crystal and the power of the battery had somehow joined together and created a freezing beam of light.

He started to lift his hand toward the beam to test it, but Marika grabbed his wrist. "No! Don't!"

Jake lowered his arm. The darkness hid his blushing embarrassment. What a stupid thing to do! He could've frozen his fingers right off his hand. He kept the beam pointed ahead of him. Now they had a weapon—for at least as long as the battery's power lasted. But who knew how long that would be?

"Stay behind me," Jake told Marika and Pindor. "We have to get to that far door."

He edged out into the room, sweeping his light right and left. As he neared the table, a *scritch-scritch* warned him. He danced back as another of the stingtails scuttled out from under a chair, tail high, dripping poison.

Jake fixed his light on it. Its scrabbling legs suddenly froze up, but its momentum kept its body sliding across the stone. The poison on the tip of its tail had become an icicle. Jake performed a Tae Kwon Do sweeping kick and sent it flying away.

Spinning, he searched all around with his flashlight.

If all five of Zahur's scorpions had been set free, that

left three more running around somewhere—or flying. The next attacks came from the rafters and the top of a cupboard. With a flurry of wings, the monsters dive-bombed from two different directions.

Jake couldn't stop both.

He pointed his light at one and fought to keep his beam on it long enough to freeze it. The blur of wings stopped in mid beat, and it dropped like a heavy stone to the table-top. Legs broke under it, but its body remained intact, a gruesome centerpiece.

Jake tried to swing the light around in time to freeze the other attacker, but as he turned, Pindor punched out with a fist and knocked the diving scorpion to the floor. It landed on its back, legs waving and claws clacking. As Pindor stumbled back, Jake lunged forward and used an ax kick to smash his heel through its belly.

"The door!" Jake said, and waved the others forward. There was still another stingtail out here.

Marika yanked it open. The room beyond looked like a small infirmary, with a cot, shelves of glass bottles, and a table with rolled bandages, scissors, and jars of thick pastes. The room smelled acrid from whatever medicines were used here.

Marika screamed.

Jake immediately saw why. It was the huntress, Livia, sprawled under a thin blanket on the bed. She looked as pale as a ghost. Her skin shone silvery, almost translucent in the feeble light from a tiny lamp at her bedside.

Atop her chest crouched the last of the scorpions. Its venomous tail arched high, ready to strike. Jake feared pointing the beam of his penlight at the creature. The scatter of the beam might freeze Livia, too.

"Get back," Jake whispered, clicking off the flashlight. He slipped between his two friends and crouched low as he took three slow steps toward the bed. He had to get close.

With their arrival, the stingtail had gone as still as a statue, wary, sizing up the threat. The only thing that moved were its black eyes on tiny stalks. They swiveled all around.

Jake only needed one more step—but he was too late.

The tail whipped forward like the head of a striking rattlesnake. It plunged toward Livia's thin neck. Jake thrust his arm forward and flicked the switch on the penlight. The tip of the flashlight was less than an inch from the spike as it stabbed into the woman's neck.

Marika gasped as Jake held steady. The tail yanked out, dripping blood from its spike. The scorpion scuttled backward, trying to escape the icy touch of the beam. But Jake twisted his wrist and shone the beam into its stalky eyes, toward its head. The legs suddenly spasmed and convulsed. Claws tore holes in the blanket. Then with a final tremor it simply collapsed like a puppet with its strings cut.

Jake had turned its brain to ice.

With a shudder, Jake slapped the creature off the huntress. Marika ran up to him. Pindor crossed over, too, but not before stamping his heel through the stingtail, making sure it stayed dead.

"It stung her!" Marika moaned.

Jake thumbed off his penlight and leaned over the woman in the bed. Blood dripped down her neck, but nothing spurted. Jake inspected the wound. The stinger had hit nothing vital. With a bandage, it should heal.

"The venom will kill her in a matter of breaths," Marika said.

Jake watched Livia's chest rise and fall under the blanket. "Maybe not, Mari. I did the only thing I could. I froze the tip of the tail first. With luck the poison turned to ice and remained trapped in the stinger."

Faint hope shone in Marika's eyes. "We should know in the next few moments."

They kept a silent vigil. Jake used the time to press a bundle of cloth gently against the hole in Livia's neck, but already the blood had slowed its seeping. After a full three minutes, Marika's eyes shone brighter as she glanced to Jake.

Livia's chest continued to rise and fall, weakly, but no more so than before.

"I think she's going to make it," Marika said.

Ever practical, Pindor dampened her hope. "Maybe

she wasn't poisoned by the stingtail, but those shards of bloodstone are still in her."

Confirming this, the huntress let out a low moan. One hand flew up and knocked the lamp off the bedside table. She was suddenly wild, frantic. Her eyelids fluttered open, but there was no sight. Only the whites of her eyes showed.

"We have to help her! But what do we do?" Marika searched the room, looking lost. "Where's Magister Zahur? Or even my father and Magister Oswin?"

Jake shook his head. They'd seen no sign of any of the Magisters. "Maybe they haven't gotten here yet?"

A touch of hysteria entered Marika's voice. "Even if they'd walked, we should have seen them from the chariot."

"No, I think they got here," Pindor said. He was down on his knees, recovering the lamp Livia had knocked over. He pulled a hand from beneath her bed. In his fingers he held a slender stick of wood that looked like a wand. Its crystal tip reflected the lamplight. Jake recognized the wand. Marika's father had used it to touch the bloodstone arrowhead and banish its evil.

"Papa's dowsing wand!" Marika said.

So her father *had* been here.

Marika snatched the wand from Pindor and clutched it to her chest. She turned in a full circle, as if expecting to find her father suddenly standing there. She looked a breath away from full panic.

Jake tried to calm her. "Just because his stick is here, it doesn't really tell us what happened. They could have gone anywhere." He kept himself from adding, "We've seen no bodies."

"Then who set up this trap? Who locked us in here?" Marika asked.

"Maybe Zahur," Pindor said. "Those were his sharp-tailed beasties. And he did call your father. Maybe it was to lure him here, while everyone was at the Olympiad."

Marika shook her head, trying not to believe, but she didn't shake her head too vigorously or scold Pindor for such doubts. Like Jake, she was probably brimming with suspicions. Her fingers still clung to her father's wand.

From the room outside, a heavy creak of hinges rasped, like bone scraping on bone. Everyone froze. Someone was coming.

"Stay here," Jake hissed.

He crossed to the door and peered out into the dark room. In the weak light Jake spotted a small side door swinging slowly open. It was a furtive motion, possibly someone checking to see if they were dead.

Jake slid out into the common room.

A shadowy shape pushed through a narrow door, like the one in Balam's common room. What if it was one of the Magisters? Even so, Jake still wouldn't know what to do. Who could he trust?

The door opened wider as the intruder stepped into the room. His small form revealed his identity.

"Bach'uuk," Jake whispered.

The Ur boy froze in place. He looked ready to bolt away. Jake could only imagine the boy's fear at hearing his name whispered out of the dark. Jake flicked on his penlight but kept it pointed at the floor.

Bach'uuk straightened but remained wary.

Marika appeared behind Jake. "Bach'uuk!"

Pindor stood at her shoulder. "Apollo be praised! A way out of this trap!"

Jake still kept his penlight ready. *Who's to say Bach'uuk can be trusted?*

Marika held no such misgivings. She hurried over and crushed Bach'uuk in a hug. "What are you doing here?"

Free of her embrace, he shuffled his feet. "I saw someone . . . a stranger fly up out of the cellars. I come to see if Magister Zahur had any trouble."

"He had trouble all right," Pindor mumbled.

Marika started to explain, but Jake cut her off. "What did this stranger look like?"

"He was made of shadows."

"What do you mean?" Marika asked.

Bach'uuk shuddered from head to foot. "The stranger had no form. Shadows rode his shoulders and flowed behind him like a cloak. Where he passed, the hearth-lights died, eaten by his shadows."

Jake glanced back to the darkened room. No wonder the crystals refused to glow.

"I saw only a single gleam." Bach'uuk touched his throat, as if indicating a clasp on a coat. "It shone only because it was blacker than the shadows that covered him."

Jake recognized the description. "Bloodstone."

"He ran into the castle where shadows swallowed him up." Bach'uuk shook his head, indicating he didn't know where the stranger had gone after that.

"Did you see my father? Or Magister Oswin?" Marika asked. The worry in her voice rang like a bell.

Bach'uuk frowned. "Not after this morning."

Marika looked stricken.

"What are we going to do?" Pindor asked. "Who are we going to tell? The Magisters are all gone. Everyone else is off at the Olympiad."

A weak moan whispered out of Livia's throat. It sounded as if it came from far away, as if she were already fading into the distance, crossing where they could not follow.

"We can't just leave Livia," Marika said. "We have to try to save her. Maybe she saw something."

Jake knew that was not likely, but he also read the fear for her father in the lines around Marika's eyes. Jake studied Livia. She would not last another hour. If even that. They had to try something.

He nodded, more to himself than to the others. "We'll try to destroy the bloodstone in her."

He expected some complaint, but Pindor surprised him. "What do you want us to do?"

Jake thought quickly. Pindor had longer legs and could run faster than Jake. "Bach'uuk, can you lead Pin up through your back stairs? All the way to the Astromicon? We don't want anyone to see either of you."

Bach'uuk nodded.

"Pin, I want you to bundle up that mess the Magisters made of Kady's iPod."

"You mean her farspeakers?"

"Exactly. Bring everything back down here."

Pindor nodded, swung away, and headed out with Bach'uuk.

Jake turned and joined Marika. They sat on the edge of the bed. It would be a hard wait. He stared down and found Marika's hand in his.

"He'll be all right," Jake said softly.

Jake did not mean Pindor.

She stared off to nowhere, lost in fear and grief. "He's all I have left."

Jake squeezed her fingers, knowing the pain she was feeling all too well. To lose a mother or father—it was a heartache that never went away.

I SEE YOU . . .

What is taking them so long?

Jake paced the length of the sickroom. After more than fifteen minutes of sitting on the bed, Marika had suddenly stood up and asked to borrow the bedside lamp. Jake was happy to get up, too. The tension had been building like a swollen dam inside him. So he paced in the dark, with only the coarse breathing of the huntress for company. He heard Marika rustling around in a neighboring room and thought maybe he'd heard her talking to herself in there, too.

After five long minutes, she returned with the lamp. Her face looked pale. She carried something in her other hand—one of the farspeakers. The green crystal rested in its frame, suspended by a web of tiny fibers. Jake realized for the first time that it looked sort of like a Native American dreamcatcher. Dreamcatchers were made out of a hoop of willow branch and woven with sinew and decorated with stones and feathers. Traditionally it was hung above a child's bed to trap bad dreams.

Marika lifted the woven hoop. "I found Magister Zahur's collection of farspeakers. This one connects to Papa's. There was no response. Zahur had others, too. I tried them all." She shook her head. "Everyone's at the Olympiad."

Jake understood. Most people must have left their walkie-talkies at home. But he had a more worrisome thought. "Or they might not work at all," he said. "Like the lights. Bach'uuk mentioned how the shadow man's cloak sucked the alchemy out of the lights. Maybe it did the same with the farspeaking crystals."

Marika stared down at the hoop in her hand. She sank back to the bed. One finger reached out to touch the emerald crystal at the heart of the dreamcatcher, perhaps seeking some connection to her father.

"No one truly understands such crystals," she whispered. "At least not fully."

Jake joined her, knowing she needed to talk.

She glanced at him and offered a sad, crooked smile, while worry continued to reflect in her eyes. "There are many mysteries about these stones."

"Like what?"

She stared back down at the entwined green crystal. "On rare occasions, strange voices echo out of farspeaking stones, whispery and ghostly. A word here, half a sentence there. Magisters are taught they're just ripples bouncing off the valley walls. But my father thinks they might be messages traveling from other valleys like Calypsos—towns that lie far, far away."

Like telephone wires crossing! Jake thought.

Her words stirred his curiosity. "Wouldn't it be wonderful if such places existed?" Marika said, though without much heart behind her words. "One day I'd love to see them."

A door banged open in the other room, cutting off the conversation.

Pindor rushed into the infirmary carrying a blanket tied into a sack over one shoulder.

Bach'uuk followed, bringing lighted lamps from upstairs.

Pindor gasped as he joined them. "Sorry it took so long. Bach'uuk wanted to alert his people about the intruder. In case he comes back. We should be safe."

"Good thinking." Jake held out his arms for the loaded blanket.

"What do you want me to do now?" Pindor asked, still panting.

Jake pointed to Livia. "Help Mari get that bandage off her shoulder. Find some clean water and soak her skin and wound."

As Pindor and Marika set to work, Jake untied the blanket and spread it on the floor. Kady's iPod was a disassembled mess. He fished through the wreckage and picked out the rechargeable battery pack. He hoped it still held a charge, enough voltage. A pair of wires—black and red—hung from one corner of the battery. He stripped the plastic off each wire with his teeth. He wasn't sure how much of a shock he could get from the battery pack, but Jake had once licked the end of a 9-volt battery and got quite a stinging zap.

Jake touched two wires together and a pair of sparks flashed from their ends. Satisfied, he hauled up the battery pack and crossed to the bed.

Marika held one hand to her throat and kept her other on Livia's shoulder. Pindor backed out of the way.

The arrow's wound was bloody and deep, the skin puckered and swollen around it. Spidery red traces skittered from the wound across Livia's pale skin, down her arm, up her neck. Just the look of it screamed, *Poison*.

Jake swallowed and worked up his courage. "Mari, move away. Bach'uuk, bring that light closer."

Taking a deep breath, Jake cradled the battery between his palms and aimed the stripped ends toward the bloody water pooled in her wound.

"Stand back," he warned, not knowing what would happen.

With a wince, he shoved the wires into the water and touched them together. A spat of electricity popped.

Jake held his breath, but nothing more happened.

He raised the wires out of the wound. As he lifted them, the wires continued to spark and pop. Even after he separated them.

"Jake?" Marika asked, clearly worried.

Suddenly the wires whipped wildly in his fingers. Thin streams of blue fire flowed out the stripped ends and zapped the wounded flesh. Jake backed away, hauling the battery with him. But the streams of electrical fire continued to suck out of the wires and into the gash. He retreated all the way until his back hit the wall. The other three scattered to the sides, fearing the twin frazzles of lightning flowing from the batteries to the woman.

Livia began to quake under the covers. Her head arched back in a silent scream. She was going into a full seizure.

"The blanket!" Jake yelled. "Pull it over her shoulder! Break the connection!"

Marika and Pindor skirted the sides of the bed and grabbed the opposite corners of the blanket. They yanked it up and over Livia's head, slicing through the electrical fire.

Jake felt the interruption like a kick to the gut. The backlash knocked him into the wall again. The battery pack gave off a loud bang and began to pour out black smoke. Fearing it might be toxic, Jake flung the whole thing out into the other room.

Jake rushed back to the bed. Livia was still covered by the blanket, like someone who had recently died. And maybe she had. Her body lay flat and unmoving under the blanket.

Jake pulled down a corner. Her face was slack, her eyes open.

Marika and Pindor stumbled away in shock. Her eyes were solidly black, like polished bits of obsidian. Had they killed her?

A hand suddenly lunged from beneath the sheets and snatched Jake's wrist. Fingers clamped, strong enough to grind bone. Livia's body sprang up like a jack-in-the-box, her nose only inches from Jake's. Her black eyes stared at him, shining with evil.

"I see you . . ."

The words were not Livia's. Jake recognized the voice from when he'd been transported here. It was the voice from an open crypt, hoary and ancient, rising from a place where screams and blood flowed equally.

Before Jake could even struggle to break free, the hand went limp and fell from his wrist. Livia slumped into the bed.

Backing up a step, Jake rubbed his wrist. What had just happened? He remembered the ruby crystal burning through the table. Had the electricity released the evil of the bloodstone shards all at once? If so, now what? Were they gone, consumed and burned up? Or were they more powerful?

From the bed, a hard gurgling cough shook Livia—

followed by an impossibly huge gulp of air, as if the huntress were surfacing after a swim to the bottom of the deepest sea. Her eyes wobbled in her head and slowly steadied. They were no longer black, but an icy blue.

"Wh-where am I?" she asked hoarsely.

Marika stepped into view. "Huntress Livia, you're in Calypsos."

"I know you. . . ." She coughed heavily as if trying to clear something foul. "You're little Mari. Balam's daughter."

"That's right!" Marika said, sighing in relief.

"What happened?"

"You were poisoned by a bloodstone arrow."

Her eyes widened, as if suddenly remembering a nightmare. With a weak, wobbly effort, she pulled the blanket from her shoulder. The wound remained, but the angry poisonous red lines were gone.

"I think you did it," Pindor said at Jake's side.

Jake felt a burst of relief and pride, but those black eyes still haunted him.

Livia seemed to find little comfort in her survival. If anything, her expression grew more anxious. Behind her eyes, Jake could see blank spaces of her memory filling, like water pouring into a glass, faster and faster.

Livia reached for Marika and snagged the edge of her sleeve. "How long have I . . . what day is it?"

Marika tried to calm her. "It's the Spring Equinox."

Livia reacted as if someone had stabbed her in the belly.

"No!" She tried to pull herself up, but she was plainly too weak.

Marika knelt next to her.

Livia grabbed her again, more forcibly. "He's coming."

Jake jolted at her familiar words.

"The Skull King," Livia pressed. "I captured a grakyl in the sucking bog of Fireweed. Before I slit his throat, he told me. Of a huge attack. To come on the night of the Equinox."

The words of the huntress were full of dread and certainty.

"The Skull King comes this night!"

21

RUMOR OF WAR

A few minutes later, Jake stood out in the common room with Marika. "It's probably just a nightmare," he said, "but we should still get word to the Elders."

Marika glanced over to where the dead stingtail still rested atop the table like some macabre centerpiece. It was a deadly reminder of the danger swirling around them. "But I still don't understand," she said. "The great temple protects our valley. Whether the danger is from sky or land. It has shielded us for hundreds and hundreds of years. The Skull King's armies can't get through."

Jake pictured the monstrous grakyl writhing against that shield. He shrugged. "Like I said, the huntress may be mistaken. It could all just be a hallucination. No telling what sorts of nightmares were triggered by that poison."

Marika sighed and grew more troubled. She was plainly scared to death about her father, but she knew her duty to Calypsos. She would not let her father down by dissolving into a weepy mess.

The narrow side door swung open. Bach'uuk returned with two taller Ur, a man and a woman. They were dressed in crudely sewn hides that still somehow looked neat and well trimmed.

Bach'uuk lifted an arm. "They will attend to Huntress Livia after we leave. Keep her safe."

Pindor crossed out of the sickroom. "Are we ready? Huntress Livia is not happy to be left behind. Keeps trying to get out of bed. But I promised I would get word to my father."

Bach'uuk spoke to the other Ur in his own tongue, a mix of guttural sounds combined with tongue clicks. The pair nodded and crossed toward the sickroom.

Pindor said, "The Olympiad must be over by now. All the Elders will be heading over to my father's house for his traditional Equinox Night celebration."

"Then that's where we'll meet them," Marika agreed.

Jake and Pindor followed with Bach'uuk in tow. They needed him to tell his part of the story, about the strange shadow man.

Once out in the courtyard, Jake was shocked at how late it had become. The courtyard lay in deep twilight. Only the very top of the giant corkscrew tree was still in sunlight. The nesting dartwings were all huddled up there, soaking in the last warm rays of the day.

Off to the west, the sun had already half sunk into the

jagged ridgeline. On the opposite side of the valley, a heavy full moon lay low on the horizon, ready to herald the coming night.

"It'll be faster on foot!" Pindor called out, and waved toward the courtyard gates. "We'll cut across High Street Park."

Jake remembered the park from the trip to Bornholm two days ago. It lay outside the castle wall and overlooked the town below. They ran as the sun continued to sink.

As they exited the gates, sounds of revelry echoed up from the city: shouts, laughs, ringing of bells, blasts of horns, bleating of saurians. Wagons and chariots, festooned with lights, moved in the beginnings of a makeshift parade. Jake imagined that after sunset the entire place would be aglow.

Or at least Jake hoped it would be.

The four of them ducked into the park and allowed Pindor to lead them through the maze of gravel paths. Under the tight tangle of branches, night had already come to Calypsos.

As they hurried through the forest, they startled a pair of young lovers who were locked in an embrace. The pair quickly shoved apart and pretended to be extremely fascinated by the twist of tree roots near their bench.

Jake and the others continued onward. They flashed through a meadow of knee-high wildflowers as they sprinted by the lookout spot where they'd stopped yesterday. The coliseum in the distance was sunk fully into darkness.

Jake wondered where Kady was. Had she returned to Bornholm? If Calypsos was attacked, at least she was surrounded by some of the city's best warriors. Still, Jake wished she were here with him now. Worry made him stumble.

Pindor misinterpreted his staggering step for exhaustion. "Not much farther," he promised, pointing vaguely ahead.

After another two twists of the trail, the trees spread wider apart to reveal a manicured lawn. Shrubbery had been carved into fanciful spirals or perfect spheres. Atop a small hill rested a white house with a peaked roof and a double line of pillars fronting it. It reminded Jake of a mausoleum.

"That's where I live," Pindor said as he ran.

In preparation for the celebration, small tents had been set up in the garden, and long tables held mountains of food and pyramids of wine bottles.

People were already here, early arrivals of the larger party to come. They wandered in small groups or pairs. Pindor searched among them as he crossed the yard. Near a large statue of the god Apollo, someone lunged out and grabbed him.

"Pinny! Can you believe it?"

Pindor shook free and backed a step away. The attacker,

an older boy, didn't seem to notice. His face was flushed red with wine and excitement.

Jake recognized the fellow as one of Pindor's earlier tormentors.

"Believe what, Regulas?" Pindor asked, letting his annoyance ring.

"We won the Torch! By a single point!" He clapped Pindor on the shoulder. "You should've seen your brother, snuck it right past those Sumerians and through the ring. *Whoosh!*" The boy pantomimed shooting a ball from his arms.

Pindor turned to Jake and exclaimed, "We won!"

"Pindor!" Marika snapped, drawing his attention back to the matter at hand.

Regulas's excitement refused to dim. "Heron was carried out of stadium on the Roman team's shoulders. And those shapely huntresses led us all in song. . . ."

The boy had to be talking about Kady's new cheer squad. Jake stepped in closer. "Do you know where the huntresses went?"

It was Jake's turn to get his shoulder grabbed. "Ah! That sister of yours. If Heron weren't whistling at her . . ."

Jake shoved Regulas off. "Do you know where she is?"

"Into the woods! For the bonfire! Last I saw, she and Heron were hand in hand." He ended this with a wink.

Marika pulled Jake away. "Another tradition. The winning team has a big bonfire to represent the Eternal

Torch out in the Sacred Woods." She rolled her eyes. "But mostly it's a chance to have a big party."

Jake glanced in the direction of the forest that surrounded the temple pyramid. His fear for Kady grew to fill his chest. He lost his ability to speak, to question.

Pindor filled in the gap. "Regulas, have you seen my father?"

He frowned. "Off in the atrium. Or maybe down in his cellars. He's entertaining his closest friends. Sharing the best wine with them!" This lack of democracy seemed to wound the boy.

Pindor pushed past him and led the others toward the porch steps. "We'll have to get my father alone . . . along with the other two Elders."

At the top of the stairs, a tall figure blocked their way. "So there you all are!" Centurion Gaius towered, his face as red as the plume on his helmet. "I've spent the afternoon looking for you. Missed our victory at the Olympiad because of you!"

Pindor stammered, intimidated.

Marika stepped forward. "Centurion Gaius, I apologize for our subterfuge," she said formally. "But there was good reason. We must speak to Elder Tiberius."

"If you think you'll find any mercy from the Elder—"

"No!" Marika cut off the tall man. "None of that matters. You must stand aside!"

Gaius's face went even redder. Jake suspected it was

more from embarrassment at being rebuked by a girl who stood barely taller than his waist. Gaius spoke with his teeth clenched. "Marika Balam—"

"It concerns Huntress Livia!" she interrupted again, almost yelling now. "She's awake and has a message for the Council that must be heard immediately."

Gaius studied Marika as if trying to judge the truth of her statement. Another voice cut in, coming from behind the centurion.

"What news is this of my sister?"

Centurion Gaius stepped aside and revealed Elder Ulfsdottir. She had been standing just inside and had overheard Marika's outburst.

"What news do you have of Livia?" the Elder asked. Her eyes sparked with concern. "I was on my way from Bornholm to check on my sister. I tried calling the Magisters on the farspeakers, but there was no answer."

Marika bowed her head once. "She lives. And wakes with a story of a great danger to Calypsos."

The woman's eyes closed for a moment in relief and silent prayer, then opened and revealed a steely resolve. "Of what danger does she speak?"

"Perhaps Elder Tiberius and Elder Wu should also hear this story," Gaius offered, still glancing at them all with a measure of doubt.

"Yes, of course." The Viking leader led them into the inner courtyard. She lowered her voice to Marika. "I thought my sister was doomed, poisoned by splinters of dark alchemy."

"It's a long story," Marika answered, and nodded to Jake. "But it was the newcomer's sy-enz that saved her."

The Elder turned her blue gaze upon Jake with a warmth that made him stand a little taller. "I owe you a great blood-debt, Jacob Ransom. And by the keel of the Valkyrie, it will be honored."

They reached the center of the courtyard and found Pindor's father talking to the Asian Elder. The bald man had waxed his thin white mustache so that it glowed in the lamplight.

The smile on Tiberius's face fell when he saw his son. "Pindor! Where have you been? Do you know what trouble you've caused Centurion Gaius?"

Gaius stepped forward. "Perhaps you should hear the boy out."

Pindor glanced back to Marika for help. She gave him the barest nod, her instruction simple to read. *Tell your father.*

Pindor swallowed hard and stiffened his back. He started slowly, stuttering here and there, but as the story continued, his voice found its firmness. By the time he finished, the squeaky nervousness was long gone.

His father's expression also transformed: from anger and doubt to concern and apprehension. The others were questioned, even Bach'uuk, who answered most inquiries with a single word.

"This must be venom-addled madness," Tiberius said. "The temple's shield protects us."

"Perhaps the Skull King plans on laying siege around us," Elder Wu said. "Thinking to starve us out."

"But we've plenty of food," Elder Ulfsdottir said with a shake of her head. "And fresh spring water bubbles out of the rock."

As they continued to discuss the likelihood of an attack, the sky turned from dark blue to indigo. The sun sank away. A few stars began to shine in the east. Jake's fear for his sister—somewhere out in the woods—grew to a fiery lump in his heart. He could remain silent no longer.

"I'm sorry to intrude," Jake said.

Eyes turned to him, but he didn't back down.

"From what Bach'uuk saw, you have at least one of the Skull King's men already in your midst. Who knows how many others? And now the three Magisters have gone missing. I don't think you should take Livia's warning as just madness. And the longer you wait, the less time you'll have to prepare a defense."

Tiberius nodded. "The boy is right. To attack on this night, when most of the town is celebrating and when many will be deep into their bottles of wine—there is a certain wicked strategy to it."

"Then what do we do?" Elder Wu asked.

"I will alert the People of the Wind. We'll get their

entire nest into the air to watch the skies all night. On the ground, we'll rouse the Saddleback forces into patrols and scouts."

"And the townspeople?" Wu asked.

Elder Ulfsdottir answered, "I will rouse all of Bornholm. We can begin to shift the townspeople into the castle. It was why Kalakryss was originally built. As a final line of defense if all else should fail."

Tiberius turned and stared at Jake and his friends. "Centurion Gaius, I think it best if you take these four back to Kalakryss. Once there, spread the word and rally your guards to the walls."

Gaius struck a fist to his chest in acknowledgment. He turned and swept an arm toward his charges, ready to herd them off.

Jake ducked under his arm. "Elder Tiberius. My sister . . . she's gone off into the woods. I believe with your son and the Roman team."

The older man frowned, not comprehending.

"The bonfire," Pindor reminded him. "In the Sacred Woods."

Tiberius slowly nodded, and lines etched his brow.

Elder Ulfsdottir answered instead. "I will send a runner out to them. You have saved my sister. I can let nothing happen to yours."

Jake let out a sigh of relief. The assurance by this stolid woman helped to smother the worry inside him.

But only slightly.

With the matter settled, Gaius gathered Jake, Pindor, Marika, and Bach'uuk and headed toward the exit. The centurion grumbled under his breath. "And this time, no running off on your own!"

No one argued.

22

FIRST BLOOD

By the time they reached the parkland again, the sun had fully set. Stars filled the heavens, and the white road of the Milky Way blazed across the sky. The full moon hung over Calypsos, shining brightly on the merriment below. Music drifted up from the lower levels of the town, along with songs in a chorus of languages.

But how long would it last?

A giant raz flew low over them, rising up from the Tiberius estate. Jake felt the rush of its wings as it passed. It was probably a scout, sent out to raise the alarm among the People of the Wind.

"Keep moving," Gaius urged as Jake slowed to watch the bird's flight.

The gravel path crunched underfoot as if they ran over crushed bones.

With every step deeper into the forest, Jake could not escape the feeling something was watching them—or rather watching *him*. Jake searched both sides of the path. Here in the darkness, he remembered Livia's black eyes, and the words that flowed from her throat.

"I see you . . ."

The hairs on the back of Jake's neck quivered with the certainty that something frightening shared this dark forest. A shadow shifted on his left, a twig snapped.

Something *was* out there!

With a gasp, Jake veered and bumped into Bach'uuk. He was nimble enough to catch Jake and keep them both on their feet. They sped onward. Jake finally noted a break in the darkness. He hurried and took the lead. The trail flowed out of the forest and into one of the park's many meadows, the one that overlooked the city.

As he burst out, the welcome moonlight washed over him. It bathed the field with silvery light and revealed something perched at the edge of the overlook. It was black as if a clot of shadows refused to flee from the moonlight.

Jake's first thought was of the dark assassin Bach'uuk had spotted, the man with a cloak of living shadows. This illusion grew as the form heard their group's approach and twisted around, casting out wings of darkness from its wrapped body. Outlined against the stars, it was plain the wings were not made of cloth or shadow—but leather and bone.

"A grakyl!" Gaius shouted behind them.

Jake fled from the overlook, drawing the others with him. Only the centurion remained behind. Gaius yanked his sword and crouched. The beast sprang into the air, wings outstretched. With a single flap, it dove toward Gaius.

"Run!" the centurion yelled. "Make for the castle!"

They obeyed, but Jake kept half an eye behind him. The grakyl fell upon Gaius with a great thrashing of limbs. It beat at him with its wings. But Gaius danced and spun and stabbed out with his sword. The beast screamed like a rusty fork dragged over a chalkboard. Blood gushed from its wounds. But it did not try to escape. With a great shudder, it cried out and prepared to attack again.

Worst yet, its cry was answered by another scream. From beyond the lookout, a second grakyl swooped up from below and swept overhead. The pair fell upon Gaius with a storm of claws and teeth.

Then Jake dropped into another section of forest, and he lost sight of the centurion. The four of them fled, too scared to speak, only run. Once again, Jake felt that overpowering sense that something watched him, possibly hunted him. He again heard whispers of pursuit: a rustle of leaves, a crackle of branches.

They reached the bench where the young lovers had been sharing a kiss. The pair had long since gone, but something else had taken their place. It leaped off the bench and filled the trail. Wings spread and blocked the way completely. They all froze on the path.

A grakyl. Its porcine nose sniffed at them. Its ears swiveled, taking in every slight noise. It panted at them, revealing a mouthful of jagged teeth.

But this was no ordinary grakyl.

This one clutched a sword in one claw, and two spiraling horns grew out of its head like some horrible crown. It hissed at them and lowered its sword, as if trying to judge which one to kill first. Jake scrabbled for his penlight, but he'd buttoned it into another of his pants pockets, and he couldn't get it free.

Behind Jake, a snapping of branches alerted him that a second beast closed in from the rear. They were surrounded. He didn't have time to get his flashlight out. He grabbed Marika and dove to the side.

But the trailing beast simply shot past them, running low to the ground, a blur of shadows. It leaped straight into the air and struck the grakyl in the throat. Its momentum and weight knocked the hollow-boned creature onto its back. A fierce feline scream followed as saber-toothed fangs ripped deep into the tender neck of the monster.

It was the *Rhabdofelix*! The one Jake had set free. Latched onto the monster's throat, she shook and spit and thrashed until the wings of the grakyl stopped beating.

Jake urged them all to circle around the trail. "Go! Cut around that way!" He pointed and followed after them.

As he edged past the slaughter, the cat growled in Jake's

direction. Her eyes caught every bit of light under the dense canopy as she stared at him. The giant cat must have been following him all along. He read her eyes as she stared at him, sensing the bond between them. Not as pet and owner, but more like equals. *You watch my back; I'll watch yours.*

Then she leaped away and vanished back into the woods. But Jake knew she was still out there.

Jake ran after his friends. He still sensed eyes upon him, but now they offered him a measure of comfort. He felt a little less alone.

"What in all of Hades' fires was that thing?" Pindor gasped out. "It had horns! Carried a sword!"

"A grakyl lord!" Marika answered, panting. "I read . . . but no one believed they were real."

"*That* looked real to me!" Pindor said.

Jake stopped them at the edge of the forest, keeping to the shadows of the branches. Ahead, bright moonlight lit the way. But as he caught his breath, the world suddenly went a little darker.

Concerned, Jake saw that a low black cloud had swept over the face of the moon and flowed toward the castle.

Below, in the city, all music had stopped. A hush had fallen over the town.

Somewhere high above, a piercing cry screeched downward. At this signal, grakyl after grakyl dove out of the clouds.

Screams rose from the streets.

Jake pushed everyone deeper into the forest's cover.

"They're here!" Marika moaned. "Through the barrier. How?"

"I don't know, but they are."

"What are we going to do?" Pindor asked.

"Find somewhere to hide. That's what we must do first."

"What about Gaius?" Marika asked.

Jake shook his head. They could not count on help from the centurion.

"He told us to go to the castle," Pindor said.

They all turned toward Kalakryss. Flocks of grakyl already mounted its walls. A few soldiers fought on the ramparts, but they were being swamped. More grakyl disappeared into the courtyard. Beyond the wall, saurians bellowed and men shouted.

The bright blare of a trumpet sounded near the stadium.

Jake stared up again as a new force rose into the sky. The People of the Wind! A wave of the mighty raz took to the air in scores of V-shaped groups, launching from their cliffside homes. They climbed high, then dove quickly downward. Like a volley of black arrows, the birds shredded into the black spiraling cloud. With a single pass, scores of grakyl fell earthward, tumbling and trailing shredded wings. The sharp talons of the raz ripped leather and bone with ease.

But the winged riders were vastly outnumbered.

Pindor realized it, too. "They'll never last," he said. "We need more forces."

"Who?" Marika asked. "The Saddlebacks are spread all over Calypsos. The People of the Wind are only one tribe."

Pindor shook his head. "I don't know. But for now, Jake's right. We need a safe place to regroup, maybe somewhere we could rally more forces."

Jake studied Pindor. It seemed his skill at strategy was not limited to just a ball game. Did anyone else have a plan? Jake found himself studying the most silent of their group.

"Bach'uuk," Jake said. "Your caves are on the far side of the wall."

He nodded. "Our Elders wish to look upon the face of the dark forest, to not forget. That is our way."

Jake turned to Pindor and Marika. "The town's not safe, neither is the castle. Our best chance might be to hide out there."

Pindor stepped before Bach'uuk. "Would your people come and defend Calypsos?"

Jake knew what Pindor was hoping—that perhaps the Neanderthal tribe could *be* the extra forces he was talking about. But Bach'uuk would not meet the Roman boy's eye and stared down at his feet. His heavy brow hid his features.

"That is not the way of our people," Bach'uuk mumbled. "But such matters must be judged by our Elders."

"Then we'll talk to them," Pindor said. "Convince them."

The Ur boy's eyes flashed with a moment of anger, but the fire quickly subsided and his features went calm.

Pindor hadn't noticed. "How do we get all the way over there?"

"There is a way. I can take you." Bach'uuk pointed beyond the castle to the Sacred Woods. "A tunnel."

Jake stared out there. For the moment, the fighting focused on the town and the castle. The forest remained dark and undisturbed. Also Kady was out in those woods, too.

Marika frowned. "I don't remember hearing of any tunnel in the forest."

Bach'uuk pointed his arm. Jake followed his direction. He seemed to be pointing toward the stone dragon. It hovered over the treetops, lit by moonlight.

"Are you talking about the great temple?" Marika asked.

Bach'uuk nodded. "Tunnel there."

"*Inside* the temple?" she pressed.

A nod again, this time followed by an impatient grunt.

"But only the Magisters are allowed to enter the Temple of Kukulkan," she insisted.

Again fire flashed in the Ur boy's eyes. "Magisters . . . and those who *serve* them."

Marika stared at Bach'uuk a moment longer, stunned,

then over at Jake. "I didn't know."

"No one sees us," Bach'uuk said, letting some of his irritation shine more boldly. "No one counts us. We are only Ur."

Jake remembered how Marika's father seemed hardly to acknowledge Bach'uuk. Marika certainly appreciated his help, but Jake recalled her earlier description of Ur intelligence. *Papa believes there is a dullness to their thoughts, but they are strong and obey simple directions.*

Jake knew better than that. And apparently so did Bach'uuk.

"Will you lead us there?" Jake asked.

Bach'uuk nodded and turned away, but Marika remained where she was.

"Even if the Ur are allowed to trespass in the temple, we are not," she said. "It is forbidden for any but the Magisters to tread inside the pyramid."

Jake struggled not to roll his eyes. He had great respect for Marika, but she had some streaks of stubbornness equal to his own. He had to break through her rigidity. He grabbed her hand.

"Mari, there are no more Magisters in Calypsos. At least none around at the moment."

He saw how much his words wounded her, reminded her of her missing father. But they had to be said.

Jake touched the badge still pinned on his vest jacket. "As apprentices, we are the only Magisters Calypsos has at the moment."

Her brows scrunched together, digesting his way of looking at it. She glanced to the war in the sky, then finally nodded. "You may be right." Her voice firmed. "We must try."

Jake gave her wrist another squeeze, then waved for Bach'uuk to lead them.

Pindor followed, mumbling his usual dour advice. "You're Calypsos's only Magisters? Then we're doomed for sure."

PART FOUR

WHISTLING IN THE WOODS

The Sacred Woods spread like a black sea beyond the outskirts of the besieged town of Calypsos. It washed up against its walls in a twisted tangle of trees. All of the trees were giants with corkscrew trunks, like the one that graced the castle courtyard.

A path wound through the woods, lit by solitary lamp-posts of glowing crystals, but they were spread far apart, leaving long stretches of pitch-black darkness. The group raced along the path.

The temple lay in the heart of the woods, over a mile away. As they ran, they heard sounds of fighting. The war continued to spread. Other townspeople were seeking refuge in the forest. Voices called out to them from hiding places as they ran past. But they kept moving, led by a determined Bach'uuk.

Jake searched the woods for any flicker of flame. Kady

had come to this forest with her friends for some post-game bonfire. But Jake saw no sign of any fire. Either it blazed much deeper in the dense woods, or they'd doused it once the fighting started.

Worry kept his jaw muscles tight.

"We'll never get inside the temple," Marika whispered as she ran alongside him. "As the crystal heart of Kukulkan protects our valley—at least until this night—it also casts a shield over the opening to the temple. Only Magisters are allowed to pass through."

Jake pictured the grakyl at the Broken Gate, writhing against the force shield. "Are you saying there's a barrier across the entrance?"

Her face was in shadow, but Jake knew she was frowning. "What do you think I was saying back at the park? Only Magisters may enter . . . and apparently the Ur."

Jake had thought the temple was guarded by men or by mere superstition. "What if we can't get in?"

"Like you said, Jake, maybe *we* are the Magisters now, and we'll be allowed to pass. Or maybe Bach'uuk will know a secret way inside known only to the Ur. He mentioned a tunnel."

Jake nodded and increased his pace. He would cross that invisible barrier when he got to it.

They continued through the forest in silence. This deep in the woods, the whispers and calls had grown quieter. None of the townspeople hiding in the Sacred Woods had gotten this far. And why would they? If Marika was right, the temple offered them no refuge.

Jake sensed the pyramid before he saw it. The air grew heavier and somehow charged, like before a thunderstorm, when the skies were low and dark and chains of lightning crackled in the distance. His senses grew keener. His ears picked out the rustle of leaves over the canopy. He smelled the sweetness of night-blooming moss that grew with a ghostly luminescence on the twisted trunks of the trees. His skin prickled with every skittering breeze.

Then there it was.

The forest stopped a few yards from the pyramid's bottom step.

Jake stepped out into the clearing. It wasn't a wise thing to do as the war continued to roll toward them overhead. But he had never seen such a wondrous sight. There was no doubt. It was exactly the same as the golden artifact at the museum, the one recovered from his parents' dig.

Only this one is giant-sized.

Each of the pyramid's tiers was taller than Jake's head, rising higher and higher to crest above the tallest trees. And there, perched at the very top, crouched the stone dragon. Moonlight turned it silver, crisply outlining each and every detail.

The outstretched wings were inscribed with feathers. Jake stared up at it. The statue truly was a feathered serpent! No wonder Marika's people named it Kukulkan when they first came here. Then again, perhaps the myths of Kukulkan among the Maya came from this place. Jake remembered what he had spied in Magister Balam's library. It made him wonder once again: Had ancient people long ago found a way back home from here? Had they carried myths of monsters and feathered serpents from this place back to their native lands?

Jake studied the statue. The dragon's face stared toward the horizon. The face did not look quite saurian, nor did it look even reptilian, but somehow something entirely new, even vaguely human. That last sense came from the crinkled stone eyes that looked outward with such hope and seemed full of ancient wisdom.

Lastly Jake noted its tail. It curled fully around the uppermost level, as if it were protecting a nest of eggs. The tip of the tail formed a perfect circle, marking off a round door at the top of the pyramid. It looked to be the only entrance. It was at the spot where Jake had inserted the two halves of the Mayan coin into the golden artifact at the British Museum.

"This way," Marika said, pointing forward.

Down the center of that side of the pyramid, the giant tiers had been sliced through with a narrow staircase of ordinary-sized steps. The stairs aimed straight for the round entrance. She headed there.

"We'd better hurry!" Pindor added, looking over his shoulder as he passed Jake.

Jake craned up and saw the writhing storm of gra-kyl and razor-taloned raz had reached them. They had no more time. Jake hurried after Pindor with Bach'uuk behind him.

Jake hit the stairs and began climbing. He fumbled out his penlight. He wanted it in his fingers if they were attacked. He kept a thumb on the switch, but he kept the light off. He wanted to save the battery. He didn't know how long it would last. He also feared the beam might attract the wrong eyes.

But in the end, it made no difference.

The grakyl proved to have sharp vision. A few of them spotted the four figures climbing the moonlit pyramid. A screech pierced the night. Jake glanced up and saw a dozen grakyl diving toward them. The one in the lead was the largest, with spiraled horns on his head, and his black blade reflected the moonlight off its wicked length.

One of the grakyl lords.

"Everyone together!" Jake screamed.

They were only a quarter of the way up the side of the pyramid. They'd never make it. All around them, grakyl crashed to the stone sides of the pyramid. The lord of the foul beasts landed a few steps below Jake. It crouched, wings out, its sword pointed straight at Jake's heart.

Jake raised his only weapon. He pointed his penlight at the grakyl's face and clicked on the light. The glare bothered the beast at first. A wing snapped around, shielding its eyes like a cape. Then it suddenly wailed as the freezing touch of the light turned its eyeballs to ice. It fell backward, clawing at its own face, tearing gouges as it rolled down the steps.

Its sword struck the step below and rattled. Jake lunged and grabbed it before it bounced away. They needed every weapon. Jake passed it to Pindor, but he caught a glimpse of an emblem melted into its hilt. It struck Jake as familiar, but he didn't have time to examine it further.

The grakyl lord's cries had ignited a bloodlust in its brethren. They came at the small group from all sides. Jake hit two more in the face, blinding them and sending them tumbling after their lord. Pindor did his best to ward off the others with his sword. But more beasts closed in from all directions, screeching in agony and fury.

They had to keep moving.

Jake twisted and pointed his light toward the grakyl on the stair above. It hissed and hid its face. The creatures were learning. Thinking quickly, Jake aimed for its knees instead. He flashed his beam between the two bony joints.

"Run!" Jake yelled. "Follow me!"

He ran straight toward the monster ahead and hollered a challenge. The beast tried to step forward to meet Jake head-on—but its knees were frozen solid and wouldn't bend. It toppled forward, straight at Jake, ready still to rip the boy's throat out. But Jake ducked and used a Tae

Kwon Do shoulder flip to pitch the beast down the stairs. It crashed end over end. The others dodged past it and followed.

Jake took two steps at a time. Behind him, the other grakyl gave chase, scrabbling up the stairs, flapping from tier to tier, trying to cut them off. They'd never make the entrance. Their pursuers were closing in.

"Jake!" Marika yelled.

He turned. One of the grakyl had grabbed Marika by the ankle. It flapped and tried to drag her off the steps. Then Jake heard a whistling noise and something struck the head of the monster. The grakyl dropped like a rock and let Marika go.

Suddenly a great barrage of stones were pelted from the forest fringe. A group of young men in togas stepped out into the clearing below. They had slings and whipped them with expert skill.

Jake recognized a familiar face.

"Heronidus!" Pindor yelled, spotting his brother, too.

The rain of stones crashed down upon the grakyl demons from below. Bones broke and skulls cracked. The beasts sought to escape, but next came a flurry of arrows. The twang of bows sounded again and again. Behind the Roman ballplayers, a line of Viking women appeared with short bows in hand.

The fleeing grakyl were peppered with arrows and tumbled back to earth.

But the battle at the pyramid did not go unnoticed. More screeches erupted from the churning war overhead. An entire black wing of the grakyl horde swept down toward the bloodshed. More than three dozen strong. Some aimed for the pyramid, some for the forest's edge.

"*Jake!*" a call burst out below.

He tore his eyes from the skies. A woman in Viking garb waved at him, motioning him to make for the pyramid's opening.

"*Run, Jake!*"

It was Kady!

He hardly recognized her. Her clothes were ripped, her face bloody, but she somehow stood taller. In her hand, she lifted a sword and pointed it to the top of the pyramid.

"*Go! Now!*"

He watched Kady and the others flee back into the forest. Jake sprinted for the opening in the pyramid. Overhead, the stone dragon stared off into the skies, its expression never changing, aloof to the flow of blood and screams.

Jake pressed harder but Pindor had taken the lead. Jake and the others chased after him. They had to reach the entrance. It wasn't much farther. They were almost to the top.

Then a dark clutch of graykl landed on the stairs ahead—eight of them, led by another grakyl lord. They blocked the way. Pindor faced the monster with his stolen blade.

Jake pushed forward, ready to help defend him.

But Pindor sensed it was a fight they could not win. They were outnumbered. The point of his sword dropped, giving up. The grakyl lord grinned like a shark, revealing a gaping maw of sharp teeth.

But Pindor wasn't done. He lifted his other hand to his lips—and blew. Jake heard a faint high-pitched whine that faded into nothingness. Pindor had Jake's dog whistle to his lips and blew with all his heart.

The grakyl horde screamed and clutched their peaked ears, as if trying to stuff them into their own canals to shut out the noise. Their foul lord hissed in agony and jumped straight into the air. It twisted and writhed as if off balance. The others scattered, fleeing the piercing ultrasonic whistle.

With the way open again, Jake pointed. *"Go!"*

Pindor raced up with him. "They have big ears," he gasped out. "I thought maybe . . ."

"You thought good!" Jake said, knowing Pindor had saved their lives.

The four of them raced up the last few steps and leaped through the curl of tail that circled the entrance. Jake felt a slight tingle, like when he'd passed through the Broken Gate, but they weren't stopped. They ran a few more steps.

Jake paused to stare behind him. The grakyl returned,

but they hovered at the entrance. One swiped a claw at them. A small frizzle of sparks ran over its skin. But that was all. It wasn't repelled, which meant that the pyramid's barrier, like the one around the entire valley, was down.

Still, the creature pulled back. It refused to follow them into the pyramid. Others gathered outside, but none of them entered.

"Looks like they're afraid to pass inside," Marika whispered.

Afraid of what? Jake wondered with a trickle of fear.

"Scared or not, they're also not leaving," Pindor said.

It was true. More and more grakyl gathered outside. Jake pictured the entire pyramid crawling with those monsters. Maybe they were trying to get enough nerve to storm inside. Jake wanted to be gone when that happened.

"Where to now?" Jake asked.

Bach'uuk waved and led them forward. The entrance tunnel slanted steeply downward, heading toward the center of the pyramid. The way was dark, but light glowed at the end of the passageway.

They had no choice but to face what lay ahead.

SHADOW IN THE MACHINE

As Jake moved through the tunnel, he ran a finger along one wall. The stones fit perfectly, but rather than stacked, they were fitted together like pieces of a jigsaw puzzle, each block an irregular shape. Still, the stone seams were so smooth that he doubted he could slide a razor blade between any of the blocks.

The light grew brighter ahead. Jake felt a pulse in the air, as if something were squeezing his chest, releasing it, then squeezing again. With each step, the sensation grew.

Pindor rubbed at his stomach, feeling it there. Despite the danger, Marika's brow pinched with curiosity. Only Bach'uuk seemed unfazed. But he had been here before.

The hall continued to angle downward, but the end appeared to be just ahead. The pulse grew more intense, the glow even brighter as the passageway opened into a cavernous chamber, domed like the Astromicon.

Jake stopped, awestruck by what lay ahead.

A perfect sphere of crystal hung in the center of the chamber. It spun slowly in place, suspended in midair under the roof of the dome. It glowed steadily, but Jake felt that pulse burst out with each full spin.

The crystal heart of Kukulkan!

The pulse was its heartbeat.

As Jake's eyes grew accustomed to the glow, he saw something else that surprised him. The sphere was really *three* spheres, one inside the other, like Russian nesting dolls. Two layers spun in opposite directions: one spun left to right, the other right to left. The third spun from top to bottom. Strange letters were carved across the surface of all three spheres and spun to form all manner of combinations, like some crystal computer.

Marika crept forward and passed between Pindor and Bach'uuk. Her eyes were huge. The floor sloped down to form a bowl under the crystal heart. Below the spinning sphere were three miniature versions of the larger one. One emerald, one ruby, one sapphire blue.

The three primary colors of light again.

Jake glanced at his silver apprentice badge. The same three stones formed a triangle around the diamond. He realized the pattern must be a miniature version of the layout here. The diamond represented the crystal heart. The colored gems stood for the three smaller spheres.

Fascinated, he stared back at the center of the room.

Below the giant crystal heart, the small spheres spun in place, like small moons trapped in orbit by the larger planet above—or rather *two* of them spun.

The emerald crystal seemed to wobble, and while the others glowed with their own inner light, the green sphere was dull and dark. Something was definitely wrong with it.

The cause for that became apparent when shadows boiled out of a hallway on the far side of the dome. They fluttered around a humanlike shape, but details were impossible to pick out. They cloaked the figure completely and spat around him like black flames.

It had to be the assassin Bach'uuk had seen fleeing Kalakryss.

Jake withdrew to the shelter of the passageway and drew Marika with him. The shadowy man—if it was a *man*—knelt by the green crystal and placed two hands over its surface. From his fingers, darkness flowed and sank into the emerald stone. The wobbling grew more erratic.

The assassin was doing something to restrain or possibly destroy this one sphere. But why? To what end? Jake remembered Marika talking about *the gifts of Kukulkan,* her description of the field cast out by the pyramid, how it granted a common language to all, protected the valley against dangers, and kept the crystals in the valley powered.

Three gifts . . . three colored spheres

Two gifts still worked—language and the power of the crystals—but not the third. Not the barrier. Jake now knew how the Skull King's forces had penetrated the valley's defenses. He was staring at it. This creature had weakened the barrier at its source—he had poisoned the emerald sphere.

He had to be stopped or the entire valley would be destroyed.

Jake stepped out. He rose to his toes and flicked on his penlight. If he moved quietly, he could catch the shadowy assassin by surprise. And with the reach of the penlight's beam, he wouldn't even have to get that close. It was worth the risk.

Jake lifted a hand to warn the others to stay back. He had continued a few steps farther when a piercing cry rose from the grakyl horde outside. Jake cringed at the triumphant keen to their wails. He feared what that might mean for everyone in the valley. But at the moment, it meant disaster for Jake.

The shadowy figure, perhaps curious about the noise, glanced toward the entrance. His swirling face swung straight at Jake. Jake froze as if struck by the beam of his own penlight. The creature sprang up, carried by the shadows beneath him. He rushed straight at Jake.

Jake finally reacted and raised his penlight. He shone it straight at the pool of shadows that hid the figure's face. The freezing light burned through the shadows. The darkness flowed away from the beam like water.

The creature shied to the side. Jake almost caught a glimpse of the face behind the mask—then the beam from his penlight flickered and died.

Panicked, Jake shook the flashlight. He got it to shine for another second, then it blinked off again. The shadows poured back over the face and swallowed the features away.

The figure cast up both arms and shadows boiled out from his form and washed over Jake's lower body. His legs went immediately cold. The shadows thickened to the consistency of tar. He couldn't move.

"Jake!" Marika cried out to him.

"Stay back!" he yelled. *Or we'll all be trapped.*

The creature seemed to have no trouble wading through the shadows toward Jake. Though the figure had no face, Jake imagined a vicious smile.

Words flowed out, muffled by the shadows: "You survived my trap. My master will be pleased. He has grand plans for you."

Jake didn't know what the creature was talking about.

He frantically shook his penlight, but the batteries had completely failed.

Jake heard feet running behind him. He glanced back and saw Marika, Pindor, and Bach'uuk sprinting to his aid, aiming straight for the pool of shadows. They hadn't listened to him. Emotions warred inside him. He was both selfishly relieved, while at the same time terrified for his new friends.

Pindor hit the pool of shadows first, and his legs went out from under him. He fell face-first into the black pool. Bach'uuk and Marika used the boy's body like a bridge. Bach'uuk was in front and when he reached Pindor's shoulders, he twisted, grabbed Marika by the waist and threw her toward Jake. She flew over the pool and landed two steps behind him—then she sank to her waist like Jake.

She tried to take a step, hauling her upper body, but she could not move. The entire bit of their gymnastics seemed only to amuse the shadowy creature. A muffled chuckle flowed, but it held no warmth, only ice.

"The Magister's daughter and the Elder's son. And a young Urling. You few think to thwart the Skull King?"

Again that dark laugh.

"Jake . . ." Marika said behind him.

He glanced back. Marika held one hand to her throat and tapped a finger under her chin, as if signaling him. He didn't know what she meant. Her other hand rose from behind her back. In her fingers, she held a long slender rod, tipped by a fiery crystal. It was her father's dowsing stick.

She held it out toward Jake, out of sight from the shadowy creature. Marika again tapped at her throat.

Then Jake remembered. Bach'uuk had described one feature that his sharp eyes had picked out of the shadowy form as the assassin fled Kalakryss. A clasp at the throat, decorated with a chunk of bloodstone.

Jake turned and faced the sculpture of shadow. Marika slipped the wand into the hand Jake hid behind his back. He lifted his chin and stared as the figure closed the distance.

"Though the master wants you," it hissed, "that doesn't mean I can't make you suffer for your trouble. And what better way to make you suffer than to see one of your friends die?"

The creature pointed an arm. Jake risked a glance and saw Pindor struggling to pull himself out of the black pool. He had got his head out and gasped for air. Then the shadows rose over his friend's body, flowing up and filling his nose and mouth, leaving only his eyes above the darkness. Pindor twisted in fear. His mouth stretched in a silent scream as he tried to draw air.

Jake shoved around and faced the shadow-cloaked monster. "Let him go!"

Jake drew back the creature's attention. It wanted to savor his pain. But when it turned its head, Jake spotted the glint buried in the shadows. A chunk of blackness darker than any shadow. The bloodstone clasp.

Jake whipped his arm around and stabbed out with Balam's dowsing stick. The crimson crystal cut through the shadows and reached the black stone. With a touch, the bloodstone seemed to jump. A tiny scream flowed as a fiery light burst from the wand's tip. Jake blinked away the glare and saw the chunk of bloodstone had gone dead white, drained of its power.

"*No!*" the creature moaned, echoing the cry from the stone.

The shadows collapsed like a wash of snowmelt after a sudden thaw. Jake stumbled free as the pool around him turned from tar to thin air. He fell back into Marika, but they kept their footing. Pindor coughed and choked, but he was still alive. Bach'uuk helped him to his feet. Pindor picked up his sword and lunged groggily forward. He pressed the tip of his sword over the heart of the assassin.

With the bloodstone clasp undone, the shadows melted away from the cloaked figure. Blackness flowed down and revealed a pale face and an overly large belly.

"Magister Oswin!" Marika gasped.

He showed no remorse, only disdain and disgust.

"Why?" she begged.

"Why not?" he scoffed, curling a lip.

"But you've always served Calypsos."

A hard laugh escaped him. "No. I've always served

Kalverum Rex, my true master. Since I was an apprentice, I served him, recognized his brilliance. Someone not frightened to delve into alchemies that others shunned. He found a dark path to godhood, and I was allowed to follow him."

"Then why didn't you leave with him when he was banished?" Marika asked, her face pale and sick.

Again that wicked smile bloomed. "While others were allowed to go with him, he forced me to remain behind. To be his eyes and ears. To bide a time when he could again return!"

"So you were his spy!" Pindor said, and poked his sword enough to get the prisoner to wince.

"And his saboteur," Jake added with a nod toward the murky emerald sphere.

"All these years . . ." Marika said.

"Such gullible swine." He spat on the floor. "You know nothing about this land here! Nothing about the forces that close even now around you. With but a word—" He suddenly twitched and gasped. He stared down at his feet.

The shadows had pooled there like a discarded cloak. But they did not lie limp. Around the Magister's feet, the shadows began to churn like a whirlpool.

"No, Master!" he moaned.

Oswin's legs began to sink into the inky whirlpool. His eyes got huge and panicked. His face suddenly twisted in pain. A scream burst from his throat. Not pleading this time—pure agony. Oswin attempted to lunge out of the churning pool, but he was caught as surely as Jake had been before. He sprawled on the floor.

They all backed away.

The black tide pulled his body deeper, sucking him away. His fingers clawed at the smooth stone floor, but he could gain no purchase. His face screwed up into a mask of pain and terror.

"No! Not like this!"

Marika took a step toward him. Jake held her back. The fiend might drag her with him.

"My father," she pleaded. "What happened to him?"

Oswin seemed not to hear her, or simply didn't care. His fingers left bloody tracks as he was sucked into that black churning maw. He vanished with one final scream of terror.

Marika turned away and pressed her face into Jake's shoulder. He put an arm around her. The whirlpool continued to churn, but like water flushing down a bathtub drain, it was quickly gone, leaving nothing but the smooth stone floor.

They all took a moment to steady themselves. Pindor poked his sword at the floor, as if testing its solidity. Jake kept his arm around Marika. They moved shakily forward and passed under the crystal heart of the temple. Jake knelt by the emerald sphere. It no longer even wobbled.

Deep within the stone, where the other spheres glowed, this crystal was dark—no, not just dark, it was *black*.

A solid piece of shadow rested at the heart of the stone.

Jake carefully placed a palm on the surface. It was cold, but nothing more. He placed his other palm on it. He could fathom no way to clear out the poisoning darkness within. There was no way of reaching it with Balam's dowsing stick, not through solid crystal. And Jake's penlight had no more juice. They could not even try shocking it.

Jake glanced to Marika. She shook her head. They needed a true Magister, not two apprentices.

Pindor stared back toward where Oswin had been sucked away into the void. "He betrayed us all. But I guess it makes a certain strategic sense."

Marika snapped at Pindor, "Sense? How does any of this make sense?"

Pindor waved an arm around the chamber. "The Skull King needed a Magister. Only a Magister could pass through the barrier that locked the temple and bring down the shield that protected our valley. It was no wonder the Skull King accepted his banishment so easily. He knew he could return to the valley whenever he was ready."

Jake stood back up. "But that doesn't mean we have to let him." He nodded to Bach'uuk. "We came here with a plan—your plan, Pin—to find a place to regroup and seek more allies."

Marika joined them. "We can't let him win."

"We won't," Jake promised—though he hoped it was an oath he could keep.

As they set off, a screech blasted outside the temple. It was so loud that it hurt Jake's ears even inside the temple. He swore it shook the floor under them.

Jake remembered the cries of triumph that had excited the grakyl horde a few moments ago. He suspected that the cause of that excitement had just arrived.

"Has he come?" Marika asked, voicing what Jake feared. She didn't need a name. They all knew to whom she was referring.

"Let's go," Jake said.

WORLD ENOUGH
AND TIME

Bach'uuk led them to the tunnel beyond the crystal heart. It opened into a twisted set of narrow stairs that headed down into the lower levels of the pyramid. They went single file. Jake realized they had to be *beneath* the pyramid by now, or maybe the pyramid was actually larger than it appeared from above. Maybe what was on the surface was just the tip of a much larger structure.

Around and around they went.

Finally the stairs ended at another room, flat roofed but circular in shape. Giant stalactites of crystals hung from the high roof like the fangs of some colossal fossilized beast. They glowed and illuminated the space ahead.

Jake followed Bach'uuk into the chamber as he headed toward yet another tunnel on the far side of the room. It looked like more stairs—heading down again.

How far down does this place go? Jake wondered, but his full attention remained on the room. His feet slowed.

Marika and Pindor kept close to him.

On the floor rested a giant device. It was a circular wheel, made out of pure gold. It lay flat on the floor and stretched ten yards across. Its inner edge was notched like a gear. A second wheel was fitted inside the first one.

As Jake watched, the larger gear revolved a few degrees with a loud snap, turning the smaller gear inside. Then it stopped, as if marking time. And maybe it was. Jake walked around its outer edge. Though there were no marks on it, Jake recognized the shape.

Marika realized the same as she followed behind Jake. "It's like our tribe's calendar wheel."

Jake nodded. The Maya had developed a detailed calendar using wheels fitted together like gears. Again he wondered which came first. Had the Maya built this? Or had some ancient Maya stood where they were now and returned home with the knowledge? Jake continued around the edge. According to Marika, the pyramid had been here long before any of the tribes had arrived, even before the Neanderthals had made their home here in the valley. Jake began to suspect he was looking at the possible source of all ancient science, knowledge found here and taken back home.

Bach'uuk, who'd seen all this before, waited at the entrance to the far tunnel.

Jake began to head over when he finally noted the curved walls of the room. Row after row of ancient script covered the walls from floor to ceiling, so crisply inscribed, it could've been cut with a laser. Jake scanned the ancient writing.

What language was it? Who wrote it? Jake ran his fingers along the letters. It had to be the builders of the pyramid. Possibly the same ones who drew the Lost Tribes of Earth to this wild land.

He continued along the wall and crossed toward Bach'uuk, whose brows grew heavier with impatience. They had to keep going. But as Jake continued around the room, a drawing appeared ahead. It had been carved in a blank space on the wall. It showed three circles with shapes sticking out, creating a shadowed bas-relief.

Jake moved away to view it full on—then stopped in midstep. He gawked at the first circle, unable to speak. He edged closer. Though the detail wasn't great, the shapes looked like a crude map of Earth. He drew a finger along the forms carved within the first circle, whispering the names of the continents.

"Africa, South America, Australia . . ."

The next circle showed those same continents moving closer together, fitting together like a jigsaw puzzle. The bulge in South America fit into the curve of Africa. And so on.

The last circle showed all the continents fused into one whole.

Jake gasped and moved away again to take in the whole view. He began to understand what he was seeing. Back during the time of the dinosaurs, the world was just a single large supercontinent. But a great cataclysm and the forces of flowing magma eventually broke apart the single large landmass and formed today's seven smaller continents.

Jake swallowed and mumbled the scientific name for that supercontinent drawn in the last circle. "Pangaea."

Pindor stood at his shoulder. He looked oddly at Jake. "I didn't know you spoke Greek."

Jake frowned at him. "What?"

"*Pangaea*. It's Greek. I studied it in school."

Jake felt a creeping sense of realization. Pindor was

right. The word *Pangaea* was actually formed by two words in Greek. He pictured it in his head.

Pan = all

Gaea (Gaia) = world

So *Pangaea* translated as "All-World."

Jake frowned. All-World was also the name for the universal language used by everyone here. It couldn't be a coincidence, could it? He glanced at Pindor and the map. Then he turned in a slow circle as an icy realization struck him. His friends weren't speaking All-World, they were speaking Pangaean.

A shudder passed through Jake as he faced the map again. Pangaea was a prehistoric world full of dinosaurs and primitive plant life. Like here. He raised his arm and placed his palm on the supercontinent.

Could this be where I am?

If he was right, he was staring at the shape of this world. All along, he'd been asking the wrong question since he and Kady had landed here. The question wasn't *where* they were, but *when*. Jake was still on Earth—but two hundred million years into the past.

"This is Pangaea," he said aloud.

Marika seemed mystified by his stunned response to the drawing. "Jake, what's wrong?"

He shook his head. He didn't have the time to explain, and he wasn't sure they would believe him anyway. At least not yet.

Pindor pointed his sword toward Bach'uuk. "We should be going."

Jake allowed himself to be guided away. He moved on legs numb with shock. A loud snapping *click* drew his gaze over to the clockwork mechanism on the floor. It turned another notch. The smaller inner wheel rotated. Jake glanced back to the wall, to the map of Pangaea.

It's all about *time.*

Jake knew that was central to the mystery here. As he began to turn away, a rolling bit of gold on the floor caught his eye. The turning of the inner ring had bumped something that lay within it. It looked like a fat gold coin. It rolled to a stop inside the ring and bobbled a bit.

Jake stepped toward the pair of gears. *Is that . . . ?*

"We have to go," Pindor insisted. He shifted his sword between his hands, clearly worried about his people, his town.

But Jake leaned out over the outer ring and squinted at what lay within the smaller ring. It wasn't a coin. Jake recognized the shape. He crossed over the outer ring, careful of the toothed gears, and gently stepped into the inner ring. He bent and picked it up.

He was right. It was an old dented pocket watch. Jake examined it, flipping it between his fingers. His father had one just like—

Jake discovered an inscription on the back. His vision darkened at the corners as he read what was written there.

To my beloved Richard,
A bit of gold to mark our tenth revolution
around the sun together.
With all the love under the stars,
Penelope

Jake felt the room suddenly tilt as a life he'd thought long dead momentarily came back. He stumbled to the side, tripped over the ring's edge, and landed hard, but he didn't even feel it. His world had become the watch—and the words written on it.

"Jake?" Marika hurried to his side. She held out a hand to help him up.

He ignored her and stared at the watch resting in his palm. His fingers closed over the gold case. It was cold and hard—and very real. He whispered the miracle, fearful of raising his voice and making it all go away.

"This is my father's watch."

Jake had no real recollection of how he ended up in a long narrow tunnel cut crudely out of volcanic rock. He remembered being dragged to his feet and guided by gentle prods and cautious words. He recalled more stairs, and a slab of stone that Bach'uuk and Pindor had to shoulder open. The passage lay beyond that stone, a secret tunnel. Bach'uuk led the way with a chunk of glowing white crystal raised in his hand.

They continued in silence. His friends sensed Jake had become a pond covered with a fragile sheet of ice. They trod carefully. Marika kept to his side, waiting for him to be the first to speak.

Jake carried the pocket watch with both hands. It was a weight he couldn't bear with only one arm. It took his whole body to carry it.

"What does this mean?" he finally mumbled, more to himself than to Marika.

The question was a tumbling grain of sand that, once let loose, became an avalanche. *Why is the watch here? How did it end up here? And when?* Had his father and mother been to this land? Or did the watch get sucked here, like Jake and Kady, purely by accident and chance? If his parents had been here, why hadn't anyone told him, mentioned them?

Questions swirled amid mysteries and the unknown.

Jake shuddered and finally let one last question rise. He fought against it because there was too much pain and fear around it.

Could my parents still be alive?

It was a dangerous subject. If Jake allowed himself to believe it and was proven wrong later, it would be like losing his mother and father all over again. Jake did not know if he could survive that.

Still . . .

He stared down at the pocket watch. He felt the heft

of it, rubbed a thumb over one of the dents. This wasn't a child's fantasy, some hope without substance. This was his father's watch . . . in his hand.

Jake gripped it and came to a realization. For now, that would be enough. He could know no more. His father had warned him against letting his imagination run wild. He said that a real scientist balanced hypothesis against tested reality.

Jake took a deep breath. He would do that here.

He'd found his father's watch.

It was real.

What it meant remained unknown.

For now.

With his heart more settled, he allowed the words on the back of the watchcase to warm through him like a soft smile from his mother. *A bit of gold to mark our tenth revolution around the sun together.*

Jake's focus broadened. He began to note the drip of water along the walls. He smelled a slight rotten-egg smell to the air. Sulfur from the volcanic vents. The passage grew warmer, even steamy.

He heard Pindor tell Bach'uuk, "We must be a league under the jungle by now."

Bach'uuk shook his head. "Not much farther to go."

"You keep saying that!" Pindor griped.

Jake swallowed and stared down at the pocket watch. He used a fingernail to crack it open. He felt strong enough to do that now. The watchcase was crooked, the hinges tweaked. But Jake cranked it wide. The crystal face of the watch was in no better condition than its gold case. A skittering crack split the surface. The damage flamed the fear in his heart. How had it become so beat-up?

But this fear quickly dimmed as he watched the slender second hand sweep around the dial of the watch. It shouldn't have been moving. The watch was one of the old-fashioned ones that had to be wound with the tiny stem that stuck out at the top. But that wasn't what truly mystified Jake and forced him fully back to reality.

The second hand spun slowly and surely.

But in the wrong direction.

Counterclockwise.

The watch was running backward!

Before he could ponder the significance, Pindor called, "The way out!"

Jake became aware of a roaring sound. Bach'uuk lifted the crystal higher to reveal a heavy cascade of water flowing over the mouth of the tunnel. No wonder the path had remained a secret. Its end was hidden behind a waterfall.

They hurried forward together.

Marika glanced over at Jake.

He closed the watch, slipped it into his pocket, and buttoned the pocket tightly shut. He kept his palm over it, not wanting to be far from it. But he met Marika's gaze and nodded. He understood what was at stake. As war raged above, the mystery of the watch would have to wait.

Still, he remembered the second hand sweeping around and around, running backward. In his head he heard the click of the golden clockwork calendar as it turned. He pictured the bas-relief showing the breakup of Pangaea.

The key to all these mysteries was one word.

Time.

And Jake knew one thing for certain.

They were running out of it.

THE LONG COUNT

Spray soaked Jake to the skin.

Bach'uuk led them behind the waterfall along a thin ledge of rock. He kept a hand on Jake's wrist. Jake, in turn, grasped Marika, who grabbed Pindor. Any misstep and they'd all go tumbling to the sharp rocks below.

But that wasn't the only danger.

Though the falls filled the world with their rumble, beyond them the jungle croaked, roared, bellowed, hissed, buzzed, and screeched.

At last they reached the edge of the waterfall, and the ledge widened underfoot. Pindor shook his hair like a wet dog. They all caught their breath for a moment.

The full moon had risen high as midnight drew near. Scents of night-blooming flowers and dark rich loam mingled with the sweet rot of the ancient forest. Here was a primeval world where nature first practiced with seed and leaf, with tooth and claw, with root and vine.

It was a riot of new life.

Jake stared out, still reeling from what the temple had taught him. He now had a name for this world.

Pangaea.

At this moment, Jake understood why the Neanderthal tribe chose to live on this side of the ridge. There was great beauty here, savage yet wondrous.

Bach'uuk got them moving again toward a steep-walled cove, pocked with caves high up the walls like windows on a skyscraper. Some openings were dark, while others glowed with firelight—real firelight, not glowing crystals, shimmering, flickering, dancing flames.

Jake counted in his head. There were well over a hundred caves, maybe twice that. This wasn't some little Ur village, but more like a thriving metropolis.

"I never imagined . . ." Marika said.

"It's so big!" Pindor exclaimed.

Jake heard the hope in Pindor's voice. If the tribe could be convinced to come to the town's defense, there might be some chance of driving off the Skull King's forces.

Bach'uuk pretended not to hear their words or the awe behind them. But he did walk a bit taller.

Crude ladders connected the various dwelling levels, while vine ropes draped between them, holding baskets, buckets, and hooks. It was like a city turned on its side, where traffic didn't flow east and west, but up and down. Still, it was clear the Neanderthals respected the jungle's dangers. The lowermost caves were high above the ground and rows of sharpened logs poked outward like thorns.

A tall shaggy figure dressed in sewn leather garments stepped out of the first cave and spoke to Bach'uuk in the Ur tongue. His expression was not welcoming. Bach'uuk pointed to their group and answered. A short argument followed, but eventually the tall man grimaced and walked back inside.

Bach'uuk returned. "Kopat will gather our Elders. They know of the attack, but the Ur do not make rash decisions."

"What's there to decide?" Pindor asked. "The Skull King will bring this war to your caves once he's finished with Calypsos."

Bach'uuk shrugged.

With no choice but to wait, Jake's mind pushed aside the mysteries of the day and turned to a more immediate worry. Kady. He had no idea where his sister was or how she was doing. He began to conjure up horrible scenarios, and his breathing grew heavier with his fear for her.

Before he descended into full panic, the large man returned. This time he spoke in All-World. "Come. The Elders will listen." His expression was no more inviting, but he turned and led them all inside.

Bach'uuk lifted up an arm and barred Pindor from stepping across the threshold. "As an outsider, you may not carry a weapon in the Elders' presence." He held out a palm for the grakyl sword.

Pindor's shoulders slumped, but he passed the blade over.

With the sword in hand, Bach'uuk led the way inside. Jake quickly became lost in the maze. Along the way, he spotted more of the Ur. Most shied away but curiosity kept them close by.

Suddenly the tunnel opened into a natural cavern. A small pool of water lay in the middle, reflecting the flames from a small fire. The firelight also glowed over the walls. A vast landscape had been painted, showing a wild jungle where giant saurians lumbered and all manner of beasts roamed, flew, slithered, and crawled. In the flicker of the flames, the animals seemed to caper and dance.

Marika passed along the wall with her neck craned. Her eyes shone with wonder.

From a tunnel behind the fire, three shapes emerged from the shadows and into the light. Their backs were bent with arthritis, and their hair had gone white with age. They hobbled on thick staffs, which had been decorated with glowing crystals and polished bronze bangles. The bangles reflected the firelight and caused the painted animals on the wall to dance even more.

Their eyes seemed nearly blind, only able to see light and dark. They sank heavily to the rock floor near the flames. These were not just *Elders*, but more like *ancients*.

The one in the center spoke in native Ur to Bach'uuk,

who bowed his head and answered. Three pairs of eyes swung to stare at Jake. Their gazes weighed down upon him. Jake had never felt such intensity—it was almost as if they were trying to peer into his mind.

"Why do you come to us?" the middle Elder asked.

Jake swallowed. "We come to see if you will join in the battle against the Skull King."

Those eyes merely stared.

"Calypsos will fall without additional aid," Jake pressed.

"All things come to an end," the Elder to the left whispered hoarsely.

"All life exists only in the short time," the Elder to the right added. "Marked by the beating of the heart."

The center Elder finished what sounded like an ancient proverb. "Only one heart marks time in the long count." He lifted his ancient hand and formed a triangle with his bony fingers.

He must be referring to the pyramid and the crystal heart that pulsed in the center of it.

The Elder lowered his hands. "And only the temple will be here when we are all gone. So it is spoken from the time when the Ur first came to this land and walked into its great shadow. Nothing else matters."

Jake recalled Marika's story about how the first of the Lost Tribes discovered these people already here. The Neanderthals must have also been snatched from their homeland—and time—and brought here. But how long had the Ur settled here before the other tribes arrived?

"So you won't help us?" Pindor snapped off angrily.

There was no hesitation. No apology. Not even regret. Just a swift "No."

"But you must," Marika pleaded.

"That is not our way," the center Elder intoned, echoing the same words Bach'uuk had used before. "We are not Calypsos. Such a struggle in the short time is of no concern to the Ur. We serve only the temple as it marks the long count."

Jake understood. The temple had protected the Ur when they first came here, and reverence for it had been deeply instilled.

"What will come will come," the Elder finished with a note of finality. "But the temple will always be."

Plainly the town of Calypsos could expect no help from the village. The Ur were set in their ways.

Then again, maybe not *all* the Ur.

Bach'uuk stood straighter. "This is wrong."

The Elders turned to him slowly, clearly showing surprise.

Bach'uuk continued, "I have seen much this past day. Flesh turned to ice. Men who walk in shadows. Monsters who carry swords." Bach'uuk hefted the weapon they'd taken from the graykl lord. "And I've seen the heart of the temple darkened with poison."

At these last words, the centermost Elder waved for Bach'uuk to bring the sword closer.

The others seemed less impressed. "The pyramid will always be," one intoned, and the other nodded.

The Elder in the middle examined the sword after Bach'uuk carried it to him. From the Elders' reactions, Jake suspected Bach'uuk might be arguing along the right track, warning of a threat to the temple.

His eyes were drawn to the sword. As Bach'uuk turned it in the firelight, he revealed a symbol melted into the hilt. Earlier, Jake had caught a glimpse of the sword's mark as he'd passed the weapon to Pindor, but he'd forgotten all about it in the excitement that followed. The symbol glowed in the flames. Stunned, Jake recognized it. He'd seen the symbol before, back in his other life. It had been stamped on the bottom of Jake's invitation to attend the show at the British Museum. It had been sculpted into a steel tie tack worn by Morgan Drummond, their bodyguard in London.

Jake struggled to comprehend what he was seeing.

It was plainly a griffin—the mythological beast with the head, wings, and claws of an eagle and the body, hind legs, and tail of a lion. But it was also the corporate symbol for Bledsworth Sundries and Industries, Inc.

What is it doing here?

Jake moved closer to the fire to examine the mark. Bach'uuk noted his interest, and Jake pointed to the hilt.

The Elder narrowed his eyes. "A mark of corruption. It is a monster made from the parts of many beasts."

"It is also the mark of the Skull King," Bach'uuk said.

Jake remembered Marika's story, how Kalverum Rex used the bloodstone to corrupt and taint animals into foul creations. One only had to look at a grakyl to see the result of his evil alchemy. Even the griffin symbol looked a bit like a grakyl.

Jake's mind churned as Bach'uuk continued speaking in low tones to the Elder. What was the connection here? With every new discovery, the mystery deepened. Jake's hand drifted to his pocket and clutched his father's watch. Threads between the modern world and Pangaea were weaving tighter with every new discovery.

But what did it all mean?

Jake stared at the griffin. Though he couldn't prove it, he knew something more was afoot here in Pangaea, something connected to the Bledsworth corporation.

Across the fire, Bach'uuk had become more animated, pleading his cause using the Ur native tongue. Jake didn't understand, but he heard the word *science* mentioned. Bach'uuk pantomimed using a flashlight, relating the story of its freezing beam.

All three Elders scrunched their heavy gray brows.

Bach'uuk suddenly pleaded in All-World. "We Ur shared our valley, offered its protection to the other tribes, like a mother to a child. Yet now we will sit in our homes and let them die. That is not right. A mother does not abandon a child."

The Elder in the middle shook his head. For the first time, there was true regret in his voice. "Lives are short. Do not fear. Fear exists only in the short time."

Jake stepped forward, sensing Bach'uuk needed support. Searching for a way to prove his friend's argument, Jake showed them his penlight and firmly stated what he was growing to believe. "This object comes from beyond any *short* time," Jake warned. "It comes from a *long* time." *A very, very long time*, Jake added silently. *Two hundred million years in the future, to be exact.* "And I believe the new danger to the temple may stretch from that same long time."

The Elders stared at the penlight, not so much fearfully but with curiosity. Jake needed to convince them of the danger. He screwed off the top of the penlight and shook the batteries into his palm. "These hold both alchemy from *your* time and science from *my* time. And in the wrong hands, the combination threatens all. Even the great temple."

Jake threw the batteries into the fire. He needed the ancients to understand the full threat. If he was right—if there was any connection between his world and Pangaea—then something had to be done before it was too late.

The batteries heated up, and Jake waved everyone back. Though the AAA batteries had no juice, they were still dangerous. Exposed to flame, they could—

Both batteries exploded at the same time, popping with

less force than Jake had hoped. Still, the secondary result far exceeded Jake's expectation. Apparently a little of the freezing alchemy from the blue crystal remained stored in the penlight's battery. The flames blew out. The red-hot embers went instantly black and cold. But even more dramatically, the pool next to the fire crusted over with a solid sheet of ice.

No one moved, stunned by the display.

Before anyone could speak, a commotion at the entrance to the chamber drew their attentions. An Ur tribesman led in a young woman wearing the bloodied uniform of a Roman scout. Another two Ur carried a second soldier—an older man in centurion armor. His leg was broken, and his head lolled—he was barely conscious.

The scout noted Jake and the others. Her only reaction was a twitch of surprise that she quickly suppressed. She spoke to the Elders.

"The valley has fallen. Kalakryss belongs to the gra-kyl horde. The People of the Wind have been chased out of the valley, and the last of the Saddleback riders barely escaped through Serpent Pass. Calypsos is now in the hands of the Skull King."

After several minutes of frantic questions and confusion, Pindor finally asked, "What of my father?"

"I can't say," the scout answered. "The town is locked down by the horde. Most hide in their homes and attics. Little is known. But word has come of a demand.

From the Skull King."

"What demand?" Marika asked.

The woman glanced at Jake, then away again. "To give up the newcomers. We have until sunrise to obey. Already they prepare to lay torch to the Sacred Woods to smoke out the girl. But if we fail by dawn's first light to bring forth both, the horde will begin slaughtering the townspeople."

All eyes turned to Jake. He read the question in their expressions: *What did Kalverum Rex want with Jake and his sister?*

He wasn't any the wiser and shook his head, admitting his confusion.

The scout spoke. "Elder Tiberius sent us to speak with the Ur. To seek their aid."

Pindor said, "That's why we came here, too."

"But they will not help us," Marika added. "It is against their way."

The scout studied Jake with hard eyes. "Then perhaps my journey here was not in vain. If the Ur cannot help, the only hope for Calypsos lies in obeying the Skull King's demands. At least for now."

Marika gasped. "What? You can't be thinking of turning Jake and his sister over to—"

Jake touched her arm, silencing her. If there was any hope to avoid a massacre in Calypsos, Jake would have to give himself up to the Skull King.

But a hoarse voiced interrupted, fierce and uncompromising. "No." Jake turned to find the Elder pointing at him. The ancient's voice lowered into a deep warning. "A great storm builds across time. Sweeping up from the past and down from the years yet to come. It swirls around this boy. This we have suspected from our reading of the stars. It is why we set Bach'uuk to watch over him."

Jake stiffened in surprise.

"The newcomer must not be tossed into the darkness," the Elder finished.

"But Calypsos . . ." Jake said.

The ancient Elder pointed his staff at the frozen pond. "With this you have proven who you are. You are indeed of the long time. Like the temple." He stamped his staff once on the stone floor. "To preserve both, the Ur will rise up against the shadow that has fallen over the valley."

"Then you'll fight?" Pindor asked.

Marika's eyes brightened with hope.

"To follow the way, we have no choice." Jake felt naked under the ancient's gaze. "The great storm is upon us all."

SERPENT PASS

The full moon silhouetted the eastern gateway. Unlike the Broken Gate on the western side of the valley, this gateway had not fallen. A stone sculpture arched over the pass, black and foreboding. It formed the looping curls of a snake with two heads, one pointing south, the other north. Jake had seen the same shape drawn on the map in Magister Balam's library, and he'd seen it sculpted in gold at the British Museum.

Jake hurried up the trail, following the Roman scout and the massive Ur warrior named Kopat. Marika trailed Jake, along with Pindor and Bach'uuk. Behind them stretched a long line of Ur tribesmen, all carrying weapons: pole spears, stone axes, crude bolas made of stones threaded on leather ropes.

Jake moved around a shoulder of rock that blocked the trail. Down a gully in the path ahead, a dozen saddled fleetbacks clustered, clearly nervous. The riders huddled near their mounts. The Saddlebacks were all young men and women, just a little older than Jake. And fear made them look even younger.

Kopat headed off to the side, gathering the Ur tribesmen together. The Roman scout led Jake and the others over to her group of fleetbacks.

"Where's Centurion Portius?" one of the riders asked.

The scout answered, matter-of-fact, "His leg is broken. He will not be able to ride. The Ur will care for him."

"Then who will lead us?" another asked. He seemed to find little hope in Kopat's forces with their crude weapons. Like most of Calypsos, he must not hold much stock in the Ur's abilities, beyond menial tasks.

The Roman woman turned to Pindor. "With Centurion Portius down, we have an empty saddle."

Mumbles passed through the riders.

"It's Tiberius's son . . ."

"No, not Heron—the other one. . . ."

"We *are* cursed. . . ."

Pindor pretended not to hear them.

The woman crossed to a fearsome-looking fleetback with a ragged scar that blinded one eye. It stood off from the others and kicked a clod of rock and mud.

Jake backed away. If this was the centurion's mount, no wonder his leg got broken. The sick expression on Pindor's face was easy to read, even in the dark.

Before he could move—either toward the abandoned mount or away from it—a horn sounded behind them all. The low moan of its call set Jake's teeth on edge.

Turning, Jake saw all the Ur had gathered on the lower trail. There were over fifty men. It was a large number, but only a fraction of the Ur village.

Where are the others?

Kopat stood atop a boulder with his legs widely spaced and some type of curled shell lifted to his lips. He blew again, and the long sustained note sailed toward the moon with a plaintive call.

And it was answered.

Out in the jungle, another horn blew. From the dark canopy, a large snaking head rose from the trees and pushed up into the moonlight. It climbed at least ten stories into the air. Jake recognized that long neck and blunt head. It was a brontosaurus, one of the giants in a land of giants. It began to lumber toward them.

Behind it, out in the forest, another head rose up . . .

and another . . . and still another. Like a lawn growing dandelions, a herd of brontosauruses rose into sight. Seven of them! And they all began shifting forward. The first and closest climbed out of the lower forest and began to plod up the trail toward the pass.

Ur warriors rode atop its long body and hung from its flanks in rope harnesses. Like fleas on a dog. One brave warrior sat in a high saddle behind the beast's head, swaying with the brontosaurus's strides. The other brontosauruses followed, equally draped with warriors.

The Roman woman shouted to the Saddleback riders. "Mount up!"

A few responded to the sharpness of her voice, but the others looked unsure—fearful of venturing back into the valley.

Marika pulled Pindor and Jake off to the side.

"Can you believe what we're seeing?" Pindor gasped out, still staring at the lumbering brontosauruses.

Marika drew them another step off. "The surprise of the attack will surely shake the grakyl horde, but for how long? The Skull King has more fearsome demons at his call. Worse than grakyls."

"But what else can we do?" Pindor asked.

Marika stared at Jake. "Our only chance for a true victory is to raise the temple's shield. Without that, we're doomed."

Jake pictured the darkened emerald stone, poisoned by

shifting shadows at its core. "But how?"

"Can your sy-enz help us to cure the stone? To cast out the shadows at its heart? Can you not summon the power of your *elektra-city*?"

Jake shook his head. "I have no more batteries. No way to generate electricity. And even if I could, I'm not sure it would heal the emerald stone."

Still, Jake refused to give up. He ran through all the possible ways to produce electricity: wind, steam, coal, geothermal, solar. All were beyond his abilities and certainly beyond the level of technology here.

There had to be an answer. His hand drifted to his pocket and touched the watch. If his father were here, he'd know what to do. But he wasn't.

Jake's fingers tightened over the gold case. Could his parents still be alive? Jake had no way of knowing, but he knew that he first had to survive to ever hope for an answer.

"There must be a way to cast the shadows out of the stone," Marika repeated.

Jake barely heard her. But a corner of his mind took in her words. They stitched across the surface of his brain— *cast the shadows out*—while at the same time he kept churning through all the ways electricity was generated.

Coal, wind, steam, nuclear . . .

Then he suddenly knew. He tensed—hard enough that Marika noticed.

"Jake, what's wrong?"

He was afraid to speak or lose his train of thought. He ran it through his head a second time. He pictured the bronze bangles on the Ur Elders' staffs, the dancing reflections across the painted walls. He had to close his eyes.

"Jake?" Marika pressed.

He calculated what it would take—the slant, the angle, the distance.

"It will take three of us," Jake decided aloud.

"What will?" Pindor asked.

Jake turned to his friends. "We must get back to the pyramid."

By now, Bach'uuk had joined them. He had been watching the approach of his people with a proud reflection in his eyes.

"Bach'uuk, can you guide us back to the temple?"

He nodded. "If you wish."

"Before we head out," Jake added, "we'll also need some armor."

Marika grabbed his arm. "Jake, what are you planning? Do you have a way of healing the emerald crystal?"

"Maybe."

It was a long shot, but if Jake was right, it also helped explain why Kalverum Rex had waited until the *night* to orchestrate this attack. The Skull King had been taking no chances.

"How are you going to heal it?" Pindor asked. "With what?"

"With the world's oldest and largest battery," Jake answered.

As he laid out his plan, Pindor's eyes glazed over a bit.

"Do you think it will work?" Marika asked.

Jake saw no reason to lie. "I don't know."

"What if it fails? What if you're wrong?"

"Then we'll be doomed." Jake shrugged. "But as you said, Mari, we're doomed anyway."

"Will you both quit saying *doom* so much?" Pindor groused at them. He did not look well.

Jake asked, "Does anyone have a better plan?"

No one spoke up.

Jake began to elaborate on the details, but Pindor cut him off.

"What you're planning to do—it'll take perfect timing."

Jake nodded.

". . . and a distraction might help," Pindor added.

Before Jake could agree, his friend glanced to the gathered Saddlebacks, who were reluctantly climbing into their seats. They wore expressions varying from *hopefulness* at the approaching Ur tribe to *hopelessness* at what they faced in Calypsos.

Pindor spoke with his head still turned. "Jake, you said you needed three of us. Can Bach'uuk take my place?"

Marika touched Pindor's elbow. "Pin, we need you."

He stepped away. "You need three people. Not me. Is that right, Jake?"

Jake heard the strained tones in his friend's voice. He knew it didn't rise from fear, but from determination. Pindor wasn't trying to avoid this dangerous mission. He intended to throw himself into a hotter fire.

"Three should do it," Jake answered.

Pindor nodded. He clutched the whistle Jake had given him like a good-luck piece and headed toward the Saddle-backs.

"Pin!" Marika called.

Jake put a hand on Marika's elbow. "He knows what he's doing."

Jake remembered Pindor's skill at strategy. He had spotted the weak point in Jake's plan and sought to fill it. To have any chance of pulling this off would take precise timing. And a distraction at the right time could prove the difference between success and failure.

"Listen for the horns!" Pindor called back.

The Roman woman still sought to control the giant scarred fleetback as the other riders mounted up. As Pindor stepped up to the stubborn beast, a few derisive snorts followed in his wake.

The fleetback stamped a foot and came close to taking off all of Pindor's toes. But Pindor didn't flinch. Instead he raised a palm and placed it on the leathery neck of the mount. His other hand pocketed the whistle.

"Stamp like that again, Scar-Eye," Pindor said, "and I'll make my next pair of sandals out of your scaly hide."

The fleetback swung its boxy head and fixed its good eye on Pindor. The two stared each other down. The saurian was the first to blink.

Pindor jumped, caught a toe in a stirrup, and hauled into the high saddle. He moved like he'd done it a thousand times—and Jake imagined his friend had done just that, if only in his head.

Twisting in his saddle, Pindor called to his fellow Saddlebacks. "What are you all waiting for! We have Calypsos to rescue!"

The Roman scout gaped at him for a breath longer, then dashed to her own mount and flew into her saddle.

With a wave of his arm and a shout of encouragement, the Saddlebacks began moving up the trail as the Ur forces followed atop their brontosauruses. The parade ascended slowly toward the giant archway carved into the shape of a double-headed snake.

Jake turned to Marika and Bach'uuk. It was now just the three of them. His doubts grew sharper. How could they hope to defeat the Skull King by themselves?

But Marika's eyes shone with hope, and Bach'uuk matched his gaze with a stoic determination. Jake drew strength from his friends. He lifted an arm and pointed back along the cliffside trail.

"We'd better hurry."

LAST STAND

Dressed in bronze armor that Bach'uuk had borrowed from a blacksmith shop at the Ur village, they made their way back to the pyramid. It seemed to take three times longer than before. The pressure of time grew to such a sharpness that Jake swore he could almost sense the sun pushing around the Earth and climbing toward a new day.

The weight of the breastplate alone reminded Jake of the burden of his responsibility. Worry grew with each heavy step.

What if I fail?

What if I'm wrong?

At long last, Bach'uuk led Marika and Jake back into the pyramid's lower levels, and they began a rapid ascent toward the chamber of the crystal heart. As Jake passed through the room with the gold Mayan calendar, his eyes traveled over the strange language on the walls, the map of Pangaea, and the two gear wheels on the floor. His hand cupped the watch in his pocket. He wanted to stop—his feet even slowed—but the mystery would have to wait. He forced himself to hurry up the stone stairs to the room above.

The main chamber had not changed. The strange pressure again pulsed with each turn of the three-layered crystal heart. The odd glyphs spun and rolled in thousands of combinations as the sphere hovered in the center of the domed space. Beneath the massive sphere, two smaller ones glowed—a rich crimson, a vibrant silvery blue. The emerald had grown so dark that it almost looked black.

Jake dropped to one knee for a closer look, while Marika hovered at his shoulder.

"Does it look like we're too late?" she asked.

Jake studied the stone. "I don't know."

The core of the emerald sphere swirled with dark shadows, an inky whirlpool that screamed of corruption and death. They didn't have much time.

Jake straightened and glanced up to the pyramid's main entrance. The tunnel angled upward, dark as pitch. At any moment, he expected to see demonic grakyl come pouring out.

"C'mon," he said, and led them to the mouth of the tunnel, then turned to Marika. "You stay here in the chamber. I'll bring Bach'uuk farther up the tunnel. You know what you have to do?"

Marika's eyes were wide with fear—some of it reserved for Jake. "Be careful."

Jake nodded, but his plan was the farthest thing from *careful*. As he began to turn away, Marika suddenly lunged forward and hugged him tight. Then she let him go.

Jake warmed and blushed. He opened his mouth and found no words.

"Go!" she said, and pushed him away. "What are you waiting for?"

Jake blinked. He still had no words. So he swung around and hurried up the slanted tunnel. His heart pounded in his chest, but in a good way.

Once he was halfway up and almost out of sight of Marika, he halted again and told Bach'uuk, "You have to stand ready here. I must go up alone."

Bach'uuk reached over and grasped Jake's forearm in the typical handshake of the Ur. Jake returned the shake. They were all taking a huge risk, one that could cost them their lives.

Jake continued up the last part of the tunnel on his own. The dark passageway grew lighter as the opening appeared ahead. A starry sky filled the pyramid's round opening.

He slowed his approach—and with good reason.

Shadowy shapes blotted out the stars. Jake heard hisses and squeals, along with the leathery beat of wings and scrape of claws on stone. The grakyl horde gathered just beyond the opening.

Jake edged forward until a strange tingle swept over his body. It stood the hairs of his arms on end. He had felt the same when he'd jumped through here before, like he felt when he'd passed through the Broken Gate, what seemed like a lifetime ago. Only now the tingle was barely a whisper of its former strength. It was all that remained of the shield. But it still seemed strong enough to keep the grakyl horde out of the temple. At least, Jake hoped so.

He just waited, bathed in that tingling.

Jake stared out over the valley. From his high vantage, he could see all the way over to the eastern wall. The skies had already begun to lighten. He had no more time to spare.

Jake cupped his hands over his mouth. "Hello!" he shouted.

In response something huge dropped from above the doorway and landed on the step below the opening. The dark shape swung around and brandished a long black blade that looked like a glassy shard of obsidian. Wings unfurled and cut out the sky.

A grakyl lord.

Jake dropped to his knees, making sure to stay within the tingle of the fading shield. Pinched black eyes stared back at him.

"I am Jake Ransom!" he yelled out, hoping the bat-faced monstrosity understood. "One of the newcomers."

The grakyl lord climbed the step to stand at the threshold. Jake was close enough to note the cracked yellow nails of its claws and the squashed snout of its nose. Its sword rose to point at Jake's chest.

Jake shivered in his armor, but he had to buy an extra moment. So he reached to his sides and unbuckled the bronze breastplate. He let it clatter to the stone in a clear sign of surrender.

This last idea had been Marika's. As Jake stared at the razor edge of the grakyl lord's sword, he began to doubt the wisdom of her strategy. But he was committed now. There was no turning back.

Jake lifted his arms. "I surrender!" he yelled out to the monstrous figure. "But only to your master! Only to Kalverum Rex!"

The grakyl lord leaned closer. Its slitted nostrils flared open and closed. Beyond its wings, the eastern sky continued to brighten as sunrise neared. Dawn had been the deadline set by the Skull King for the surrender of Jake and Kady.

They had no more time.

"I give up!" Jake yelled. He coughed to clear his throat. His chest had seized up in fear. Still, he repeated his one ultimatum. "But I'll only surrender to the Skull King!"

The grakyl lord studied Jake a moment longer—then swung around with a sweep of its bone and leather wings. An ear-shattering cry erupted from its ghastly mouth and echoed out over the valley.

The call was repeated by others in the horde. Soon the whole valley rang out with the horrible cries. The message was being spread.

But would it be answered?

Yes or no?

Both answers terrified Jake.

The waiting stretched to an agonizing length. Jake's heart climbed into his throat and pounded there. To make matters worse, he felt the tingling fading from his skin as he knelt at the pyramid's opening. The shield was almost gone.

The grakyl lord kept his distance on the outer steps, but for how much longer?

How much time do I have left?

Jake studied the sky. To the east, a rosy glow seeped upward from the horizon. Sunrise was fast approaching. The deadline given by the Skull King was about to pass. Jake's fear grew sharper. His worry for Kady weighed like a cold stone in his belly.

All he could do was wait.

In a matter of moments, the first rays of the sun would shine brightly upon the pyramid's entrance. Despite his pounding heart, Jake remembered the significance of such an orientation, something he'd learned from his father. All Mayan temples were built to greet the first light of the new day. And for that matter, the great stone cathedrals of Europe also faced their front doors to the east.

As Jake knelt, he wondered if that tradition traced its origin to here, to this very structure. Before he could ponder the mystery any further, the cries of the grakyl horde cut off. The sudden silence felt like a blanket thrown over the entire valley.

Concerned, Jake climbed to his feet. Out on the steps, the grakyl horde ducked low and bowed their heads. Their wings folded behind their backs. Jake spotted something sweeping across the sky. The breadth of its wings stretched impossibly far—and it grew larger with each beat of Jake's heart.

Like some saurian jumbo jet.

How could something so immense stay aloft? It seemed impossible. And what made its approach especially creepy was its utter silence. It glided toward the temple without a sound, as if it were more shadow than substance.

The creature sank lower until it was a dark silhouette racing over the treetops of the Sacred Woods. It looked like the monster of all winged dinosaurs, the pteranodon. As it flew toward the pyramid, the forest canopy rustled in its wake as if the trees themselves shivered.

Then it suddenly twisted and shot upward, so high and fast that Jake lost sight of it. The muscles of his legs twitched. He came close to stepping out of the doorway's shadow to keep it in sight. Instead he tensed his entire body and kept his post.

And lucky he did. . . .

A moment later, the pterosaur landed on the side of the pyramid, filling half the steps. Grakyl scattered to the sides. One was crushed under a heavy leg. Squirming and screaming, it died.

Jake forced himself to remain in the doorway. Everything depended on him keeping his place.

The pterosaur lowered its neck and stretched its wings as if hugging the temple. Though the creature was massive, Jake had a hard time seeing it clearly. Shadows clung to its form, flowing over its body.

Its long narrow head ended up coming to rest only a couple yards to the left of the doorway. Draped in shadows that looked like a lion's mane, the head ended in a crocodilian snout rimmed by crooked pointed teeth. Jake had seen enough pteranodon fossils to know this was no ordinary pterosaur. For one, pterosaurs didn't have *teeth*.

But it was the eyes that truly set Jake's jaw to clench. Two black orbs stared at Jake, like polished black diamonds. They were empty and bottomless tunnels to places were screams always echoed and blood flowed like rivers.

But even that wasn't the worst.

From behind the saurian's neck, a clot of shadows dropped away and struck the temple stairs. The other grakyl fell back, scrambling over one another to keep out of its way. On the steps, the shape straightened and formed the figure of a man.

He was massive, at least seven feet tall. He wore a suit of black armor that covered him from head to toe. It was crowned by a helmet bearing a pair of horns, but unlike those on the Viking helmets, these horns were kinked into savage twists and curls, as if grown from the skull of a beast that had been tortured its entire life. The figure stalked up the steps, moving with a deliberate determination toward Jake.

Jake tried to spy any features, but beneath the helmet lay only shadows. Still, Jake knew who climbed the temple.

Kalverum Rex.

The Skull King.

As the dark shape neared the entrance, Jake realized one error. Kalverum Rex wore no armor. What covered his body were dense shadows. They flowed over his form, shining like black oil on skin. But rather than billowing and wafting about, the shadows wrapped tight to his body, as if the darkness were scared of what lay hidden at its heart and attempted to hide the horror from the world.

For the Skull King, shadows were his armor.

Though there were no eyes, Jake knew the fiend stared straight at him. His skin crawled with a burning itch that had nothing to do with the temple's shield. He wanted to run—and keep running. But Jake didn't move. More than bravery, terror kept him rooted in place.

The Skull King climbed to the top step and towered across the threshold. Jake leaned away as an arm stretched toward him. He knew a single touch and he would be dead.

The hand edged closer, reaching for him, cautiously, as if testing unknown waters. As it crossed into the weakening shield, emerald fire danced over the black fingertips and stripped the shadows away. From out of the darkness appeared fingers covered in gray-green scales and tipped by long yellow claws.

No *man* had hands like that—at least no one that was still human.

A rustle of satisfaction shook through the shadows that covered Kalverum Rex. He knew the shield held no power that could stop him. All that stood between the Skull King and the heart of the temple's power was a boy from North Hampshire, Connecticut.

Recognizing this, too, Jake took his first scared step backward.

Kalverum's satisfaction melted to dark amusement. With the shield down, nothing could stop him. Jake had nowhere to hide.

Words flowed out that turned the marrow of Jake's bones to ice.

"Come to me . . ."

FIRE AND SHADOWS

Any sane person would run when faced by a tower of shadows. But Jake held his ground. The Skull King took another step toward the threshold. More shadows stripped from his limb, revealing scales and a ridge of thorns.

Jake feared what else would be revealed, what else the shadows hid. But he couldn't turn away, trapped between horror and fascination. Still, there were limits to what curiosity could bear. Jake finally flicked his eyes away from the peeling shadows.

It proved to be a mistake.

His gaze fell upon the breastplate of bronze armor he'd abandoned at the threshold. At the same time, Kalverum's left foot bumped against it. The armor rattled with a ringing tone and drew the monster's attention to the ground.

Kalverum stopped. He glanced down, then at Jake, then down again. His posture was one of caution and suspicion. Jake held his breath. Then the Skull King did what Jake had dreaded. Kalverum turned to the side and stared over a shoulder to the east, to where the sun was just cresting over the horizon. The first rays of the new day speared outward and aimed for the pyramid.

The Skull King's entire body stiffened. *"Clever boy . . ."*

The fiend lunged down and snatched the breastplate.

"No!" Jake yelled, and tried to grab it, too.

But Kalverum moved with a speed born of shadows, a flicker of darkness against the new day. He reached the plate first and snatched it away.

Jake saw all hope yanked out of reach. His heart sank with his failure—but he'd forgotten one thing, something vital and important.

He wasn't alone.

Across the valley, a piercing volley of horns heralded the sunrise. It rang out loudly, echoing and bright. Roman bugles blasted as Ur horns blared. The cacophony sounded like a legion of thousands.

Pindor!

His friend had come with the last of the Saddlebacks and the Ur army—and as promised, Pindor let it be known.

All around the pyramid, the grakyl rose like a flock of crows startled from a cornfield. Even the Skull King turned to the north to assess this new threat.

It was all the distraction Jake needed.

He leaped forward and grabbed the bronze piece of

armor out of the shadowy grip of the Skull King. Dropping to a knee in the doorway, Jake turned the polished surface of the breastplate, shiny as a mirror, toward the first rays of the new sun. He caught the light, twisted to the side, and angled the reflection down the throat of the tunnel behind him.

"Now!" Jake yelled.

Far down the slanted passageway, the reflected sunlight illuminated Bach'uuk. Bach'uuk lifted his shield of armor into the light. It sparked as brightly as a piece of the sun, which in fact it was. He tilted his plate and reflected the brilliance farther down the tunnel—toward Marika.

Would it work?

Marika had given Jake this idea, a way to rid the emerald shieldstone of its poisonous shadows and possibly raise the valley's protective barriers. The plan had started with her statement *There must be a way to cast the shadows out of the stone.* The answer was obvious. What was the best way to chase away a shadow?

To shine a light on it.

Also at the time, Jake had been struggling to think of a way to use electricity to jump-start the stone, to fuse modern science and Pangaean alchemy. With his flashlight's batteries gone, he had needed a new source of power. And what was world's largest power source? The answer rose into the sky every day, warming the Earth.

The sun.

Even Marika's father had stated the connection between the crystals and sunlight. They'd been in the Astromicon, watching the dance of crystals across the sunlit slits of the dome. His words had stayed with Jake.

All alchemy starts with the sun.

So Jake hung his hopes upon the new day, the rising of the sun. He sought to reflect its brilliance down into the heart of the temple, to cast out the shadows from the stone and use the sun's energy to fire the crystal back to life. The problem was getting the energy down there.

The bronze bangles hanging off the Neanderthal Elders' staffs had reminded Jake.

Mirrors reflect sunlight.

All he needed was to bounce the morning's light from one mirror to the next, from Jake to Bach'uuk to Marika. She could then reflect the sunlight into the heart of the pyramid and bathe the darkened crystal in the sun's brilliance.

But would it work?

All these thoughts flashed through Jake's mind within the blaring of a single horn. He held the breastplate steady as the grakyl horde rose up to the challenge from Pindor's army. Down the tunnel, Bach'uuk was bathed in sunlight and reflecting its brightness deeper into the heart of the pyramid.

But also from the corner of his eye, Jake noted the Skull King swinging around. Kalverum lunged toward him.

Then time froze. He saw his father sitting under a tree, explaining about Isaac Newton, how the scientist discovered gravity in the falling of an apple. He had told Jake at the time that the greatest gift of the human mind was its ability to ask one question, one word. All of human history traced back to this one question.

Why?

His father's words echoed to Jake now.

The discovery of truth is what we all seek. And it is the good man who stands behind the truth and defends it with his life.

So as the Skull King attacked, Jake did not flinch. Bathed in sunlight, he held the breastplate steady. He must trust he was right. Even if it cost him his life.

Claws reached for his throat. Nails touched his neck and burned his skin, blistering on contact.

Then the tingling over his body suddenly burst into an emerald blast of blinding force. The explosion blew Jake back into the tunnel as if he'd been shoved in the chest. Kalverum was thrown the other way, down the pyramid's steps.

Jake landed hard on his back. The breastplate got knocked from his hands and went banging down the slanted passageway. Jake gasped air back into his shocked lungs and fought to his feet. He scrambled back to the threshold.

He felt the pressure of the shield as he neared it. Even

a yard away, the hairs on Jake's arms quivered with its energy. He pushed far enough into it to view the lower steps. The Skull King stared up at Jake, his shadowy fists clenched. Hatred pulsed off his evil form.

Jake sensed a storm building within that shell of darkness, readying to hurl itself against the reborn shield. But thunder rumbled overhead. Both Jake and Kalverum turned to the sky.

When the rumble of thunder repeated, with it came an arc of energy, an emerald fire across the roof of the valley. The energy seemed to set fire to the volcanic ridges. It pooled across the sky like an aurora borealis.

The shield! It was re-forming over the valley!

Against this fiery backdrop, the grakyl horde flew in ragged formations.

Then the lightning storm truly began, crackling with sharper blasts of thunder. A forked bolt lanced down out of the sky and froze one of the grakyl in midair. Then the emerald lightning snapped back into the sky—taking the grakyl with it. The beast was torn out of the valley and flung high into the air. It tumbled end over end, tossed far beyond the new shield.

Other bolts fired downward, zapping some of the grakyl with such force that they fell dead to the earth. But most were grabbed and fired out of the valley with such force that they quickly vanished.

Down the steps, the Skull King recognized the tide

of battle had suddenly shifted. He turned his gaze again toward Jake. For the first time, Jake saw his eyes. They were spats of black flame. Jake imagined the fire rising from a core of pure bloodstone.

It was like staring into the eyes of something ancient and evil, something far older than any Calypsian Magister gone bad. Behind that black gaze hid the nameless beast that forever haunted nightmares and prowled shadows and dark spaces, something that had been lurking at the edges of humankind since the beginning of time.

Jake felt a scream trapped in his throat.

Then that dreaded gaze fell away. The Skull King flowed down the steps to his shadowy mount and flew up into the high saddle. Wings rose like great sheets of night. The beast bunched its massive bulk and leaped skyward.

Jake watched the mount circle into the sky with mighty beats of its wings. Lightning crackled all around mount and rider, stabbing and bursting against the shadows. Unlike the grakyl, the Skull King bore some alchemy that kept him from being immediately flung out of the valley. But from the rapid ascent, Jake guessed such protections would not last long. The beast's dark form fought for the clear skies and climbed higher.

With one final burst, the Skull King broke through the shield with an explosion of green fire and flew off.

It was over.

Still, Jake felt little relief. He remained cold and

trembling—and he knew why.

Just before the Skull King had turned away, Jake sensed a wordless promise: *This was not over between them.* In this cusp of a new day, where light and darkness balanced, Jake had made a choice to stand in the sunlight. And from this moment onward, the darkness would be watching him, waiting for him to slip.

Jake might have quailed and lost all heart right then, even with victory near. But he remembered something vital and important.

He wasn't alone.

Bach'uuk came running out of the heart of the pyramid. Marika came with him. She gripped Jake's hand, all warmth and sunshine. Jake put his arm around Bach'uuk, too. He needed their solidity to remind him that the world was far more than shadows.

Together, they listened to cheers rising from the town.

"You did it," Marika breathed.

"*We* did it," Jake added, but his lips refused to add what he also knew to be true.

For now.

It did not take long for the skies to be cleared of the enemy. In a matter of minutes, only shimmers of emerald fire remained. Then even this blew out, and wide blue skies beckoned.

"We should get back to town," Marika finally said. She

lifted a hand and tested the shield ahead of them. Whispers of emerald energy danced over her fingertips.

"Can we get out this way?" Jake asked.

"I think so. We should be able to pass through to the outside."

Marika stepped forward and drew Jake along. Jake felt the tingling sweep over his body—then they were through and stepped out of the shadow and into the fullness of the morning.

Bach'uuk followed after them.

Curious, Jake reached back toward the doorway again. The shield pushed against him, crackling with a fierce fire. It had let them out, but it wasn't going to let them back in.

Satisfied the heart of the pyramid was safe for the moment, the trio hurried down the stone steps and reached the path that crossed the Sacred Woods. They hadn't taken more than a couple dozen steps along the trail when they were surrounded.

He recognized the mix of Norse gear and Roman attire—battered, bloody, and torn.

"Jake!"

He turned to see Kady push forward. Of course, she hadn't gone far. She must have thought Jake had been trapped inside the pyramid this entire time.

Jake let go of Marika's hand and ran toward his sister. Kady ran toward him. They crashed against each other.

Kady hugged him tight. They were silent for a full breath, allowing themselves simply to be brother and sister, to let the warmth of family melt away the rest of their fears.

"I thought . . . I didn't know . . ." she said, squeezing the breath out of him.

"I know," he gasped out. "Me too."

She broke away and stared at him sternly. "Don't ever do that again!"

"Do what?"

She seemed at a loss as to how to answer that. Her fear was nameless. She managed an exasperated "Scare me like that."

But Jake knew the words failed to truly hold all she felt. He felt the same way, a swirl of emotions that could not be contained within words. It was relief and terror, chaos and security, happiness and tears. It was both the most painful thing and the most wonderful.

It was simply family.

With one final squeeze, they let go of one another. Everyone was watching. But Jake kept near her. He reached into his pocket and removed the gold watch.

"I found this," he said, reverting to English, though it took concentration.

Kady's face crinkled with mild curiosity—then widened and ran through a whole series of emotions, using every muscle in her face. Shock, disbelief, bewilderment.

"Is that—" She stopped, choking, unable to bring herself even to voice it aloud.

"Yes." He turned and showed her the inscription.

She leaned close and read each word. When she lifted her face, there were tears in her eyes. "When . . . where did you find it?"

Jake didn't think it was a good time to explain about the map of Pangaea and all he'd discovered and learned in the great temple, but he pointed his arm back to the pyramid. "In there."

She turned her gaze to the steps leading to the round opening. Her brows arched in bafflement. "But how? What does it mean?"

"I don't know."

At least not yet, he added silently.

Kady's eyes went into a thousand-mile stare, trying to fathom the implication of the watch's discovery here. He imagined his own expression hadn't been much different.

Jake remained silent. He had no words that would ease her heart. It would take time to absorb this shock.

Perhaps sensing Kady's distress, Heronidus stepped out of the Roman group. He limped on his right leg, and the left side of his face bore a wicked scratch that looked like it had come close to taking out his eye. But before Heronidus could speak, a new blare of horns and bugles sounded from the other side of the city. It was a triumphant noise.

"Who is that?" Heronidus asked, cocking his head and listening.

"Pindor," Marika said with a proud grin. "Leading the Ur forces."

Heronidus looked at her in disbelief and turned away. "If you don't know, just say so."

He stalked off, collecting Kady gently under one arm. She leaned her head on his shoulder, needing consolation that Jake could not provide. Still, she took a moment to glance back toward her brother. She gave Jake a rare sad smile.

For the first time in a long time, Jake recognized how beautiful his sister was. He saw something beyond the usual lip gloss, eye shadow, and perfect hair (which was presently in shambles and with bits of leaves stuck in it). For just a moment, he saw who she might become. And a warm thrill of pride rushed through him. Along with a trace of sorrow. In that same brief expression of affection, he recognized one more thing: a ghost of their mother's smile, shining from one generation to another.

As a group, they headed back to the gateway into Calypsos. Already cautious celebrations were under way. Though no one knew the source of their last-minute salvation, the empty skies and brilliant lightning display let them know the most important thing: *they were safe*.

Townspeople crept back out of fruit cellars and musty attics, where they'd holed up during the attack. Bells rang out, sounding the all clear from the castle. As Jake walked through the streets, calls and shouts echoed. But also tears and sobbing. Jake had passed only one body—and it had been a grakyl, lying broken in the street. But there were surely other casualties that struck closer to home and heart. How many had died? It might take days to discover that answer.

It also lightened Jake's heart to see Saddleback riders dashing around town, carrying messages, spreading the word, rallying their scattered forces. The sky was also crisscrossed with winged raz. The People of the Wind were again in the air, ready for any sign of a secondary attack.

But Jake knew that would not come. At least not for a while.

Ahead, the castle of Kalakryss appeared. The courtyard was in utter chaos. People and beasts crowded the space. Tents were already being erected to shelter the injured.

Jake almost got bowled over by a large scarred fleetback that bounded up the street and through the gates behind him. It took a second glance to recognize the blind eye of the mount—and the scarecrow riding it.

It was Pindor atop the fearsome-looking fleetback named Scar-Eye.

"Jake! Mari! Bach'uuk!" He guided his mount to a stuttering stop and slid from the saddle as if climbing off a lounging chair. Whatever fear he'd had before was lost in his excitement. Pindor rushed over to them and hugged and pounded them and shook hands—sometimes all at once.

"You chased them off!" Pindor announced. "You got the shield raised!"

His shout drew many eyes to them.

Heronidus limped forward. "Pin, is that you?" He eyed his brother up and down. He smiled, trying on an expression of pride, but it came out awkward. It was rare for Pindor to outshine his older brother.

But the shouted words drew two others' attention.

Centurion Gaius pushed through the growing throng around them. Jake felt a surge of relief. The centurion had survived the attack by the grakyls in the park. But he was bloody and carried one arm in a sling. Still, he cleared the way for the man behind him.

Elder Tiberius leaned on a staff. His leg was bandaged from ankle to midthigh. Each step clearly pained him. But his voice was as hard and firm as always. "What's this about the shield?" he asked.

Pindor made a move to run and hug his father, but then caught himself. He wasn't a boy any longer. He struck his fist to his chest in a Roman salute. "Father, sir, it was Jake Ransom who was able to raise the fallen shield around the valley."

Tiberius turned that stern countenance upon Jake. "Is this true?"

Jake nodded, but added. "I didn't do it alone." He waved to include Pindor, Marika, and Bach'uuk. "It took all of us."

Tiberius stared at them with an appraising eye. Then he turned and headed toward the castle. Without a word or a gesture, it was clear they were to follow him.

"I will hear more of this in private," he said. "The Magisters will also want to learn what was done."

Marika tripped a step next to Jake.

"Clear the way!" Gaius shouted, fighting a path through for them.

In the confusion, Marika wiggled up next to Pindor's father and tugged at his sleeve. "Elder Tiberius, what do you mean by *Magisters?*" Fear trembled in her voice. "It was Magister Oswin who betrayed us."

Jake moved closer, growing concerned. After all that had happened, had the traitor survived?

Tiberius nodded at Marika's words. "We are well aware. Your father and Magister Zahur have already informed the Council of his treachery."

"My father . . ." Marika clutched Jake's arm to keep from falling. "He's alive?"

Noting her relief, Tiberius slowed and reassured her. "Of course he's alive. Oswin cast some shadowy spell upon the two other Magisters, knocked their wits to senselessness, and bound them in one of the empty cellars down below. Once awake, they were able to escape."

By now they had reached the timber doors of the main keep. Inside the main hall, Marika had proof of the Elder's story.

"Mari! Thank all the stars . . ."

Balam had been standing off to the side with Zahur. Turning at the commotion by the door, he had immediately spotted his daughter and rushed to her. The relief that rang in his voice was the same as his daughter's a moment before. He had also changed. His usual easy aplomb had gone stony. Dark circles haunted his eyes. But his face brightened and cracked, like a sun through dark clouds. He hugged Marika tightly.

"I thought you were dead," she mumbled into his chest.

Jake watched their reunion with mixed feelings. Most of him rejoiced, but he could not ignore a bitter sliver of jealousy. He would do anything to have his own father back from the dead.

"I don't think Oswin would have killed us," Balam consoled her. "While he had the chance, he didn't. I think perhaps a part of him was still loyal in its own crooked way."

Zahur had joined them. The Egyptian had a different take on the matter. "Or maybe he just kept us alive so he could gloat."

Balam frowned at this assessment, clearly preferring his own. Still, it was plain to see Marika's father had been deeply wounded and shaken by the betrayal of a close friend.

Jake stepped away and allowed father and daughter to have their moment alone. Even the taciturn Tiberius lifted a welcoming arm and hugged his youngest son.

Jake turned away. Though he was happy for his friends, it was also too painful to watch. Jake's hand reached to his pocket and squeezed the gold watch.

For now, this would have to be enough of a reward.

But only for now. . . .

TIME AND TIME AGAIN

The new Council of Elders filled the two rows of the high bench. Once again, Jake and Kady were the center of attention of six pairs of eyes. Across the top sat the same three Elders as before—Tiberius, Ulfsdottir, and Wu—all bruised, bloodied, and older.

It had been three days since Jake had raised the valley's shield. It had been three days of questions and more questions. The townspeople had to face a hard truth. Though their valley was safe for now, such security was not permanent. They would have to be more vigilant from this time forward.

Balam stood up from his center seat on the lower level of the bench. He was flanked by Magister Zahur on his right and a new Magister on his left.

Balam began solemnly, "Our new Magister has requested a small private ceremony to honor the five who protected both our valley and the great temple."

Balam motioned to his left.

The newest member of the Council of Elders pulled himself to his feet using his staff. The bronze bangles hanging on the wooden shaft danced in the lamplight and tinkled like wind chimes. The Ur Elder nodded to the five who gathered at the foot of the bench.

Behind Jake and Kady stood Marika, Pindor, and Bach'uuk. They were all wearing their finest clothes and stood stiffly. Jake and Kady had donned their safari outfits, freshly laundered and pressed. It was as formal as they could manage. None of them was sure what to expect.

The Ur Elder—named Mer'uuk—clumped out from behind the bench and crossed slowly toward the five of them. The old tribesman was the first of the Ur to be appointed a Magister on the Council of Elders. The lofty position was a reward for the Ur's part in saving Calypsos and a long-overdue recognition. The Ur and the townspeople could no longer afford to ignore one another. Not if they wished to survive. The Skull King would attack again, and when that happened, the entire valley needed to be united.

Mer'uuk waved for the five of them to line up. After a bit of shuffling, the Elder started at the end farthest from Jake. He reached out and took Pindor's left arm and bared his wrist. Then Mer'uuk lifted high a single bangle of silvery metal so all could see.

"From the night sky, this metal fell in a blaze of fire," the

Ur Elder intoned. "It holds a rare and potent alchemy—one of *binding*. To bring you all together as one."

Stepping forward, Mer'uuk snapped the bracelet around Pindor's wrist, then moved down the line to Bach'uuk. Another band was fastened around the Neanderthal boy's wrist.

Marika stood next to Jake. She watched as Mer'uuk snapped a third bracelet around Kady's left wrist. The bands all appeared identical. A moment later, Marika fiddled with the band around her wrist.

"Must be forged out of lodestone," she whispered.

Lodestone was an old-fashioned word for "magnet." Jake guessed the bands were probably made out of magnetite, which had natural magnetic properties.

Jake held out his arm and slipped up his sleeve. Mer'uuk pulled out a fifth band. It was open and hinged. The Elder dropped it over Jake's wrist and snapped it closed.

"So completes the binding," Mer'uuk finished. "You are now one."

Jake studied his band. He turned the bracelet around his wrist and frowned. He could find no hinge, not even a seam where the two halves had snapped together. It was perfectly smooth, as if forged new around his wrist. Jake lifted his arm and squinted harder. He could find no breaks in the band's perfect surface, but he did discover something else. Strange letters had been inscribed very faintly along the outer edge of the band. Jake recognized the script. It was the same language that appeared throughout the pyramid.

Bewildered, Jake lowered his arm and looked up. Mer'uuk still stood before him and wore a ghost of a smile.

The wizened Elder leaned closer to Jake and spoke softly in his ear. "To know the truth, you must stop living in the short time."

With those cryptic words, he straightened and thumped his way back to his seat on the bench.

As they waited, Jake stared down the row. The five of them all wore matching bands. *You are now one*, Mer'uuk had said. What did that mean, that last whispered comment? *To know the truth, you must stop living in the short time.*

Tiberius finally spoke. "Are there any last requests before we adjourn for the day?"

The question was directed at his fellow Elders, but Jake stepped forward and lifted a hand. The Ur Elder's words continued to echo in his head. Especially the word *time*. It reminded Jake of the weight of his father's gold watch in his pocket. And where he'd found it: within the gears of the giant Mayan calendar as it slowly ticked away the days.

Everything—all the mysteries of this place—seemed to boil down to one concept.

Time.

Tiberius nodded to Jake. "You wish to speak, Jacob Ransom?"

"I would ask a favor. If I could."

Tiberius motioned for him to continue.

"I would like to visit the pyramid once more," Jake said. "To return to where I found my father's watch."

Kady joined him. "As would I."

The two of them had already talked about it. Kady wanted to see the chamber for herself, and Jake sensed there was a clue that had escaped him during his earlier rush through the pyramid.

Tiberius frowned at the two of them. "While I appreciate all you've done for Calypsos, to trespass within the temple remains forbidden. Especially now. But I will leave it to the Magisters to decide."

Balam lifted a hand. "On a point of order, *only* Magisters are allowed within the great temple. That is clear and should remain firm."

Jake felt hope slipping away.

"However," Balam continued, "there is nothing to say that the Magisters need only number *three*. I put it to the vote of the Council that we grant to these two, for the status of one day, the title of *Junior* Magisters. By a show of hands?"

Six arms lifted into the air.

Balam rapped a fist on the table and offered Jake a secret wink. "So it has been approved."

Two hours later, Jake and Kady stood at the top of the pyramid. Overhead, the stone dragon continued its silent vigil. A step ahead of them, Balam had both palms raised against the invisible shield that sealed the round opening.

"It remains strong," Balam said with a sigh of relief.

Even from where Jake stood, he could feel it. A force, like a wind, tried to push against him. He shifted his pack higher on his shoulder, anxious to get inside again.

"First, we'll have to all hold hands," Balam said. "So I can usher you both through."

Kady gripped the man's hand, then held hers out for Jake to grab. But instead Jake turned away.

Marika, Pindor, and Bach'uuk waited on the step below. They weren't going to be allowed back inside, but his friends had come anyway. They knew how important this was for Jake.

He jumped down and gripped Pindor's forearm in Roman fashion. "Thanks for coming," he said. "If it wasn't for you—for *all* of you—I don't know where I'd be."

Pindor blushed a deep red. Compliments had been rare for his friend, but Jake suspected Pindor would have to get used to them from here on.

Jake shook Bach'uuk's arm in the same fashion, but when he tried to shake Marika's hand, she brushed his arm aside and hugged him instead.

"We'll be waiting for you out here," she said into his ear.

Her breath tickled his neck. Jake's face heated up, and probably turned as red as Pindor's. "We might be in there a while," he mumbled as he stepped back.

"We'll still be here," Pindor said. He glanced at the other two, who both nodded.

Jake smiled, knowing it was crooked and goofy but it was real. He'd never had friends like these. Only at this moment did he recognize what had been missing in his life. For the past three years, he had been so focused on following in his parents' footsteps that he'd forgotten that such a road was best walked with friends at your side. But like Pindor with compliments, Jake suspected he would just have to get used to it.

"Are you coming?" Kady asked with a long, exasperated sigh.

Jake hopped up, waved to his friends, and took his sister's hand. With Balam leading, they stepped across the threshold. Again, a wave of tingling swept over him and the hairs all over his body danced. Then they were through and heading down into the pyramid.

Balam spoke to Kady as they walked, but Jake barely heard them. His mind was already on the chamber with the Mayan calendar. He had missed something down there, he was sure of it . . . but what?

Once they reached the heart of the pyramid, Kady took

in the immense crystal sphere. It spun and churned, forming combination after combination of strange letters.

"I can feel it beating!" Kady said with wonder.

Jake felt it, too. That throbbing pulse of power emanated from the massive sphere. Below it, the other three crystals spun happily. The emerald sphere looked as bright as the ruby and sapphire ones.

Balam noted Jake's attention. "The taint of shadows caused no permanent damage. It was pure brilliance on your part to think to reflect sunlight upon it. Pure brilliance!"

Jake dismissed the praise. "I got the idea from Mari. And from what you taught me."

Balam raised an eyebrow.

Jake explained, quoting the Magister's earliest lesson. "'*All alchemy starts with the sun.*'"

Balam laughed. "So someone *does* listen to me once in a while. Still, it was brilliant on your part to concoct such a plan." The old man tousled Jake's hair. It was a fatherly gesture that sent a wave of warmth through Jake's body.

"And I suppose," Balam continued, "you're anxious to continue on to the chamber below."

"Yes, sir. And would it be possible for Kady and me to go by ourselves?"

Jake wanted privacy when he explored the room. If he had any questions, he could always come back up and ask.

Balam had no problem with this plan and shooed them away. "I have plenty to do here. When you're ready, come back up."

Jake forced himself not to run. He led Kady to the far opening and down a spiraling stair. The round chamber with the Mayan calendar looked exactly as he'd left it. On the floor, the two gear wheels shone in lamplight.

Kady gasped again—but for the wrong reason. "So much gold! It must be worth a fortune."

"That's not why we came here," Jake said.

Kady rolled her eyes at him. "I know, but that doesn't mean I can't look."

"Just don't touch anything."

Jake crossed into the chamber. He wanted to take everything in again, slowly, meticulously. His father had warned him. *Attention is in the details.* It was the responsibility of all scientists to work painstakingly when faced with life's mysteries.

Jake pulled out the pocket watch.

Here was one mystery he didn't want to get wrong.

"Where did you find Dad's watch?" Kady asked.

Jake pointed to the inner wheel. "It was lying on the floor there."

"Just lying there?"

"Yes, what did I just say?"

Kady held out her hand. "Let me see it."

Jake hesitated. He'd kept the watch with him, on his

person. He didn't like it out of his sight. So Kady hadn't really had a chance to examine it herself.

With some reluctance, Jake placed the watch in her hand. "Be careful with it."

She rolled her eyes again and turned away. She left Jake's side and went to explore on her own.

Jake focused his attention back on the room. The walls were covered with writing. Surely there were some answers locked in that unknown language. He had asked Balam, but no one in Calypsos could translate any of it.

Jake's gaze swept over the lettering and settled on the three maps carved in bas-relief into one section of the wall. His legs carried him closer of their own accord. Something about the maps . . .

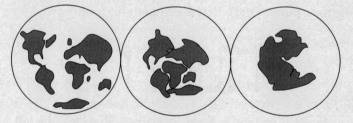

He again stared across the three of them, studying how the modern-day continents merged together like a jigsaw puzzle into one huge landmass named Pangaea. What was it about these maps that kept nagging him?

Only then did Jake notice the lettering *below* the map.

Earlier, he had been so shocked by his discovery that he was in Pangaea that he'd failed to note what was written below it. Then again, it was just more of that strange lettering.

ᚠᚓᛁᛚᚠᚾᛏᛚᛩ

It meant nothing to him. He returned his attention to the round maps. His gaze swept back and forth. Seven continents formed one supercontinent. But he couldn't quite let go of the letters below. They hovered at the corner of his eye. Eight letters in all. Eight pieces to the puzzle. Jake watched Pangaea pull together one more time, merging into one. Then the letters again.

What if . . . ?

Jake pushed the letters together in his mind's eye.

ᚠᚓᛁᛚᚠᚾᛏᛚᛩ

Something tried to form. Something that looked familiar. His brain tickled with the mystery.

Jake reached into his pocket and removed his mother's sketchbook. He tore out a page near the back that was still blank and slipped his mother's charcoal pencil from the book's binding. With the page pressed to the wall, Jake scribbled the pencil across its surface to make a rubbing of the letters.

Once done, he had a copy of the letters etched on the paper. He knelt down and creased the paper between each letter, so that he could accordion them all together into one piece. Just like the continents had formed Pangaea.

With great care, he merged all the letters together until they formed a single word. Jake stared down at what he'd created.

ATLANTIS

Shock drew Jake back to his feet. The paper began to tremble in his hands. He now understood what had nagged at him to return here. In his head, he broke the letters into shapes that were more familiar.

ATLANTIS

He read it aloud. "Atlantis."

Jake backed away from the wall. Could it be true? Could the pyramid and the knowledge displayed here trace back to Atlantis, the mythological island, where an advanced race once ruled? He struggled to recall all he knew about Atlantis. The earliest stories were written by Plato, one of the most famous Greek philosophers. He claimed to have visited Atlantis, seen its wonders. And according to his stories, the island was violently destroyed, broken apart, and sunk into the sea.

Jake stepped back to the map. He touched the surface of Pangaea. The supercontinent *did* look like an island. Was this what Plato had seen? Had the Greek philosopher been brought here . . . the same as Jake and Kady? And was Plato being poetic when he said Atlantis vanished into the vastness of the seas? Maybe he had meant the civilization had vanished into the seas *of time*.

It was too much to absorb. Jake fell back. He turned, dazed, staring at the walls, picturing the crystal heart above. Was all this built by the lost civilization of Atlantis? Was it their technology that drew the other Lost Tribes back in time to Pangaea? Or were the Atlantean people the first of the Lost Tribes? Did they start all this? If so, where did they go?

Question after question filled his head.

Jake pressed his palms against his ears. He had solved one riddle only to have it shatter into a thousand other mysteries.

"Jake!"

The shout cut through the flurry in his head. He turned to Kady. She stood in the center of the inner wheel and held the pocket watch in her hands. She had popped the watchcase open, as if checking the time, but she squinted at something inside that bothered her.

Jake was glad for the distraction. He crossed over and

joined her in the inner ring. "What?" he asked.

She tilted the watchcase at an angle and pointed to the underside of the lid. Jake reached to her hands and moved the watch more fully into the light. A shape had been crisply carved into the gold surface.

Jake recognized the shape. It was an *ankh*, the Egyptian symbol for "life." It was one of the most important symbols of ancient Egypt, carried by pharaohs during important ceremonies.

"And look at this," Kady said. She pulled the watch closer to her. "The second hand is spinning *backward*!"

Jake had already noticed that, but he'd forgotten to tell Kady. It was a minor mystery when compared to the discovery of their father's watch.

Jake tried to pull the watch back toward him. He wanted a closer peek at the ankh.

Kady fought him. "I don't get it. What's wrong with Dad's watch? Maybe if we reset it."

Jake, still struggling to get a better look at the Egyptian symbol, took an extra beat to hear what Kady had said.

Especially one word.

Reset.

He was too slow. Kady already had her fingers on the watch's stem. It was used to wind the watch—but also to adjust the *time.*

"No!" Jake warned.

For just a moment, he remembered the adage Balam had taught Marika: *Look twice and step once.* It was a bit of wisdom that urged restraint and caution.

Kady hadn't learned it. She pulled the stem out.

Instantly a great grinding of gears sounded. It rose not from the watch, but from the golden wheels around them. The Mayan calendar wheels began turning as Jake and Kady stood in the center. The movement was slow at first, then faster and faster. The gears churned so rapidly that any misstep by Jake or Kady could cost them a foot. And the spinning grew even swifter, turning the wheels into a golden blur.

Jake still held Kady's hands, clutching the watch between them. As the gears whirled into oblivion, Jake felt force building under his feet.

A shout of warning formed on his lips. "Hang—"

White light blasted upward and consumed them. The brightness instantly blinded Jake. Though without sight, he sensed that he was shooting skyward; it felt like being in an elevator strapped to a rocket engine. It all lasted less than an instant.

Then it was over.

He blinked against the residual glare as thunder rumbled around him.

Thunder?

The blinding light faded into ordinary lightning.

As his vision cleared, Jake stared dumbfounded around him. Kady crouched next to him, equally frozen in shock. To all sides stood glass display cases and pedestals holding up ancient artifacts. A step away, the golden pyramid with its jade dragon rested on a stand.

They were back in the British Museum!

Back home.

Has it been all a dream?

Jake still held Kady's hands. Their father's pocket watch rested in her palm. The metal bands encircled their left wrists.

Before he could make sense of it, a yell made them both jump.

"*No!*"

Jake swung fully around. A bull of a man ran toward them. It was Morgan Drummond, their assigned corporate bodyguard. Just seconds before they'd vanished, Drummond had been rushing toward them and yelling.

Just like now.

"Get back from there!" Drummond scolded. But the man pulled up short, scratched his head, then stared around the place as if sensing something was off kilter.

But after a breath, he settled his gaze back on them. His expression was vaguely suspicious.

"What were you two doing?"

Jake slipped the gold watch from Kady's fingers and showed it to Morgan. Before the man could get a good look, Jake dropped it into his own pocket.

"I was just checking the time," Jake said, and secretly nudged Kady.

She jumped, then nodded vigorously, unable to speak yet.

"If you were checking the time," Drummond said, regaining the brusque command in his voice, "then you know you've both had plenty of time in here alone. With the eclipse over, the museum patrons will want their turn up here."

Jake looked to a window. *The eclipse?* If it was just ending, then no time had passed here in London at all. They'd spent more than a week in Pangaea . . . and returned back to the very spot where they'd started.

Both in space and time.

Drummond scanned the room, as if searching for something. His eyes remained narrowed, and he focused back on Jake and Kady. "Did you touch anything in here?"

"Of course not," Jake said, pretending to be offended.

Kady also shook her head.

"And nothing strange happened?"

Jake frowned. "There was lightning. And thunder. The

lights went out." He shrugged. "But it's not like we're scared of the dark or anything."

Jake kept his expression bland, but he stared extra hard at the man. Jake remembered his earlier suspicions about Morgan Drummond. The bodyguard had claimed Jake and Kady were brought to London as a publicity stunt to draw media attention for the exhibit. But what if there was a darker purpose? Something more sinister? Had Drummond's boss hoped they would open a portal to Pangaea? Was that the true reason they'd been brought here and left alone in the museum?

Drummond's eyes shone with a growing suspicion, but a commotion by the door drew his attention around. Excited voices rang out. Men and women dressed in fine attire flowed into the room.

Drummond scowled at the newcomers. His voice grew tinged with disappointment. "I suppose it's time I got you both back to your hotel. You have an early flight back home in the morning."

Jake glanced to Kady. He tugged his sleeve to hide his metal wrist band. Following his example, she did the same. Jake had already told her about the symbol he'd seen on the grakyl sword and his suspicions about the Bledsworth corporation.

Even now, as Drummond turned to face the approaching crowd, a silvery flash drew Jake's eye to the man's steel tie tack. The small griffin with its talons bared was the symbol for Bledsworth Sundries and Industries, Inc. And likewise for Kalverum Rex, the Skull King.

Drummond swung toward them. Another tinier flash drew Jake's attention back to the man's pin. Jake might have missed it if he hadn't already been looking. The eye of the griffin sparked with a bit of dark fire. Jake had noted the eye during the limo ride across London. At the time, he'd thought it was a tiny black diamond.

But now he knew the truth.

Jake recognized the gem that made up that black eye. It was a tiny speck of *bloodstone*, the crystal forged by the dark alchemy of Kalverum Rex.

Jake fought against a shudder of revulsion. Here was positive proof that some connection existed between the past and the present. But what was that link? Jake forced his gaze away, keeping his knowledge hidden.

"So are you all done here?" Drummond asked.

Jake shared a glance with Kady. As the shock faded, a

fire had entered her eyes. He read the answer to Drummond's question in her face. It matched his own.

Are they done here?

For once, Jake and Kady were united in their answer.

No . . . *we've only just begun.*

A NOTE FROM THE AUTHOR

Over the years, I've always included a note at the end of my thrillers, where I address what's true and what's not in my novels—so I thought I'd do the same here.

But before I get started, a bit about myself. Though I earned my degree in veterinary medicine, I've always been an armchair archaeologist. I've loved all things buried and lost to time. In fact, I maintain a Cabinet of Curiosities at home, where I display all manner of the weird and strange: from giant fossilized specimens to tiny, pinned insects. And gracing the top of the cabinet is a massive 100,000-year-old mammoth tusk from China. Every day, the cabinet reminds me of that joy of the grand adventure that is life in this world.

So as you might guess, the young adventurer Jake Ransom is close to my heart—and for Jake, I saved my wildest and best adventure of all.

In a nutshell, Jake's who I was as a kid. Someone ever

curious about the world, a bit impatient, bold at times, wary at others, slightly geeky but knowing it and unable to change. He also is plagued by an older sister who thinks she knows more than she does. Growing up with three brothers—and three sisters—I understand that relationship all too well. The arguments, the resentments, but ultimately a deep and unshakable bond of family.

But back to Jake. At heart, Jake is a true adventurer, someone ready and willing to take the path less traveled . . . no matter how much trouble he might get into.

Like Jake, I love to travel and I love archaeology. But like Jake, my travels over the years have gotten me into a few jams. I've swum in jungle rivers only to discover a crocodile basking in the sun on the riverbank. I've gotten myself trapped—in caves, hanging from ropes, and jammed in a crack unable to move. While scuba diving, I've come close to stabbing my hand on one of the most poisonous spiny fishes in the world (one poke will kill you in seconds).

Jake is just the same—maybe a bit too adventurous for his own good—and he'll get himself into just as many scrapes as close calls. It will take all of Jake's ingenuity, skill, and friendships to pull him through the dangers and adventures to come.

The series is chock-full of the fantastic, but it's also grounded in reality. Each novel centers on a different lost culture from Earth's past. First up are the ancient Maya.

Throughout the book appear various Mayan glyphs, the symbolic writing of these Mesoamerican people. The glyphs in the book are real, and each plays an important role in the adventure. Likewise, details of the Mayan culture—from the clothing they wear to their astounding skill at astronomy—are all factual and integral to the story. Additionally there are several fun facts, too—like how the ancient Maya invented chocolate and chewing gum.

As to the science in the novel, all the dinosaurs that appear are real creatures from the fossil record, and the discussions about spectrums of light, refractions, and mixing of colors are all based on fact.

Lastly, for this series, I've also created my own cryptic language, snatches of which appear in this novel. The alphabet breaks down to English equivalents, so the more industrious readers can translate these bits of language to reveal secret messages.

So that's just a hint of the truth behind the fantastic world of Jake Ransom. I hope you grab a backpack and come join me—the adventure is just beginning!

—James Rollins

EXTRAS

JAKE RANSOM
AND THE SKULL KING'S SHADOW

An Interview with Pindor Tiberius

An English-to-Atlantean Translation Guide with an Encrypted Message from the Author

A Sneak Peek at *Jake Ransom and the Howling Sphinx*

An Interview with Jake's Friend Pindor Tiberius

Hi, Pindor, we've come to Calypsos to ask you a few questions. To start with, can you tell us what Jake Ransom is really like?

Jake? He's my friend, so I don't want to say anything bad about him. But between you and me, that guy likes to get into way too much trouble. He's always sticking his nose into places it doesn't belong. I prefer sleeping late, eating a big breakfast, maybe going to see a game at the stadium. That's excitement enough. But not for Jake. He's all about playing with fire, poking monsters in the eye, and running from certain death. Hmm. Now that I think about it, why am I his friend? He's going to get me killed!

We know that Mari loves hot chocolate. What is your favorite food?

I have to pick just one food? That's hard. I like fried beet wort, poached blowhorn eggs, pickled pike's tongue, warm oat bread with honey, mushberry pie, porridge with sliced kwarma bean . . . great, now I'm starving. Did you bring anything to eat?

EXTRAS

When you first brought them to the city, you told your older brother, Heronidus, that you thought Jake and Kady might be spies—did you really believe that or were you just trying to impress him?

I really wasn't sure, but it's always better to be safe than sorry. Plus I had borrowed my father's spear. Figured in all the excitement, no one would notice. But that didn't work out so well, did it?

We know that you used to be scared of mounts, but you were able to get past that fear to help your friends when they needed it most. How else do you think you've changed since you first met Jake? What is your biggest fear now that you are no longer afraid of mounts?

Wait! Who said I was afraid of anything? Let me guess. It was Marika, wasn't it? So I sleep with a glowing crystal beside my bed. So what? Look what happened to Jake with that stingtail. If he'd had a light on, he wouldn't have gotten stung. I'm only being careful, that's all. It's not like I'm scared of the dark or anything.

What can we expect from you in *Jake Ransom and the Howling Sphinx*?

[Groan.] You heard about that? I still have the bruises from that adventure, not to mention all the nightmares. I can still picture that giant sand crab chasing me, claws snapping at my heels. And then there was that horrible monster in the desert . . . forget it, I don't even want to think about it. You'll just have to read the book.

An English-to-Atlantean Translation Guide and a Message from the Author

Be the first of your friends to write encrypted Atlantean messages with this fun English-to-Atlantean translation guide!

Practice by deciphering encrypted messages in this first Jake Ransom book, and translate a personal message from James Rollins:

[encrypted symbol text]

Turn the page to see if you're right!

Translation

Dear Reader:

I hope you have enjoyed this adventure. The next road leads to Egypt in *Jake Ransom and the Howling Sphinx*. Grab a backpack and get ready for more fun and magic!

All the best,

James Rollins

Don't Miss This Sneak Peek at
Jake Ransom and the Howling Sphinx!

PROLOGUE

VALLEY OF THE KINGS

No man could survive such a storm for long.

Clouds of red sand blasted out of the Sahara Desert and swept across all of Egypt. The storm darkened the sun and grew so vast it could be seen from orbiting satellites. And it was no better on the ground. For those unlucky enough to risk the storm, the winds scoured any exposed skin like coarse sandpaper.

But the man had been summoned and knew he had to obey.

Professor Hiram Bellach was a senior curator at the Cairo Museum and the leading expert on the Old Kingdom of Egypt. The curator hunched against the stinging sand. His face was covered in a scarf, his eyes hidden behind goggles.

He fought the storm as he hiked through the Valley of the Kings. He could barely see past his own nose, but he knew his way. Every Egyptian scholar did. Egyptian pharaohs had been buried in this maze of limestone hills and sandy gullies for millennia, including the famous boy-king Tutankhamen.

But Hiram's destination lay much farther out, beyond

where most archaeologists searched. He fought deeper down the valley toward a new excavation. To anyone looking, it appeared to be nothing more than a well being dug, a project to help bring water to the parched land. Permits, uniforms, and equipment all bore a black griffin, the familiar logo of the company who funded this excavation.

Bledsworth Sundries and Industries, Inc.

The corporation financed many such humanitarian enterprises throughout the region. But Hiram knew the true goal of this particular project and had been paid well to keep its secret.

And now he had been summoned.

Had the others found what they sought?

Surely that was impossible . . .

Despite the hot breath of the sandstorm, Hiram shivered as he reached the dig site. All the workers had fled with the storm, leaving the place dark and empty. Hiram crawled and wiggled through the abandoned equipment to reach the hole in the hillside, framed by timber and sealed with a steel door.

Under the rap of his knuckles, the door swung open. He hesitated at the threshold. Even with the storm howling at his back, he balked at entering the tunnel. The passageway dove steeply downward, lit by flaming torches set into notches in the walls.

Swallowing back his fear, Hiram ducked through the door and entered. A gust of wind slammed the door closed behind him with a loud clang. Startled, he hurried forward.

The quicker he was done here, the sooner he could get home.

The way led deeper and deeper. The walls changed from raw limestone to stone blocks. Ancient steps appeared and led downward yet again. Hiram kept to the torch-lit path as the walls squeezed tighter on either side.

At last, the tunnel emptied into a cavernous space. It was a vast domed chamber. Other passageways led out from the room, but Hiram's eyes were drawn to the black statues that lined the walls. They were perfect renditions of ancient Egyptian warriors. Each man was unique in shape and size, but they all had one feature in common: their faces were masks of terror. Their horrified gazes all focused on the head of a stone serpent in the center of the room.

It stood as tall as Hiram. From the flare of the hood behind its head, it was plainly meant to be a cobra. But this cobra had *three* eyes: two carved out of limestone and a third that rested atop its skull. This last one reflected the firelight. It was a giant gem cut into the shape of an oval orb.

Hiram approached in disbelief.

A voice stopped him. It came from one of the other tunnels on the far side of the cavern. The speaker remained hidden in the shadows of the passageway; only his words scratched out of the darkness.

"You know what it is..."

Hiram recognized that voice. It had summoned him to this secret meeting. The voice came from the man who had bought Hiram's silence by paying for his dying wife's medical treatment. The money had saved her life. As such, Hiram had never regretted the pact he had made.

Not until this moment.

Since the beginning, Hiram had been certain that what the man had sought was pure myth, an object out of dark legend. What harm was there in letting the man dig in a place no one valued, to hunt for an artifact that few thought was real? He never thought they'd succeed in finding it.

"You recognize the eye..."

Hiram did. It matched the description in the ancient Book of Thoth. He named the gem. "The Eye of Ra."

"Bring it to me..."

An arm extended out of the tunnel's shadows. An iron gauntlet hid the hand. Fingers creaked open.

Unable to refuse, Hiram stumbled to the statue. He reached toward the bright eye. His fingers hovered over the gem. His hearted thundered in his ears, but he still heard the order repeated.

"Bring it to me..."

Hiram gently lifted the gem out of the stone eye socket. He stepped back and stared down at what he held.

The gem was twice the size of his fist. The firelight

flowed over its polished surface, bringing out a thousand jeweled shades. Hiram had studied enough geology to recognize a fire opal, a gem rare for this region and priceless at this size. It was perfect, except for a single blemish along one side. He ran his thumb over the elliptical vein of black obsidian that coursed over one surface of the stone.

It made the gem look like an eye.

Hiram glanced up at the statue.

Perhaps a serpent's eye.

Beyond the statue, the man who had hired him flowed out of the tunnel. Shadows cloaked and swirled around his shape, hiding his features.

Shocked, Hiram took a step back. Despite his terror, one certainty crystallized in the curator's mind. If even half the stories were true about the Eye of Ra, he could not let anyone possess the gem, especially this shadowy man.

A cold chuckle flowed from the figure, as if reading Hiram's thoughts. "There is nowhere to run . . ."

Hiram tried. He turned toward the tunnel that led to the surface. He had to get the Eye of Ra away from this monstrous man. If he could reach the surface, get it back to his museum . . .

He took a step—or at least *tried* to take a step. But his feet suddenly went dead cold and refused to obey. He stared down, then gasped in disbelief. His shoes had turned to stone and had melded to the limestone floor.

No, not just his shoes.

A coldness traveled up his body. He watched his legs turn to stone, then his waist. He fought to move, to twist away. Then the coldness swept over his belly and chest— and out along his arms.

Stone fingers now clutched the fire-opal eye.

"No," he moaned out in horror.

He stared across at the row of Egyptian warriors. His expression now matched theirs, full of terror. He suddenly understood why he had been summoned here.

"The curse . . . ," the figure rasped at him, ". . . upon whoever tries to take the Eye from its resting place."

The voice drew up behind him. Hiram could not even turn as the petrifying coldness froze his neck. He had been tricked, drawn here to break the curse.

Hiram fought against it, gasping out, "YOU MUST NOT—" But his plea died as his tongue turned to stone.

"Ah, but I must . . . ," the figure whispered in his ear.

An arm reached around, and iron fingers settled to the fiery gem. The Eye of Ra was lifted free of Hiram's stony grip. As the curse consumed him fully, Hiram heard these last words before his ears turned deaf.

"With this, I will make Jake Ransom suffer."